UNDER A DANCING STAR

◆

More from Laura Wood

A Sky Painted Gold

UNDER A
DANCING
STAR

◆

LAURA WOOD

Random House
New York

Text copyright © 2019 by Laura Wood
Jacket art copyright © 2021 by Yehrin Tong

All rights reserved. Published in the United States by
Random House Children's Books, a division of
Penguin Random House LLC, New York.
Originally published in paperback by Scholastic Ltd., London, in 2019.

Random House and the colophon are registered trademarks of
Penguin Random House LLC.

Visit us on the Web! GetUnderlined.com

Educators and librarians, for a variety of teaching tools,
visit us at RHTeachersLibrarians.com

Library of Congress Cataloging-in-Publication Data
Name: Wood, Laura (Laura Clare), author.
Title: Under a dancing star / Laura Wood.
Description: First American edition. | New York: Random House, 2021. |
Summary: In 1933, seventeen-year-old Bea is invited to visit her bohemian
uncle in Italy, where she meets Ben, a brash young artist, who challenges
her to create the perfect summer romance.
Identifiers: LCCN 2020032728 (print) | LCCN 2020032729 (ebook) |
ISBN 978-0-593-30957-5 (trade) | ISBN 978-0-593-30958-2 (lib. bdg.) |
ISBN 978-0-593-30959-9 (ebook)
Subjects: CYAC: Dating (Social customs)—Fiction. | Love—Fiction. |
Italy—History—1914–1945—Fiction.
Classification: LCC PZ7.1.W652 Un 2021 (print) |
LCC PZ7.1.W652 (ebook) | DDC [Fic]—dc23

The text of this book is set in 11.5-point Sabon.

Printed in the United States of America
10 9 8 7 6 5 4 3 2 1
First American Edition 2021

For Paul, because of love

I know you of old.

—*Much Ado About Nothing,*
act I, scene 1

UNDER A
DANCING
STAR

♦

PART ONE

England
JUNE 1933

CHAPTER ONE

◆

"That's it," I murmur as I creep closer. "Nearly got you. . . ."

My hands are steady, and I hold my breath, waiting for precisely the right moment to pounce. With a twist of my wrist I manage to trap my elusive prey, and I screw the lid on the jar with a flourish.

Victory surges through me. I close my eyes and lift my face to the sun, enjoying the warmth as it ripples across my skin. Nearby, a garden warbler is singing, the melody dancing through the air as the bird marks his territory.

For a moment all is right with the world.

"Beatrice! Not again!" A dismayed voice drags me from my thoughts, and I open my eyes to see a figure stalking furiously down the path toward me.

"Hello, Mother!" I exclaim. "Sorry, I was miles away." I see her jaw tighten. "What are you doing out here? Shouldn't you be getting ready for the party?" Mother has been talking about nothing but tonight's dinner party for months.

"I *am* ready for the party," she replies frostily, and now that she is closer, I can see that this is true. My mother always looks very elegant, but she is more dressed up than usual thanks to the rope of pearls around her neck and the dusty-pink evening gown that—though it has seen better days—still retains an air of faded glamour.

My mother is a delicate woman—willowy and elegant and rather tired, like the sort of hothouse flower that droops easily. She is lovely-looking now, but I've seen the pictures and I know that she was very, very beautiful when she was my age. She still carries that beauty around in her bones in a way that makes people turn in the street to look at her. She can occasionally be found flicking through the pages of old fashion magazines with a mournful sigh, gazing longingly at the images of immaculately turned out debutantes.

"Oh yes," I say, with what I hope is a pacifying smile. "You look very nice." Mother's disapproving glare somehow snaps straight to the jam jar, which is concealed by my dress and would be completely invisible to any other person but her.

"And is there any *sensible* reason," she asks, her voice dangerously calm, "why you are standing barefoot and covered in filth in the middle of our lake?"

To be fair, it's really more of a large pond than a lake, but I cannot deny that I am certainly in it. And that my feet are bare and covered in mud and weeds. As are my legs. And a fair few inches of my dress. The woman in front of me definitely wouldn't see the appeal of removing her stockings to feel the mud squishing between her toes.

I clear my throat and try the smile again. I aim for the sort of soothing tone one might employ upon a highly strung horse. "*Lampyris noctiluca.*" I hold the jar forward and tilt it slightly. "Absolutely fascinating."

Mother's face remains stony.

"They'll be more interesting later on," I explain. "They're currently in their larval form, but I want to observe the bio-luminescence more closely once they graduate to adulthood." No response. "They glow," I add, a little desperately now. "They're glowworms."

"Of course." Mother's voice is flat. "You went into the lake to get glowworms."

"Yes." I nod encouragingly. "Lovely, magical glowworms."

I hope that some of my enthusiasm might prove conta-gious, although if history is anything to go by it is unlikely that the woman in front of me is about to suddenly develop a keen scientific interest in the natural world. Far *more* likely that I'm about to receive a lecture. These can last quite a long time and require minimal input from me, and so I keep a wary eye on her but turn my mind to the question of what I should feed the larvae while they remain in my care.

Mother lifts her hands weakly to her head, rubbing her temples: a weary gesture that I am all too familiar with.

"And did the hunt for these magical . . . *worms* . . . drag you through some kind of swamp?"

"Well, you see . . . ," I begin carefully, "I initially went out searching for butterflies, and I was on the trail of quite a sweet chalk-hill blue when I slipped and fell in the lake. Only *then*, as luck would have it, I spotted the glowworms." I pause, considering her words. "But, and I just want to be *completely* clear about this, Mother . . . glowworms aren't actually worms at all, you know—they're beetles, in the order Coleoptera."

"I see." Her voice is painfully reasonable, a fact that I know means she is working herself into a towering temper. "And presumably it is this fall that explains the *foliage*." Her gaze flickers to the top of my head, and I reach up to find a long, green strand of algae clinging to my dark hair.

"Mmm." I make a noncommittal murmur of agreement, then, "Snails!" I exclaim, as the answer to my problem flashes across my mind.

"What?" A look of disgust flickers on Mother's face, and she takes an uneasy step backward. "Where?"

"Oh, no, sorry, I wasn't talking to you; I just remembered that in their larval forms, glowworms are particularly partial to snails, and I'll have to try and find one for them." I begin wading toward the grassy bank, scanning the ground, my eyes lingering on the wall around the flower beds—currently covered in riotous overhanging greenery, and the perfect spot for a lurking *Mollusca gastropoda*.

I glance back up and notice that Mother's mouth opens and closes, but no noise comes out. I instantly attempt to arrange my features into an expression that is winsome and respectful, because I have observed this phenomenon before, and it is generally followed by a rather lengthy fit of hysterics, which I am—naturally—keen to avoid.

Mercifully, at that moment we are interrupted by enthusiastic barking, and I just have time to register the look of horror on Mother's face before Eustace comes crashing through the hedgerow.

In theory, Eustace, the scrappy terrier before us, is supposed to be a working dog: a ratter who lives in the barn with the horses. I christened him Eustace after the patron saint of hunters in an attempt to encourage him to embrace his destiny, but it was not to be. Eustace is, it seems, dreadfully afraid of rats, and fonder of sleeping at the bottom of my bed than concerning himself with matters in the stables. At this exact moment he is grinning—yes, actually grinning—at my mother, his pink tongue lolling out of the side of his mouth as he gathers himself in preparation to hurl his mud-sodden body at her. For some reason (possibly because she actively dislikes him), Eustace is loopy for my mother, head-over-heels devoted to her.

"Beatrice!" the object of his affection shrieks, and I drop the jar onto the grass, lunging across the pond to intercept the filthy dog cannonballing toward her evening wear.

Clutching the yelping creature to my chest, I mutter soothing words into his ears, scratching him in just the right place so that he settles down to enjoy the fuss, only occasionally casting yearning looks at Mother.

"We will discuss this another time, Beatrice," she says tightly. She has obviously decided that the party is the priority at the moment, and that fact has earned me a reprieve. "The most important thing is to try to get you looking vaguely respectable."

Her eyes travel over me with a look of exhausted despair, and a shudder passes through her fine-boned body. I can only assume that the addition of a mud-splattered terrier has done little to improve my appearance, but at least he has distracted her from the matter of the glowworms. It's important to look on the bright side in these situations.

"The guests will be here soon," she continues, an edge of panic creeping into her voice. "Go and clean yourself up *right now*."

"Of course," I murmur obediently. I tuck Eustace under one arm and, while her back is turned, scoop up the jam jar, then follow her meekly inside.

"Evening, Hobbs," I sing out to the stony-faced butler, who stands looking creakingly proper in the great hallway. It is, I notice, slightly less shabby in here than usual. There are several large vases dotted around, full of blooms offered up by the garden and hiding the worst of the peeling paint and moldering woodwork.

"Good evening, Miss Beatrice," he intones gloomily. Not by so much as a flicker of one winged white eyebrow does he register my disheveled appearance.

"Did you adjust the seating plan, Hobbs?" Mother asks anxiously, and while they are both distracted I slip up the sweeping stone staircase, a wriggling Eustace still gripped firmly in my arms.

Langton Hall is my family's ancestral home, and you would be hard-pressed to find a more crumblingly Gothic monstrosity in all of England. One particularly dissolute member of the family tree gambled away the Langton fortune a few hundred years ago, and the following generations have survived on increasingly tight purse strings. This means that there are whole sections of the rambling old building that are completely uninhabitable—by humans, anyway, although we've got our fair share of bats and mice. We also have the cobweb-filled hallways, glowering gargoyles, and ominously creaky floorboards that add up to make a storybook-worthy ghostly mansion. As a matter of fact, the first time I read *Northanger Abbey,* I wondered if Jane Austen had ever been a guest at Langton Hall herself.

What we *don't* have here is comfort or warmth, either literal or metaphorical. It may sound exciting, I daresay even *romantic,* to live in a decaying stately home, but let me tell you there's nothing romantic about rotting windowsills, and freezing cold baths, and damp wallpaper. Even the most Byronic of brooding heroes would quake in the face of the groaning, ancient plumbing system. It's less like having an actual home and more like living in a badly run museum.

Add to this the fact that the estate is about to run completely and utterly out of money and you'll get a sense of the perpetual state of gloom that hangs all over the place like a fine morning mist. Unless our luck changes, and soon, we'll have to sell everything when Father dies. As far as I can tell, there are no practical solutions under consideration—my suggestions that we sell off land or that I get a job have been met with a level of horror that one might typically associate with Herod's slaughter of the innocents.

I have a terrible suspicion that their hopes are pinned on my own matrimonial prospects. The fact that I am only seventeen and have no interest in getting married, settling down, or remaining at Langton once I do doesn't seem to be of much importance.

I, for one, would be more than happy to live somewhere where I could have a nice warm bath on demand, but Mother and Father see things quite differently. They understand their lives only in the context of this big, crumbling house and its acres of land. We're not alone in this—what few family acquaintances we have seem to be in a similar situation, though, generally speaking, with a bit more money to throw at the problem.

All these grand, ancient names with drafty old houses to care for—it reminds me of the story of the king of Siam, who used to gift courtiers with white elephants. A white elephant was sacred, and so on the one hand the gift represented an enormous honor, but on the other the extortionate expense of keeping the animal was enough to bankrupt a man. That's what these houses seem like to me: great lumbering white elephants hunkered down in the land.

Don't misunderstand me: I do sympathize with my parents. It's been just the three of us and a few lingering and ancient retainers rattling around this big house like the last sad pennies in an old tin for my whole life. I think they rather assumed they would have a brood of like-minded sons to save the estate, rather than one wayward and slightly baffling daughter just as they had given up hope of having any children at all. As far as my parents are concerned, daughters aren't a terribly useful asset. I'm not supposed to go out in the world and actually *do* things. They'd like me to be more . . . ornamental. I'm just too big, too loud, too clever— *too much*.

Upon reaching the bathroom I deposit Eustace in the ancient tub and do my best to wash him off despite his vigorous protests. (And, really, who can blame him? Even in June the water in this house feels like it has been drawn from an Arctic glacier, and I shudder as I contemplate my own looming ablutions.) When Eustace is relatively clean and has had a good shake, spraying me with even more water, I let him flee downstairs, where he will no doubt get in everyone's way and try to pinch the food intended for the dinner table.

I put my *Lampyris noctiluca* specimen on the shelf I keep for my discoveries, alongside my fossil collection and the carefully mounted skeleton of a raven that I unearthed, wonderfully complete, in the garden a couple of weeks ago. Mother said she thought the thing was morbid, but I think one could say the same of the decaying family crest that we were standing beneath at the time. Anyway, I don't think it's morbid; I think it's quite beautiful, and I have named it Edgar. My eyes stray once more to the jar of larvae and from there to the desk, buried under piles of scribbled notes.

A bell rings downstairs—a long, shrill ring that somehow

conveys a sense of panic. I sigh. Mother will be frantically summoning Hobbs to deal with some tremendous domestic emergency—a crooked dessert fork, perhaps. The bell rings again, with an increasingly hysterical urgency. Poor old Hobbs can't move as fast as he used to.

There really is no time to begin my observations of the glowworms now. Mother is already having palpitations over this dinner party, and if I'm late it might well send her over the edge. I have learned the hard way that if I want to study in peace, it's best to cultivate at least an appearance of interest in these social activities.

Catching sight of myself in the mirror, I am forced to admit that the look of despair that I received earlier might have been warranted. My long, dark hair is bundled on top of my head in a style that most closely resembles the rooks' nests that tangle in the treetops outside my window. The ends that have tumbled down from the hastily inserted hairpins are sodden, dripping onto the soft material of my dress—once a pale blue, but now a dirty gray, and streaked with grass stains, dark swaths of mud, and several paw prints. The dress is old, like everything else in my wardrobe, and slightly too small for me, pulling tight across my chest and hips. Unlike my mother, I am built on sturdy lines, more a reliable workhorse than a high-bred filly.

I turn away from my reflection and prepare to do battle with my appearance. I have less than thirty minutes before the guests are due to start arriving, and the thought is not a particularly inspiring one. At least this dinner party will be something different, I tell myself, aiming for optimism. At least it will actually involve *other people*. Perhaps it will be a resounding success and my parents will be so delighted by my model behavior that I'll avoid a further scolding over the glowworms and the lake and the bare feet.

I fall to my knees and lift my hairbrush to my lips before raising it aloft, pledging my troth like a knight of old. "I solemnly swear," I say, "that this time nothing will go wrong and I will be a perfect daughter."

Full of hope and good cheer, I clamber back to my feet and head for the bathroom to wash off the grime from the lake and transform myself into a proper young lady.

CHAPTER TWO

◆

It is exactly twenty-six minutes later, and all is going according to plan. I am as neat and tidy as it is possible for me to be. My clean, brushed hair is swept back in a long, smooth braid, and my soft lilac dress is perfectly acceptable, if an inch or two too short and a deep breath or two too tight. I am standing next to Mother in the hallway, greeting guests with a charming smile and making the sort of small talk that not even our fusty old vicar can find fault with.

He is, of course, in attendance, with his equally sour-faced wife. Their attitude toward my family is a confused mix of deference to our ancient name and spiteful pleasure in our reduced circumstances. They are vocal in their disapproval of almost everything I say and do, and, unfortunately, the vicar's disapproval often comes in the form of lengthy Bible quotes.

Now, though, I am listening sympathetically as they tell me about one of their horrible children, who has a head cold.

"Yes," I murmur, my mind more than half on the snail hunt I'm going to have to perform under cover of darkness later on. "Summer colds really are the most upsetting."

I feel Mother start to relax beside me, and her voice becomes increasingly musical as she falls into the role of hostess that she so enjoys.

"Ah, Philip," she exclaims happily. Philip Astley is our nearest neighbor—his far more financially secure estate borders our own, and he is a perfectly nice, if deeply boring, man who has known my parents for years and years and doesn't know how to deal with me now that I am no longer a small child that he can pat on the head.

After clapping the top of my arm enthusiastically enough to leave a bruise while muttering, "Capital, capital!" he leans in to press a perfunctory kiss on Mother's cheek.

"Looking beautiful, Delilah, as always," he says gallantly, and Mother makes a pleased humming sound at the back of her throat before her eyes fall on the young man who is following in Philip's wake.

"Thank you, Philip." Her voice is a smile now; she looks just like the proverbial cat presented with a very large dish of cream. "And this must be your nephew. I'm so glad you could come along and join the party. You haven't been here since you were a boy. We're sadly lacking in young company, and I know Beatrice will be thrilled to see you." Her eyes meet

15

mine and she lifts her eyebrows. Something in her gaze immediately puts me on guard.

I behold the vision before me. Philip Astley's nephew is around my age, about two inches smaller than me, and possessed of the sort of blank gaze more typically found in grazing animals. None of that matters to my mother, of course, because I realize that standing before me is the heir to the Astley fortune.

It feels suddenly as though a lead weight has settled in my stomach. This whole dinner party is a matchmaking trap, and I have tripped into it as blindly as any blissfully ignorant woodland creature. I briefly squeeze my eyes shut, hoping that when I open them the scene around me will have magically resolved itself into something else. My heart pulses erratically in my chest as I conclude that my parents have moved past heavy-handed hints about marriage and decided to take action.

"How do you do?" I manage, holding out my hand while shooting a quick glare at Mother, which she blithely ignores. Frustration hums inside me.

"Hello," the nephew says, offering up a damp, limp handshake. "I'm Cuthbert."

Despite the terrible circumstances, I feel a pang for him then. The poor boy never stood a chance—however is a person supposed to distinguish himself when saddled with a name like *Cuthbert*?

"Beatrice," I say, shaking his hand, then surreptitiously wiping my palm on my dress.

"Well," Mother says brightly, "don't let us keep you hanging around here in this drafty hallway, Cuthbert. I'm sure that you young folk have lots to talk about. Beatrice will show you in and get you a drink, won't you, darling?"

"Of course, Mother," I grind out.

"Capital, capital." Philip Astley beams, rocking back on his heels and tucking his hands into his pockets.

I lead Cuthbert through to the drawing room, wishing that my bones would crumble to dust so that Hobbs could sweep me up and dispose of me in his typically discreet and efficient manner and I wouldn't have to participate any further in this scene. There are around a dozen people in here, locked in the never-ending cycle of small talk. Father is presiding over the drinks trolley, and he gives me a knowing look that indicates this is part of a tremendous scheme and he's very pleased with its progression. He stops just short of rubbing his hands together in glee. I lift my chin and treat him to a cool, quelling stare. His expression falters a little.

My father is bluff and hearty, with a bristling mustache and watery blue eyes. He taught me to ride, one thing that we both love, although he was disgusted by my refusal to join the hunt on the grounds that I thought it a barbaric exercise in cruelty. And I have never seen him more furious than the time I laid down false trails to draw the dogs away from the fox they were hunting, leaving them chasing their tails in circles. "What does a girl want with all those brains?" I have overheard him sigh more than once.

"Ahem!" He clears his throat now. "So, this must be the

famous Cuthbert!" He slaps the poor boy on the shoulder with such enthusiasm that he stumbles.

I think the truth of the situation is starting to finally dawn on Cuthbert, and he darts a frightened, rabbity glance between me and my father. His hand goes to his collar, as though it is too tight.

"How—how do you do, sir?" he manages, his voice feeble as weak tea.

"Let me get you a drink, Cuthbert," I say firmly, taking pity on him. I can see that it is going to be up to me to navigate us through this particular storm—Cuthbert doesn't seem like a very take-charge sort of character.

"Oh, th-thank you," he stutters, his neck flushing a mottled red as his Adam's apple bobs up and down gratefully.

While Father is occupied with someone else, I pour out two glasses of punch, stiffening Cuthbert's with a splash of something stronger, which I hope will provide him with some Dutch courage.

"Thank you," he says again, taking a deep gulp and then dissolving into a coughing fit. It's possible that I overdid it on the liquid-courage front, and I pat him on the back.

"Everything all right?" Father asks, turning back to watch us rather beadily.

"F-fine, sir," Cuthbert manages.

A loud dinner gong sounds, the noise rippling through the room and causing an already-overwrought Cuthbert to jump several inches in the air.

"Better knock the rest of that back," Father says jovially,

pointing at Cuthbert's drink. As he turns away for a moment, I whip the glass out of Cuthbert's hand and empty the remains into a nearby potted fern.

I am rewarded with a grateful, if tremulous, smile, and—much to Father's obvious delight—Cuthbert offers me his arm to escort me into the dining room.

Dinner is just as painful as I anticipated. The food is marginally better than usual, as we are out to impress, but our cook has never met a vegetable she couldn't boil into submission. I am seated between my mother and Cuthbert, and Mother keeps chivying our talk along with encouraging little conversation openers.

"Beatrice, Philip tells me that Cuthbert is a keen philatelist; isn't that *fascinating*?"

"Yes." I wade in grimly. After all, none of this is Cuthbert's doing. "Do you have any particularly interesting stamps in your collection?"

"Er . . . not really," Cuthbert mutters, the mottled flush making another appearance. "I don't really collect them myself, you see. Uncle just gave me some of his old scrapbooks. . . ." He trails off miserably.

"Mmm," I murmur, drawing an infinity sign in the gravy on my plate with my knife. At one end of the table I notice that Father is deep in conversation with Mr. Astley about the hunt, a subject on which they could happily spend all night agreeing loudly with each other. The vicar is making some sort of disparaging comment about the moral fiber of his parishioners to the woman next to him. The vicar's wife is telling the story of the head cold again in a rather carrying drone.

Their voices seem suddenly to clamor over one another, filling my head with the endlessly repeating pattern of polite conversation. I grind my teeth together, feeling an itch spread across my skin. A longing to jump to my feet and run as fast as I can, as far away as possible, sweeps over me.

Instead, I force myself to concentrate on the conversation on either side of me.

"Oh, Cuthbert!" Mother is saying, shaking her head, a roguish twinkle in her voice, "there's no need to be so modest; I'm sure a young man like yourself will have no trouble in running the estate. What you really need, of course, is a wife who knows how these things work: a young woman of good breeding with experience in such matters. Wouldn't you agree, Beatrice?" The look she gives me is pointed. There's steel behind her words.

"Yes, Mother," I say evenly. "Perhaps placing an advertisement in the *Times* would be a sensible way of filling the position."

Mother forces a laugh then, a shrill, nervous sound, and casts me a look of warning. We both know I'm building up to being outrageous. I was fully prepared to behave myself tonight, but this setup with Cuthbert is enough to try the patience of a saint. Really, it's her own fault.

I think I might be about to start enjoying myself.

"Ah." Cuthbert clears his throat, his uncertain gaze moving anxiously between us. "What—what do you like to do,

Beatrice?" he asks, rather desperately, as though trying to steer the conversation back to stable ground. "As a hobby, I mean?"

I lean forward on my elbows and flash him a brilliant grin. "Oh, Cuthbert," I say. "I'm so glad you asked."

"Beatrice . . . ," Mother begins, all her senses obviously awake to the danger of the situation, but it's too late now.

"Actually, at the moment I'm making a study of the *Lampyris noctiluca*, or the glowworm, as you would call it in common parlance." I sit back in my chair. "It's their mating habits that I find particularly fascinating."

My voice rings out clear as a bell in the quiet room.

"Mating habits?" Cuthbert's flush deepens, and he darts an anxious glance at my mother, whose eyes are widening helplessly. I realize that even the vicar has turned in my direction.

"Yes," I say. "Mating habits. By which, of course, I mean the sexual coupling that leads to reproduction."

Cuthbert's mouth is slightly agape, his fork hanging limply from one hand. The others at the long table sit in frozen silence.

"It's the female glowworm who emits a bioluminescence in order to attract a mate, you know," I continue chattily. "In fact, the more a female glowworm glows, the more attractive a mate she becomes, as greater luminescence indicates increased fecundity."

"F-fecundity," Cuthbert repeats in a dazed whisper.

A groaning sound comes from the end of the table, where

Father sits with his head in his hands. Mother's face is ashen. The rest of the party is staring at me with round, unblinking eyes.

"Yes," I say, turning slightly so that I am addressing all of them. "*Fecundity.*" I roll the word around in my mouth. "Or fertility. Which is, of course, innately desirable in a mate when considering copulation for the propagation of the species."

"I think this conversation is unsuitable for the dinner table, Beatrice," Mother cuts in now rather raspingly, having recovered something of her voice.

"I think this conversation is unsuitable for a young lady, regardless of the time or place," the vicar thunders in his dramatic, Sunday-sermon roar, and Mother flinches.

"Oh no," I say earnestly. "Why should young women be left out of such conversations? After all, Vicar, we're the ones who must become mothers ourselves, if the human race is to continue at all. It's in the Bible, isn't it? Be fruitful and multiply and all that." I wave my hand airily. "So, you must agree that to keep young women in ignorance when it comes to acts of sexual congress is nothing less than irresponsible."

"Acts of sexual congress!" the vicar's wife whispers as Mother sways in her chair.

"Exactly." I smile at the whole table, showing off my teeth. "I couldn't have put it better myself. Wonderful dinner this evening, Mother; I must pass on my compliments to Cook." I spear a carrot neatly on my fork and pop it in my mouth as the roar of disapproval finally breaks around me.

CHAPTER THREE

◆

"I don't think it went that badly at all."

My pronouncement is met by a groan from Mother, who lies dramatically on the chaise longue.

The dinner party has limped miserably to its polite conclusion, salvaged only by Mother's overbright chatter. After she kicked me under the table, I became mutinously silent. Once the obligatory after-dinner brandy had been drunk by the men, and the ladies had had forced icy, polite conversation in the parlor, the guests all made rather hasty exits into the night and Father disappeared to his study to smoke cigars "in peace."

"*Copulation*," Mother moans, turning and flinging one arm across her forehead. The word hangs so dramatically in the air that I have to smother a laugh, turning it into a cough. "You said *copulation* in front of the *vicar*. I'll never hear the end of it. He'll work this into Sunday's sermon, and everyone will know why, and somehow it shall be all *my* fault that you behave outrageously and talk so improperly. Honestly, Beatrice, how *could* you? It's completely inappropriate for a young woman to discuss those . . . those sorts of things. Especially in polite society."

"Oh, well, it's not as if the vicar doesn't know what the word means, for goodness' sake," I say stoutly. "He and that horrible wife of his have two equally horrible children, so they must have done it at least twice."

"*Beatrice!*" Her horrified tones come from between the sofa cushions.

"And it was in an educational context," I continue. "I was simply trying to explain—"

"Yes, that's quite enough of that," Mother snaps, drawing herself up to a sitting position. "I do not wish to relive the conversation." She glares at me. "This is the final straw, Beatrice. I've had all I can take of you behaving like a hoyden, scandalizing our neighbors, scrambling around the countryside in a complete state, collecting creepy-crawlies in jars, and stuffing your head with *Latin*—and goodness only knows what *those* books are about, given the sort of conversation you find appropriate for the dinner table. . . ."

I have to contain another nervous wave of laughter at the idea of my scandalous Latin reading. (As if I don't know about the questionable romance novels she keeps hidden behind the plant pots in the greenhouse. Now, those *have* been illuminating reading.)

"Well, I *am* sorry," I say, feeling the sharp sting of regret that inevitably follows my bad behavior. "I know it was wrong of me, but I just couldn't help myself. I mean, really, Mother, *Cuthbert*?"

She regards me in icy fury. "Cuthbert Astley was your last great hope, my girl!" She waves a finger dramatically in my face.

I snort derisively, even though a cold hand clutches my heart at the desperation in her voice. "Cuthbert Astley is not likely to be described as *anyone's* great hope, Mother, last or otherwise." I keep my tone deliberately light.

"Oh, that's just like you, Beatrice," she exclaims, and I hear real worry in her voice. "You're so pleased with yourself, but what will become of you when your father and I aren't here to look after you?" She sniffs, pulling a rather crumpled white handkerchief from behind one of the sofa cushions.

I sink down onto the floor beside her and take her hand. "I'm sorry," I say. "I know you worry, but honestly, I don't think a husband is the answer. I could get a job, like I talked about—"

It's Mother's turn to snort now. "A job," she scoffs.

"Well, why not?" I say. "I could join a profession. Plenty of women work, doing all sorts of things."

"Not women in your position," Mother says firmly, and she rubs her forehead tiredly.

I know that she will never understand my desire to work. Or even to study. The thought of studying, of going to a university to learn, perhaps even about science or medicine, from real experts, is a sudden ache in my chest, and I press my hand there for a second, as though trying to contain the feeling.

I haven't even tried to talk to my parents about it. I know they wouldn't approve, and it's not as if I can afford to go anyway. Somehow I can't bear to have them dismiss this idea as they have done my others—it feels too precious.

"Please, darling, do stop teasing me," Mother continues, oblivious to my train of thought. "You know my nerves can't stand it." And she begins to cry again, real tears, which makes me feel awful.

"Now look what you've done, Beatrice!" Father booms from the doorway where he has appeared. He crosses to Mother's other side and takes her hand. "This is all your fault."

His words are like a match to the kindling, setting something big and angry inside me alight. "You two are clinging to some ridiculous version of the past," I snap, out of guilt as much as anything. I jump to my feet. "There's a whole generation of young people out there who are changing things and living exciting, modern lives, but here we are, living in this mausoleum. It's like time has stopped here, and I can't stand it!"

"Stop being so hysterical." Mother's voice is shrill. Clearly there's only one member of the family who is allowed to have nervous episodes.

"I'm not being hysterical!" I say, taking a deep, shaky breath and trying to speak more calmly. "But you two are trying to raffle me off like some prizewinning mare without any consideration for what I want—"

"We are *trying* to do what is best for you." Father's face is turning an interesting shade of puce. "Not that we get any thanks for it, and God forbid you actually honor your family and our history. There have been Langtons at Langton Hall for over FIVE HUNDRED YEARS!"

Normally, I would simply nod and think about something else while he spouts on about the family honor, but right now, suddenly, I have had enough. I have been hearing this for my whole life, and I am sick of it, sick of the weight of Langton Hall and its legacy, sick of the generations of history bearing down on me. It's as if I can feel the walls of the house pressing in, cutting me off from the rest of the world.

"I *know* that there have been Langtons at Langton Hall for over five hundred years." I am close to tears, and I try to steady my voice. "But you must see that even if I went along with your plans and married some wealthy, inbred aristocrat to prop the estate up, then—well, then I wouldn't *be* a Langton anymore."

"But you'd be able to keep the place going," Mother says.

"You'd keep the Langton bloodline alive!" Father's voice is hushed, as though he is describing something too sacred to approach at a normal volume.

I look at them now and feel a pang of sympathy. They look smaller in this moment, their eyes ablaze with fanaticism.

"I'm sorry," I say wearily. Guilt sits heavily in my stomach.

"I don't know what we're going to do with you, Beatrice, I really don't," Mother replies, and her voice sounds sad and quiet, as though she's given up on me somehow. The ache inside me grows. I made fun of Cuthbert, but the bleak truth is that they are probably right. My future as it stretches out in front of me looks horribly empty. I can't carry on like this forever. Maybe Cuthbert—or someone like him—really is the only option.

"There, there, Delilah," Father says. He walks up and down the room a few times and then stops suddenly, looking at her. "Listen, I think . . . I think it's time for us to consider Leo's offer."

"No!" Mother exclaims. "Michael, I thought we agreed—"

Father holds up his hand and Mother falls quiet. She always does, when he says so.

"We have no choice," he goes on. "Clearly we're not getting through to Beatrice. These childish antics are getting out of hand, and now she's embarrassed us in front of half the county. Best thing for everyone if she's far away for a while, under some strict supervision. I'm sure"—he turns to me, suddenly fearfully tall, a glint of steel in his eyes—"that, given time to reflect, Beatrice will reach the same conclusions we have, and that on her return she'll behave in a way more becoming of a young lady in her situation."

"Return from where?" I ask suspiciously. "Where exactly am I going?"

"Your uncle feels that your cousin Hero needs some

young companionship. He has invited you to stay with him this summer. Your mother and I had not yet decided, but under the circumstances I think it might be a good idea."

"Uncle Leo?" I say, a sudden flare of excitement catching inside me. "Uncle Leo who lives in *Italy*?"

"It's not a holiday, young lady," says Father. "It's a chance for you to reconsider your appalling behavior."

"Oh yes," I say, my mind racing. I clasp my hands together to keep them from trembling. "In *Italy*." The feeling of claustrophobia that has been dogging me more and more these last few months loosens its grip a little.

"Leo is such an upright man," Mother says thoughtfully. "He won't stand for any nonsense, and perhaps spending time with a sweet girl like Hero will help to mend your atrocious manners. My sister—God rest her soul—was an extremely proper woman. You're right, darling—this may be exactly what Beatrice needs."

An image of gaunt, miserable Aunt Thea flashes through my mind, and I barely manage to repress a shudder. Uncle Leo always seemed pretty severe too. But still. *Italy*.

"We can tell people that Beatrice will be spending the summer in Europe," Mother continues. "Acquiring a bit of polish. That will give the talk about this terrible evening time to die down." She positively quakes at the reminder.

"And, of course," Father puts in here, "Leo lives such a quiet life in the countryside. He's going to remarry soon. A widow of good standing, I understand, who will no doubt be a sobering influence on you, Beatrice."

My heart thumps. Whatever the circumstances, the dazzling promise of summer in Italy burns too brightly to be overshadowed by either the ominous "respectable widow" or stern, solemn Uncle Leo. Still, I try hard to conceal my excitement. It won't do for my parents to think this is anything other than a just punishment.

"Very well," I say meekly, turning my eyes to the floor. "If that's what you think is best."

"I hope it goes without saying that you will be on your best behavior, Beatrice Emma Langton," Father says warningly. "You will not disgrace the Langton name abroad. You must give me your word that you won't get into any of your scrapes in Italy."

"Oh, of course, Father," I say, looking up at him now and smiling sunnily. "I promise."

PART TWO

Villa di Stelle
July 1933

There is a kind of merry war betwixt Signor
Benedick and her;
they never meet but there's a skirmish of wit between
them.

—*Much Ado About Nothing*, act I, scene 1

CHAPTER FOUR

◆

The boat chugs away, and it is not long before Mother and Father are reduced to tiny specks in the distance.

As soon as they fade from sight, I begin to feel a lightening of spirit. I am, unfortunately, accompanied by a vinegar-faced woman who is a distant relative of the vicar, and her presence is all that prevents me from dancing a little jig. (The vicar himself was, unsurprisingly, very in favor of my banishment and even bestowed a smile of approval upon Mother, an event so startlingly rare that it left her quite dazed and unable to remember the Lord's Prayer.)

The white cliffs of Dover stretch out behind me, a bleached streak daubed against a pastel-blue sky. Each inch of water that I place between myself and my home feels like a loosened button on a too-tight dress. I drag in deep breaths of the cold air and taste salt on my lips.

For most of the journey I hang over the rail on the ship's deck, feeling the sting of the water on my face, fingers of sea breeze curling around me, tugging my hair from its pins. I watch with a sort of disbelieving thrill as slowly, slowly, the horizon shifts and France comes into view.

At Calais I am bundled, like an unwanted and unwieldy parcel, into the arms of another, equally disapproving lady, who escorts me on a train to Paris. I have no time to absorb any of the sights or sounds that batter me from every side on this part of the journey, and, intrepid as I hope I am, the presence of a guide isn't completely unwelcome. I have, after all, barely left the county before this, let alone the country. The noise and the lights and the swirl of people who all seem to know exactly where they are going is unnerving. But I feel excitement too. *I am equal to this,* I think.

When we step off the train at the Gare du Nord in Paris it has begun to rain, and in the sea of unfurled black umbrellas I feel strangely anonymous. No one here knows who I am, and the thought is thrilling.

I am to continue to Italy on my own. The second disapproving woman escorts me to the train, her relief at completing her part of this task apparent. I climb carefully up the ladder-like steps, followed by a porter, who carries the capacious carpetbag that I uncovered in one of the attics at home and points me to my seat. I am still on my feet as the train pulls away, and I sway slightly as the gears grind and groan beneath me.

The whistle blows like a fanfare, and I find myself suddenly, gloriously, unbelievably alone. It is an almost frightening feeling, as though my normal life has been torn away from me—like a magician whipping away a tablecloth from beneath a full dinner service. I stow my bag in the compartment that I have all to myself, then stretch out in my seat and laugh out loud, the sound ringing in the empty carriage.

I sit with my book unopened in my lap as I watch the blurry, rain-soaked shapes of the scenery tear past the window, as day turns to night and back again. I doze briefly, but mostly I am too excited to sleep. When I navigate the single change at Milan alone, I feel something uncurling inside me, singing through my veins, and I greet it with a sense of giddy recognition—*freedom*. For a wild moment I think I could just disappear: get on a train to Spain or Switzerland or deepest Russia and never be heard from again. Of course I don't, but the mere fact that I *could* is enough to leave me breathless.

There is a sense of unreality about the whole journey. I could be anywhere. The tantalizing glimpses of the landscape that rush alongside the train are gone almost before I can make sense of them. The train compartment feels small and cramped after so many hours, and I am stiff and impatient—impatient to arrive, impatient to look properly, impatient to take it all in.

It's late evening by the time the train draws in to Arezzo. A gloomy stillness has fallen and the rain has turned into a sullen drizzle. The carriage is practically empty, and I pull down the window, surprised by the chill in the air.

Uncle Leo is meant to be meeting me at the train, but I

don't see him waiting on the platform. I gather my belongings and make my way to the door. There doesn't seem to be a steward on hand. I hesitate—my bag is quite bulky, and the steps down to the platform are high. I am about to throw the bag from the door when a boy appears with his hands outstretched. He looks like he is about twelve or thirteen, and he smiles, calling up in Italian. Gratefully, I hand him my bag before turning to clamber down the steps.

I reach the platform only to find the boy disappearing into the crowd, my luggage clutched victoriously in his hands.

"Hey!" I shout, taking off at a sprint, pushing my way past the other people on the platform. The boy looks over his shoulder, clearly surprised to find me giving chase. He hesitates for a moment, and that is enough for me to surge forward and grab the end of my bag. I tug sharply, hoping to get a better grip, and the boy pulls back, shouting and trying to shake me off.

Suddenly, from behind comes another voice, loud and carrying, also shouting angry words at me in Italian. An accomplice of this boy's, I realize, and for the first time my heart quickens with fear as well as anger. I am about to be outnumbered.

A strong hand curls around my wrist, and I just have time to register that this newcomer is tall, even taller than me, before I begin to fight back.

Relinquishing my grip on the bag, I pull my elbow back, digging it sharply into my assailant's stomach. I hear a groan as my wrist is released, and I swing around to face him. It's

36

a man, who is now bent over, winded, his arm wrapped protectively over his stomach. He foolishly lifts his face, and I have a brief impression of the kind of boyishly golden good looks typically afforded to classical statues before I spring into action.

Drawing on the information I have gleaned from reading several of Father's well-thumbed books on pugilism, I curl my hand into a fist, careful to keep my thumb outside and across the bottom of my fingers, and deliver a blow to his nose, which sends him staggering backward with an incoherent cry, landing with a thud on the ground.

Pain sings through my hand and my heart is hammering as I swing back to find my bag lying, abandoned, on the ground and the thief gone. I snatch it up. Adrenaline thunders through my veins as I turn to face my assailant again, clutching the bag in front of me like a shield, poised to run or to fight if I have to.

"Stop, stop, for God's sake!" he shouts, getting to his feet and holding his hands out in front of him in a sign of surrender. His nose is bleeding rather freely down the front of his white shirt.

I pause, thrown by his accent. He is, I realize, English.

"Who are you?" I demand, and I'm thrilled that my voice is only slightly shaky.

The young man straightens, scowling. "I'm Ben," he says acidly. "And I can only assume that *you* are Beatrice."

CHAPTER FIVE

♦

"If you lean forward and pinch your nose it will slow down the bleeding," I say.

Ben glares up at me over the top of my handkerchief. "Yes, *thank you*," he growls, batting me away. "I don't think any more of your advice is needed." He is slumped on a bench in the waiting room. After the initial confusion, our various onlookers have departed, leaving me alone with Ben—the person who, it transpires, my uncle has sent to collect me.

"I'm only trying to help," I reply.

"I think it's a little late for that," he snaps. "Perhaps if you hadn't punched me in the face in the first place . . ."

"I have apologized for that," I say, "several times, in fact." I try not to roll my eyes. He's been hamming up the very minor injuries that he sustained for quite some time. "No, don't sit up straight yet," I say firmly as he moves. "You need to give the blood time to clot."

Now that the heat of the moment is over, I can see that Ben is younger than I first thought, perhaps eighteen or nineteen. He is handsome—tall and broad-shouldered with curly golden hair that flops over his forehead and, beneath the handkerchief, a perfectly symmetrical face. Symmetry is, as I understand it, very important when it comes to beauty. The young man in front of me is very symmetrical and very beautiful—and I rather suspect that he knows it.

"Anyway," I continue, smoothing down my skirt, "it was more than a little bit your own fault, you know. What did you expect me to do when you appeared, looming over me and grabbing at me like that?"

This earns me another dark look, and Ben whips the handkerchief away from his face, clambering to his feet. I eye his nose critically and observe that the bleeding has stopped.

"I was not *looming*," Ben says with exaggerated patience. "I was trying to rescue you."

"Rescue me?" I try to keep a straight face. "I see. Did you think that I *needed* rescuing?"

"Yes, well." He grimaces, lifting a hand to his nose. "I didn't realize you were going to turn into a bloody mad-woman, did I?"

I decide it's best not to pay attention to this fit of the sullens, but instead to concentrate on the matter at hand. I take a step closer to him.

"What are you doing?" He leaps back, alarmed; the backs of his legs hit the bench, and it clatters against the wall behind him.

"Nothing to worry about," I say soothingly. "I just need to feel your nose."

"Feel my nose?" His outrage is so comical that I can't stop the laughter from bubbling out, which only makes him look even more thunderous.

"Yes," I say. "I'll just check it isn't broken. You're probably concerned about your face." I tilt my head to one side. "It *is* very pretty."

His mouth drops open at this, and he makes a spluttering noise as though he can't find the words he wants. Taking advantage of his confusion, I reach up and take hold of his nose.

We stand there for a moment as I check his perfect face for damage, and as I do so I can't help thinking how odd this is. All my life, I've only ever had polite, dull conversations with boys my age—and if I ever try to be anything other than polite and dull, the response is usually blind terror, as with Cuthbert. But Ben has talked back to me. It hasn't exactly been friendly talk, but in a strange way that's what makes it so enjoyable.

He clears his throat and I realize my hands are still on his face.

"Not even broken," I say, stepping back. "You remain symmetrical."

"There's no need to sound so disappointed."

"I've never really punched someone like that before," I explain. "I learned it from a book, you see, rather than from any practical experience." I glance down at my fingers. "Honestly, I hoped I'd be capable of doing a *bit* more damage."

"Believe me, the damage was more than sufficient." He shoots me another dark look.

"I'm sure it hurts less than my hand does," I say. "And you don't see me making a fuss."

Ben's eyes dart to my bruised knuckles, and, for a second, I think he's going to show concern for my own injuries. Then, to my surprise, he smirks. "Serves you right."

He reaches down and picks up the bag that has caused so many problems and slings it over his shoulder.

"Come on, then," he says. "Let's get you delivered to Leo in one piece. He was most concerned about you: said he didn't want you left waiting alone. Said you were a well-bred and sheltered young lady." He snorts. "And I'm the king of England." He looks at me, his eyes narrowing suspiciously. "I'd even go so far as to say you were quite enjoying yourself."

"I certainly enjoyed the part where your feet went up over your head before you hit the platform," I say sweetly.

Ben shakes his head. "You caught me by surprise," he mutters, and then turns on his heel.

I follow him outside to a battered car that looks like it's held together with nothing but rust and hope. Ben throws my bag onto the back seat and I slide into the passenger side. He starts the car, and we shudder away from the station and out into the night.

In the darkness around us, barely anything is visible; the weak arcs of light from the car headlamps achieve little except to attract every moth within a one-mile radius. The sky is still overcast, and only a few of the more robust stars are on display, while the moon drifts in and out of sight as the breeze moves the clouds across its reassuringly familiar face. It's funny that after all this travel the same moon hangs suspended in the sky—as though that too should somehow be different. The roof of the car is down and the air slipping past me is cool, carrying a sharp smell of pine needles.

I shiver a little, though whether it is from the temperature or the excitement I'm not sure.

I glimpse a rough blanket folded on the back seat beside my bag. As I twist and lean over to get it I'm forced to clamber about a bit. Ben grinds the gears rather dramatically.

"Car troubles?" I ask sympathetically, dropping back into the seat. "If it helps, I think you might be trying to change up too quickly."

"The only problem I have is you flailing around while I'm trying to concentrate," he snaps.

"I'm cold," I say. "I needed the blanket." I drag it around my shoulders, welcoming the warmth it brings.

We travel on in silence, which is fine by me—I am happy just to sit and strain my eyes against the darkness for any clues about our whereabouts. *I am in Italy,* I think, as Ben hums beneath his breath and the car heaves itself along. *I am really here; it is really happening.*

Suddenly, Ben turns the steering wheel sharply to the left,

and, as we judder along over the dirt road, a row of cypress trees appears, their knifelike silhouettes cutting dense shadows against the inky sky. Moments later, lights blaze into view: burning torches dug into the ground to reveal a rough driveway and a long, imposing wall with an arch carved in the middle. It looks like a fortress, the shadows of the trees playing eerily across the stone in the firelight. It's as though we've been dropped unceremoniously into the past.

"No electricity outside the house," Ben explains, gesturing to the torches. It must be the early hours of the morning now, and everything is silent as we trundle through the archway into a sort of courtyard. The car comes to a stop and the weak glow from its headlamps is extinguished.

I take a deep breath; there's a clinging, heavy scent in the air that's sweet, like jasmine. Ben steps out of the car and I do the same, slipping out from under the blanket and stretching my cramped limbs.

"We're here," I say into the night. I can't believe it.

Ben picks up my bag and deposits it with a thud at my feet. "What gave it away?" he asks.

I ignore him. My eyes adjust to the velvet darkness, and I make out rough walls and a tall crenellated tower that looms over us like something from a fairy tale.

Ben reaches into the car and leans on the horn for a moment. The short, sharp blast shatters the silence as definitively as a gunshot.

"They're expecting you," he says, and then he leaps back in and starts the car, drives away through another archway at the other end of the courtyard, and leaves me standing alone in the dark.

For a second, I let the sensation of finally being here wash over me. I close my eyes and listen to the crickets chirrup into the night and I breathe in that heady, perfumed air, relishing the unfamiliarity of it all. Then I reach down and pick up my bag, deciding that I've done quite enough waiting. It's time to take my destiny into my own hands, and that means finding a way into this building.

Then, as though I have summoned it myself, a light appears, a fine silver crescent carved into the impenetrable wall, widening like a waxing moon.

It is a doorway, I realize, and it is opening to let me in.

CHAPTER SIX

◆

"Bea!" A figure tumbles through the door and throws herself into my arms. I stiffen for just a moment, unused to such a spontaneous display of affection, and then close my arms around her in a tight hug.

"Hero!" My fourteen-year-old cousin pulls away, and the light from the open door spills across her sweet, pretty face, turned to look up at me.

"I can't believe you're here! I'm so happy!" She dances from foot to foot and I suddenly feel . . . *wanted*. The feeling is so unfamiliar that it swamps me, too big for me to quite understand. I suppose I'm more used to feeling like I am in the way. I swallow and give myself a mental shake. I must be overwrought from the journey.

"I'm so happy too," I say, pulling her toward me for

another hug, resting my cheek against her blond curls. "And you've grown!"

Hero laughs. "I should hope so. It has been three years, you know." I remember the last time I saw her, at her mother's funeral, pale and pinched and small under all the black clothing that hung heavy on her slender frame.

"And it's a good job too," my cousin continues now. "Fancy being stuck with a name like Hero and being so short. What an embarrassment."

Ah yes, Aunt Thea was quite a fan of the tale of Hero and Leander—especially the part where the two lovers are punished for their "promiscuity" by being killed off. That woman never missed an opportunity to revel in the misfortune of others. I glance at my cousin—her easy good nature could not be more different from her mother's.

"Don't keep her out there all night, Hero!" a bluff, cheerful voice calls, and we look back to face the doorway.

I turn and move forward to greet my uncle, heading through the open door and into a well-lit hallway that leaves me blinking as my eyes adjust. The room is chamber-like, with high stone walls and a brightly woven rug on a flagstone floor. A large wooden chandelier hangs above us like an enormous old carriage wheel: a touch of the old, though the lights attached to it buzz with electricity. Several doors lead off this room, and I'm already itching to open them and explore what lies behind. The huge stone staircase that dominates the hall climbs one flight and then forks into two different directions, smooth, broad steps snaking away into the darkness.

It is chilly in here, almost the same temperature as it is outside. I turn to face my uncle and see that he is smiling. He also looks younger than the last time I saw him, stouter and happier, with a rough red beard. I do remember him being fractionally warmer than his frosty wife, which is certainly not saying much—I think a block of ice would be warmer than Aunt Thea was—but I certainly don't remember him being as relaxed and rumpled as he is now. In my mind's eye I picture him neat and particular. I hesitate, not quite sure how to greet him, but before I can decide on the appropriate words, he folds me into a hug.

When he releases me, I catch my breath. His welcome is surprising, to say the least. We have never been particularly close, but his happiness seems genuine. His gaze moves between Hero and me with the sort of indulgent fondness I have never seen on my own father's face. I frown, trying to match the man in front of me with the reserved and formal figure of my memory.

"It's about time your parents sent you out here," he says. "This little sprite has been longing to see you." He gestures toward Hero, who is beaming and barefoot, her warm fingers clamped around my wrist, tethering us together.

"It's going to be so much fun!" she says. "The others are so excited to meet you."

"The others?"

"Bea, we have so much to talk about. Do you remember the puppies in the barn?" Hero tugs at my arm, ignoring my question, her words coming out so quickly that they fall over each other. "Mother was so mean not to let me keep one, and that scolding she gave us . . . Oh, but you got revenge, didn't you? Remember the *toad*?"

I flush a little at that, my eyes darting toward my uncle. On a long-ago visit to Langton Hall I took ten-year-old Hero to see a litter of puppies being born—an educational activity of which Aunt Thea decidedly did not approve. Following a lengthy telling-off and a sermon on propriety, I retaliated by slipping a toad into her bed. I don't regret it, but I also don't want Uncle Leo to think I'm a troublemaker. My parents have probably already hinted at that fact.

But Uncle Leo just laughs and reaches out a hand to ruffle my hair. "A pair of tearaways when you were together," he says with a sigh. "Heaven help us now that you're reunited."

"Oh, we're much older now." Hero dimples.

"And much, much worse," I finish daringly. All three of us laugh then, the sound bouncing off the walls, warming the air around us.

"I see our guest has arrived." A voice comes from the stairs behind me. "And already she is filling this old house with laughter."

I turn around and feel my mouth drop open in surprise. The woman standing there is tall, almost as tall as me, and generously curvy, with long, straight black hair that hangs down to her waist. She is wearing a decadent black silk kimono printed with red flowers, tied loosely over a red silk nightgown. Her features are large and expressive, and only the tiny spidery lines around her eyes and mouth give any indication that she's older than me. She moves with the kind of sultry grace that I have typically heard attributed to large cats.

"Ah, Fil, my love!" Uncle Leo booms.

"Filomena, this is Bea." Hero drags me forward a couple of steps. "Filomena and Daddy are getting married."

This, then, is the "respectable widow" who will curb my headstrong behavior. I hear Father's voice in my head, and just like that I am laughing again. But really, if ever there was the polar opposite of the "widow of good standing" of my parents' imagination, then she is surely embodied in the woman in front of me.

"Sorry, sorry," I splutter, moving toward the vision before me on the stairs, trying to recover my manners. "I always seem to laugh at just the wrong moment."

Filomena tips her head. "I think there is no wrong moment for laughter," she says, a smile curving her generous lips.

"Well, I'm very pleased to meet you," I manage, pulling myself together and holding out my hand to her.

But Filomena shakes her head.

"None of that." She steps forward, pressing warm kisses onto each of my cheeks, and I catch the heady scent of amber and cinnamon that clings to her skin. "It has taken me a great effort to rid your uncle and cousin of that terrible

49

English formality. I preferred the laughing." Her voice is low and musical, a slight Italian accent altering the cadence of her perfect English.

"Don't horrify the girl," Leo says, stepping up beside her and taking her hand before pressing it to his lips. "She'll run home telling her parents that we have devolved into chaos without the influence of good British manners."

"Bah!" Filomena wrinkles her nose.

"Oh no I won't," I say quickly. "Honestly, a break from good British manners sounds quite . . . wonderful."

"You see, Leo." Filomena smiles up at him. "Bea will fit in just right here."

I like that she calls me Bea, not Beatrice, using the same affectionate contraction as Hero. Somehow it sounds different in her voice: a lazy, drawn-out "ee" that tilts up at the end. At home no one calls me Bea; I am only ever Beatrice. *Bea* feels like a different person: a new name for this new place.

"Now." Filomena runs an eye over me. "This poor girl has been traveling for days on end and it is the middle of the night. Hero, I know you will want to be the one to show Bea to her room."

"Of course!" Hero retrieves my bag and begins to stagger up the stairs.

And just like that I feel exhaustion rush through my body, leaving me swaying on my feet. In spite of all the excitement, the thought of bed is overwhelmingly welcome. I follow my cousin, turning when we reach the top of the stairs to look back down to the hallway. As I do so, I am shocked to see Uncle Leo and Filomena locked in a rather ferocious embrace.

I turn the corner down the winding corridor, following the trail of lights as Hero flicks them on along the way. This is certainly not the Uncle Leo that I remember. Nor, I am sure, is it the Uncle Leo my parents imagined they were sending me to.

I smile to myself. It seems that things at Villa di Stelle might not be so respectable after all. What a pleasant thought.

CHAPTER SEVEN

◆

When I wake the next morning, I am not sure where I am. I stare up at the ceiling for a second, the events of the last few days racing around my head in a jumble of images and sensations before arranging themselves into something more orderly.

I'm here. I'm really here, in Italy, and the proof is all around me, written into the walls and furniture of this unfamiliar room. I take a moment to absorb it—the heavy, embroidered cotton of the white sheets, the wooden bed frame, and the pale green shutters that are throwing stripes of golden light across my legs.

I stand up, swinging my feet down to the floor, the cool touch of the terra-cotta tiles a shock to my warm, sleepy body. I stretch and move around the sparsely furnished room, running my hand over the rough plaster of the walls. Apart from the huge four-poster bed there is little in here—a small dressing table in one corner with a pretty, bevel-edged mirror above it and a rickety chair. There's also a large wardrobe, in which my meager collection of clothes is hanging a little forlornly, and a thin woven rug that was once probably a deep red but has now faded to rosy pink. Through a door to one side is a small, basic bathroom. I turn one of the taps, which splutters to life with—joy of joys—hot water. The villa may be old, but the plumbing is blissfully modern.

When I return to my room I make straight for the window, wrestling with the shutters for a moment before locating the catch and flinging them wide open.

All the air leaves my lungs in one dramatic rush.

The view before me is truly a fantasy made real: something that belongs in the pages of a fairy tale. It's a place of such light and lushness, beyond anything I could ever have dreamed.

I am high up, *very* high up. We climbed an awful lot of stairs last night, and I realize now that I am in the top of the crenellated tower, at the top of the house, on the top of the hill, and that the scenery has been rolled out in front of me like an offering. Directly below me is the red-tiled roof of another part of the house, and in front of that are the most spectacularly kept formal gardens: hedges divide the space into neat squares and circles, and in the center stands a huge stone fountain, with water splashing merrily from various urns held by beautiful women and babies. Beyond the gardens, the cypress and ilex trees huddle like a protective wall, sheltering the house from the undulating green-and-gold car-pet of the hills that spread out into the distance.

The rain of yesterday is a distant memory, and an endless blue sky stretches overhead. The mingled summer songs of birds and crickets and lazy bees drift through the window, along with the smell of warm, baked earth and pine needles. It seems impossible that I arrived through those hills last night, with the darkness wrapped close around me, keeping the secret of all this beauty like an elaborate practical joke.

I don't know how long I stand there, taking it in. The moment feels precious and endless. As I contemplate the view, its breadth and wildness seem to match the dizzying feeling of freedom that pounds through me. I am so far away from Langton Hall—in every way imaginable.

I'm already itching to get out there and explore when I hear the unmistakable "oop oop oop" of the hoopoe, a bird that I have never seen before, one that does not live in England, one whose call I have only read about. I rush to my bag and rummage around for my binoculars, but they're not there. Perhaps they fell out in the car last night. I tut in exasperation and return to the window, leaning out as far as I can and straining my eyes, but I can't pinpoint where the sound is coming from.

Instead I hear a shout, and over to my right I notice a swimming pool, where a man is swimming lengths. I can see the top of a golden head and a second figure, a woman, dressed in white and wearing a broad white hat, standing at the side of the pool, shouting to the swimmer and gesticulating wildly. The man's laughter cracks through the air, and for some reason I take a step back. Somehow, I know that the laugh belongs to Ben.

I retreat into my room and wash and dress as hastily as I can. Pulling on a crumpled pale-pink day dress, I lean over the mirror and tackle my long, unruly hair, stabbing at it almost at random with the pins scattered across the dressing table. My face in the mirror is a little flushed, and I take several deep breaths. My life has been so small, so monotonous, so endlessly unvarying for so long, that the utter newness of the day stretching ahead of me is almost overwhelming. *Almost.* I grin, and the girl in the mirror grins back at me, her nose scrunching up a little under a peppering of freckles, her eyes gleaming with naked excitement.

I have no idea what time it is, but I assume it must be late. I make my way swiftly, giddily along the long hallway and down the stairs, where I push one of the doors in the entranceway open at random.

Beyond it is a huge room with a high, dark-beamed ceiling. There is a gray stone fireplace stretching across one wall that is big enough to stand in, and several blue sofas and a well-stocked drinks trolley as well as a gramophone. As in my room, the walls are white and the floors tiled, spread with more rugs. This must be the living room, though it doesn't seem particularly well lived in. I listen carefully, but all I can hear is the sullen ticking of the grandfather clock in the corner, and a look at its face informs me that it is past midday.

Undeterred, I push through another door and find myself

in the kitchen, where a shrunken woman in a head scarf is bent over some dough.

"Oh, hello!" I exclaim. "Sorry, I'm a bit lost." The woman smiles at me and bustles over to the side, where she picks up a cup and saucer and pours thick, black coffee into the cup from a silver pot on the stove.

She shuffles over to me, her footsteps tiny but brisk, like a little bird, and she holds out the saucer, which I take. "Thank you," I say as she regards me through eyes set deep like dark currants in her wrinkled face.

"Il giardino," she says, gesturing to a door set into a high stone arch at the front of the room. "Filomena and Leo there," she adds in careful, heavily accented English.

"Oh, thank you," I say again. "I mean, grazie."

The woman reaches up and, to my surprise, pats me softly on the cheek. "Prego," she says, and then, as I turn to leave through the door, she makes a clucking noise to stop me and pulls a cloth back from on top of a basket full of warm, golden rolls. The smell of them is enough to set my stomach growling viciously.

"You take, you take," she insists, and I accept happily, tearing immediately into one with my teeth, chewing gratefully, the sweet dough a melting taste of sugar and vanilla. The woman nods approvingly as my greedy fingers close around another to take with me. "Bella ragazza grande," she says, beaming, and my rudimentary Italian allows me to translate this as "beautiful big girl."

When I open the door, I find myself standing in front of

the formal gardens, underneath a pergola covered in a riotous cloud of red bougainvillea and yellow jasmine, the tiny starlike flowers nodding below the sun, the scent heavy and intoxicating.

"Bea!" Leo and Filomena are sitting at the long, rough pine table stretched beneath the pergola with cups of coffee and a plate of figs between them. Leo gets to his feet and kisses me on each cheek. Filomena stays seated, smiling up at me from beneath the brim of a large straw hat.

"I see you've met Rosa." She gestures to the roll in my hand. "Her baking is wonderful. Did you sleep well?" she asks as I sit down and take a tentative sip of the coffee, the black, bitter taste a shock to my system. I'm not sure if I like it or not.

"Yes, thank you," I reply. "A bit too well. Sorry I'm so late."

Filomena shrugs, slowly, luxuriantly. "Late for what?" she asks.

"Time runs rather differently around here," Leo says, leaning back and winking at me over the top of his cup. "Takes a bit of getting used to."

"But you have missed the others," Filomena puts in. "They tend to have breakfast together before they go out to work."

"What others?" I ask, puzzled. "What work?"

"No one has told you?" Filomena asks.

"Told me what?" I'm starting to feel a little silly.

"About the artists, of course."

CHAPTER EIGHT

◆

"The artists?" I repeat, startled.

"Didn't you know?" Hero appears, throwing herself into the seat beside me and reaching out for one of the figs.

"It's my fault," Leo says, his expression not quite contrite. "I didn't mention it to your parents because I thought they might not like it, exactly."

Filomena scoffs. "What is there to like or not like? It is not their business."

"Well, it is if they're sending their daughter here to our care, love," Leo points out mildly. Filomena rolls her eyes.

"So," I say, "you have artists staying with you?"

"We do," Filomena agrees, taking another sip of her coffee.

"Filomena is a very talented sculptress," Leo says proudly, his gaze lingering on her lovely face. "We opened up the house to some of her friends. It seems the environment is conducive to producing work."

"How many artists are staying here at the moment?" I ask.

"Hmm?" Leo looks up from his rapt contemplation of Filomena's profile. "Oh, it changes. We have Klaus, a talented painter, and Ursula, a playwright, and Ben, of course, who have all been here for a few weeks, and then the others tend to come and go. Filomena is throwing a big party at the end of the summer to exhibit their work. It will be quite the occasion."

"I didn't know you were artistic, Uncle." I pull the roll apart with my fingers and dip it in my coffee. Hero snorts.

"As my daughter will be quick to point out, I am not in the least artistic." Leo raises an eyebrow at Hero, his eyes dancing. "I just happen to be in love with an artist, and I'll do whatever I can to keep her happy so that she won't leave me."

"Oh, Leo." Filomena raps his hand playfully. "What nonsense."

"And most of these arty types haven't got two pennies to rub together," Leo continues cheerfully, "so while I am no artist, I like to think of myself as a sort of sponsor, in the grand old tradition."

"Well, I love it," Hero says firmly. "It's much more exciting since Filomena came here. We have all sorts of interesting people to stay."

"Yes, it was dull for you before with only your poor old father." Leo sighs, levering himself out of his chair. "And now

I must get back to the boring world of business and leave you ladies to it." He turns to Filomena. "I will try and finish in time for drinks before dinner, my love."

"I will be working, I think, anyway," Filomena says. She barely glances at him, while his expression is one of doglike devotion. I feel a pang for my uncle.

"And you, young lady"—Uncle Leo turns to Hero— "are supposed to be working too, at your lessons. Where is Signora Giuliani?"

"She's late," Hero says smugly. But then, as though on cue, there is a clanging of the bell on the door.

"That will be her now," Filomena says.

Hero's face falls. "I wish I could spend the afternoon with Bea."

"Bea isn't going anywhere," Leo reminds her. I realize that he is right, and feel a grin stretching across my face. "There will be plenty of time for you two to catch up." He leaves, Hero trudging after him, and Filomena and I are left alone.

"Well," I say. "What now?"

"What now?" Filomena stretches, like a cat. "Why, whatever you want, Bea."

It's a perfect answer. I jump to my feet, brushing the crumbs briskly from my skirt, my mind already on the hunt for hoopoes. "In that case, I think I'd like to explore."

"Of course," Filomena agrees. "Perhaps you would like to swim as well?"

"I don't have a suit," I say, thinking longingly of the blue water.

Filomena's laugh is throaty. "This doesn't have to stop you," she says, and something in my face must betray my surprise because she laughs again. "I think your uncle is right that you will find us horribly shocking."

"Oh no," I reply. "I'm just used to being the shocking one myself."

Filomena regards me with an unblinking feline gaze. "Perhaps you have some Italian blood in you," she says, and it sounds like a compliment. "Anyway, it is no matter about the bathing suit. I will have your uncle order some things for you. And some summer clothes, perhaps." She eyes my dress rather doubtfully. "You are not too warm in that?"

The truth is that I *am* rather warm. Although my dress is cotton, it's quite thick with long sleeves, and it's also a pinch too tight. The heat here shimmers in the air, a different beast altogether from the weak English sunshine. "I suppose I am a bit," I admit, feeling a trickle of perspiration on the back of my neck. "But Uncle Leo shouldn't have to buy me clothes."

"Do not worry about it." Filomena is firm. "I will take your measurements myself later and then I will speak to him. It is fine."

"All right," I say doubtfully. I'm not sure my parents would like my uncle spending money on me, but Filomena seems very certain.

"So, you are going to explore?" she says, closing the subject.

"Yes. There's actually a particular bird that I want to find." Then I remember; if I'm going exploring then I'll need my binoculars, and that means I need to track down both the car and its driver.

"Oh." I hesitate. "Actually, there *is* another thing. The man who came to collect me yesterday—do you know where I can find him?"

"Ah!" Filomena arches a knowing eyebrow. "Another victim falls to Ben's charms."

"*Charms?*" It's not exactly the first word that comes to mind.

"It is usually the way with Ben." Filomena sips her coffee. "He has quite a reputation with the ladies, you see."

"Well, I suppose he *could* be charming," I say, a little doubtfully, "if he really put his mind to it."

"I'm sure he would be pleased to hear you say so." She sounds like she is trying not to laugh.

"I shouldn't think he'd care much for my opinion either way," I reply. "I don't think he really . . . warmed to me. To be completely truthful, we had a little bit of a disagreement."

Filomena smiles. "How intriguing. Well, Ben will be working in the grounds. When you find him, I'm sure the two of you can . . ." She pauses here, looking at me from underneath her eyelashes. "*Make amends.*"

CHAPTER NINE

◆

I trip down the steps and into the gardens. I turn, unthinkingly, to one side, choosing a path that winds through a small copse of cypress trees, stopping often to bend over and examine the various flowers that are splashed about, tumbling in a riot of crimson and violet from terra-cotta pots or growing in tangled golden constellations underneath the trees.

I follow the chirruping sound of a cricket and watch admiringly for a moment as he leaps across the path. There's a flicker of red on his abdomen—I think he may be a species that I haven't seen before. I am tempted to follow him but become distracted by a pretty little green hairstreak butterfly, or *Callophrys rubi,* who flutters around my face for a moment, her cheerful green-and-copper wings glimmering in the sun. With a sigh of happiness, I wind my way through tall avenues of carefully manicured yew hedges, my fingers running over their soft needles.

"*Taxus baccata,*" I mutter absently.

"What did you say?" a voice asks, and I look up to find that I have rounded a corner and am now standing in a large square clearing. I have found my way to the stone fountain, and the sound of the water is enticing as it splashes against the stone.

Ben stands in front of me, dressed in light trousers and a loose white shirt rolled up at the sleeves. His feet are bare, and on his head is a battered panama hat. As he lifts his face I notice a small scab on the bridge of his nose and a violet bruise under his right eye. I wince.

"Oh." His voice is cool. "It's you. I should have known you'd be the one wandering around, talking to yourself in Latin."

It is not an auspicious start. "Are you always like this?" I ask.

"Like what?"

"So rude to people you've just met."

He tips his head to one side. "I don't know." He smiles reluctantly, revealing a perfect dimple in each cheek. "Do you always greet new acquaintances by punching them in the face?"

"Oh, you can't still be angry about that," I protest. "It was just a misunderstanding. I've apologized several times as well as administering first aid and sacrificing one of my handkerchiefs in the process—a fact which would irk my mother a great deal, by the way, because I'm *always* losing the blasted things." I smooth my skirt with my hands. "I believe that continuing to dwell on it is quite ungentlemanly."

"Un . . . ungentlemanly?" Ben looks startled. "*You* think *I* am ungentlemanly?"

"Yes," I agree.

"Ungentlemanly?" he says again, a little louder.

"You don't need to keep repeating the word; I'm the one who said it in the first place." I lift my chin. "But, actually, yes. I think that your refusal to accept my apology and to move on graciously is ungentlemanly."

There's a pause as Ben seems to consider this argument for a moment. Finally, he shrugs. "Well, *I* think it's a bit rich being schooled in social niceties by a girl who chases down bandits and assaults her would-be rescuers."

I feel a smile tugging at my mouth. "Oh, but that girl sounds so *much* more interesting than a swooning maiden."

"She sounds like a pain in the neck to me." A quick answering grin flickers across his face. "And I can't imagine you're much of a swooner."

"*I* can't imagine you'll ever find out."

"Oh, really?" Something mischievous glints in his eyes, and he takes a step toward me and then another. "That sounds like a challenge."

"Is that supposed to be seductive?" I ask, entertained.

Ben blinks. "Some people might think so."

I consider the matter. "Perhaps they're just distracted by a handsome face?"

65

"That's the second time you've called me handsome." Ben is clearly pleased with himself.

I give him a long look of appraisal. "I suppose that you are quite physically attractive."

"You *suppose*?"

"I don't think I have a broad enough sample for comparison. I've had quite a sheltered upbringing, you see, and I'd hate to be inaccurate. You are, perhaps, above average," I concede.

Ben gives me a long look. "How kind of you to notice," he says at last. "But I do seem to be loved by most ladies. You, Beatrice, are the exception."

"How nice to be considered exceptional," I murmur, the dryness in my tone matching his own.

He chuckles softly, a little reluctantly. "Peace, then?" he asks, holding out his hand.

"Peace," I echo, slipping my fingers into his. The whole conversation has been strangely exhilarating.

I look past him and finally notice an easel. There are tins of paint on the ground, and a jam jar full of murky water and paintbrushes. Sitting on the easel is a canvas covered with various angular shapes, swaths of green and red and gray.

"Is this what you're working on?" I ask, moving to look at the painting.

"It is," he says. "I'm just putting the finishing touches to it."

"Mmm." I lean closer, looking at it with curiosity. Art

isn't something I know a lot about, but the picture makes me feel confused, churned up. There is nothing recognizable about the image, nothing solid to hold on to. I haven't seen anything like it before. It's certainly not like anything that has hung on the walls at Langton.

He frowns. "Don't you like it?"

"Oh yes," I say quickly. "It's very nice."

"Nice," he repeats.

A glance at Ben's face tells me that *nice* was, perhaps, the wrong word. I squint at the picture, trying to make sense of the jumbled shapes. The riot of angles and colors feels disorientating.

"I like the—um—green bits."

"The green bits," he says, sounding a little dazed.

"Yes," I agree brightly. "They're really nice and . . ."

"Green?" Ben finishes for me. He shakes his head. "You really know how to do wonders for a man's ego," he grumbles, reaching up to rub the back of his neck as he turns to look back at the painting.

"I hadn't realized that nursing your ego was my job."

Just then, I see something: the telltale iridescent cobalt shimmer of a dragonfly as it flashes in the corner of my vision. I spin around—out of habit as much as anything else—to chart its path. It lands on the edge of the fountain, its fragile wings trembling in the sunlight.

Ben is still talking. "Of course, I can't expect you to understand the work I'm doing. You obviously haven't got the first idea what you're talking about." He takes my arm and draws me closer to the painting. "Here, you see—the *green bits* are, actually . . ."

I notice a tin of paint perilously close to his foot.

"Ben," I say, "careful of the—"

Unfortunately, he's too distracted by his lecture to notice. It is this fact, coupled with the flight of the dragonfly, which conspires to create the perfect storm. The insect swerves suddenly, buzzing near Ben's face. He twists and I reach out to grab him, but it is too late. The unexpected change in direction leaves Ben off balance, his foot connecting heavily with the paint tin that I was trying to warn him about. He grasps my outstretched hand as he stumbles, and I in turn clutch at the easel.

"Oh!" I just have time to exhale and meet his surprised gaze as I am pulled forward, barreling hard into Ben and sending us both careening toward the ground.

CHAPTER TEN

◆

"Oof!" Ben's exclamation of surprise is very close to my ear. This is easily explained by the fact that I now find myself lying on top of him.

I am stunned for a second, though whether it's by the fall or by the fact that this the closest I have been to a boy—or possibly anyone—in my whole life, I'm not entirely sure. I try not to notice the feeling tightening in my stomach or the way his chest feels pressed against my own.

"Oh!" is all I manage, turning my head just as Ben lifts his. The resulting crack that takes place between our skulls leaves my ears ringing.

Ben's head falls back again and he groans.

"For God's sake!" He lifts a hand to his head. "Am I never to escape an encounter with you without some sort of horrific head injury?"

"I believe you'll find this one is your fault," I say with as much dignity as I can manage. I attempt to extract myself from the tangle of limbs, but because he is doing the same thing, our efforts rather cancel each other out and we don't get very far. "You were too busy talking to listen to me, and then there was a dragonfly—"

"Oh, there was a dragonfly. Well, that explains everything then," he mutters.

I put a firm hand on his chest and he stills beneath my fingers. I roll to one side so that I am lying on my back beside him. The sky resolves itself overhead and I find myself squinting up into the sunshine. I close my eyes for a second. When I open them, I realize Ben still hasn't moved.

"Are you all right?" I ask.

"I think so." His voice is resigned. "No blood this time, at least."

I pull myself up and look down at him. There's something staining his blond hair. "Don't be so sure," I say. I run my fingers through his hair, looking for the injury, and they come away red.

He looks startled. "Really?" he says. "Again?"

"I can't see anything wrong," I mutter, still looking for any obvious wound. Puzzled, I look more closely at my fingers, rubbing them together. There is red on my dress too. Then, in a flash, the truth comes to me. "Oh, it's just paint!" I grin down at him, and the sudden rush of relief makes me laugh. "See?" I hold out my gory hands to show him.

"Paint?" His whole body tenses. "PAINT?" He leaps to his feet with a rather startling roar, which only intensifies as he takes in the scene in front of him.

I too scramble up. "Oh dear," I say.

It seems that the can Ben kicked over contained a quantity of red paint, which, when mixed with the water from the jar that has also been knocked over, has created a rather alarming red trail, streaming merrily along the paving stones toward us. Ben's painting, now lying on the ground thanks to my desperate grab at the easel, is worryingly damp, with a long red smudge running almost horizontally across it—I'm fairly sure that wasn't there before.

Ben stares at the canvas, openmouthed.

"Perhaps it's not so bad," I say at last, reaching down to pick up the painting and place it carefully back on the easel.

"You have put it *upside down.*"

"Really?" I ask, squinting at the picture.

"This is all your fault," he says, snatching the painting up and turning it the right way around. "I never know what disaster you're going to unleash upon me next."

That's not really fair, but I don't want to argue the point. "Shall I help you to tidy up?"

"No," Ben says quickly. "Who knows what could happen next? I think I'll proceed alone, with all my limbs intact."

It is then that I remember my errand. "I think my binoculars might have fallen out in the car last night," I say. "Have you seen them?"

"Mmm," Ben murmurs, not looking at me anymore, just at the painting in an absorbed sort of way. "They were under the back seat. I gave them to Rosa this morning."

That is good news. I would have hated to misplace them, particularly in a place like this, where new and exciting discoveries seem to be waiting around every corner. With a cheery goodbye I turn away, back toward the avenue cut into the yew hedges. The air is filled with a symphony of birdsong, and almost immediately I am treated to the sight of a blue-throated keeled lizard (*Algyroides nigropunctatus*) skittering along in front of me. Surely a sighting of the hoopoe cannot be far behind? I head toward the villa in an excellent mood.

As I emerge from the gardens, the building rises from behind the trees, the earthy red facade glowing with welcome under the heavy golden sun. I make for Rosa and the kitchen. Perhaps as well as my binoculars there will be a glass of something cold. And another one of those sweet rolls. Exploring is hungry work, after all.

As I get closer to the house I spy Hero in the distance, sitting under the pergola with her books spread over the long table, and an older woman perched rigidly beside her. Hero's head turns and she spots me. She lifts her hand in greeting, leaps to her feet, and runs forward, followed by her tutor, who calls after her despairingly in Italian.

Hero's expression is cheerful, but once we get a little closer to one another, she suddenly comes to a screeching halt, naked fear and horror dawning on her face.

"Oh, Bea!" she gasps. "What has happened?"

"*Madre di Dio!*" the woman behind her exclaims, promptly dropping into a dead faint at my feet.

CHAPTER ELEVEN

◆

"And then . . ." Hero's voice is gleeful. "Bea emerged from the garden, ghostly pale and positively *dripping* with blood—"

"Paint," I put in here. "It was paint."

"Yes, yes." Hero waves a hand. "But we didn't know that *at the time,* did we? It looked like you'd been at the scene of some horrific murder; your dress was covered in blood, your hands were covered in blood—"

"Paint," I interject again.

"And that," Hero continues, ignoring me and throwing her hands dramatically in the air as though warding off evil spirits, "was when I cried out, 'Dearest cousin, what horrors have you witnessed? What on God's earth has befallen you?' "

"You certainly did not," I protest.

Hero glares at me. "And then Signora Giuliani screamed and collapsed into a swoon."

"*That* part is true," I admit.

It is evening, and we are sitting in the garden sipping on cool, pale yellow drinks that taste like sugar and sunlight and lemons. Someone has wheeled out a gramophone, and a crackling jazz record plays softly in the background. It is still warm, but the air has cooled a little. The sky is streaked with dramatic swaths of gold and burnt orange as the sun gathers its last rays for its final, spectacular display of the day—like a diva bowing offstage in a blaze of glory.

In the time since I emerged from the bushes and gave Hero's tutor the shock of her life, I have washed and changed into a pale blue dress scattered with a pattern of white flowers and closed at the side with small, cloth-covered buttons. The dress is one of my newer ones (though it is still faded and worn, it is *less* faded and worn than most of the others), and it makes me feel more grown-up.

I have worn it as armor because I have never been to dinner with a group of artists before, and I am not sure what to expect. My hair is still damp from the bath and screwed up in a knot on top of my head, and I noticed in the mirror that a little sunburn has given my cheeks and the bridge of my nose a slightly pink glow.

Ben and the other artists are yet to arrive, but Leo and Filomena are here. As Hero tells her story with relish, Leo fusses over his fiancée, wrapping a fringed and brightly patterned silk shawl around her shoulders and kissing the corner of her mouth—the kind of affectionate gestures that would never be seen in public at Langton Hall.

I watch Filomena now as she smiles and listens to Hero chatter on. The relationship between them is puzzling. They are friendly with each other—warm, even—but on Filomena's side I sense the same slight reserve that she has with my uncle—as though she's holding Hero a little at a distance.

"It sounds completely thrilling," Filomena says.

"You'd be less pleased if you were the one who had to calm Signora Giuliani down and convince her that she should stay in this—I believe she used the term *den of vipers,* but I could be mistranslating."

Uncle Leo's tone is light, teasing. At home this sort of scrape would have been met with tears and recriminations; here everyone seems to have found the slightly abridged version of events quite funny.

"Bah!" Filomena exclaims. "That woman could use some more thrills in her life."

Leo makes a funny, snorting sound at that.

"Hello," a voice calls, and I turn in my seat to see two figures moving toward us. One is a boy, lean, dark-haired, and dark-eyed, who walks with a swagger. He is perhaps a year or two older than me, and as he steps forward to shake my hand, he gives me a slightly crooked and perfectly charming smile. I notice that he has a small beauty mark at the corner of his mouth.

"Ah, Signora Bea," he says, and his voice is warm and low, with a subtle Germanic accent. "I am delighted to meet you at last. Hero has told us so much about you." He nods to Hero, who is gazing at him with worship writ large in her eyes.

"I am Klaus," he continues, and I realize he is still holding my hand. He lets go of it, but slowly, as though he regrets having to do so. It's a practiced move, I think, as smooth as a beeswax-polished floor. "And this"—Klaus gestures to the girl beside him—"is Ursula, my sister."

Ursula nods coolly. She is beautiful in an intimidating sort of way, with her brother's dark hair and dark eyes and a wide, sulky mouth painted with a slash of red lipstick. She is several inches shorter than me and slim as a reed. Her hair is cut into a short, severe bob, the strands at the front tickling her high cheekbones. Her emerald-green dress clings lovingly to her body, making me feel woefully unsophisticated.

Klaus accepts a drink from my uncle and pulls up the chair beside mine, shuffling it so that we are sitting close enough that our arms brush lightly against each other. Ursula drops into a seat beside Filomena.

"So," Klaus says, "you are from England. Is it true that all those English country houses are haunted?"

I look into his laughing eyes and find myself telling him stories about the hen-hearted ghosts at Langton, who seem only to appear in front of the most susceptible ninnies, and the scrapes that Eustace the dog has been in.

Hero then demands a retelling of the toad story, and I follow this up with an admission of several other well-played pranks.

As we are talking, several other people drift over and join the party: two older men, who sit in a corner, arguing in low tones and making dramatic gestures at one another; a willowy blond girl with an air of extreme, cultivated fragility; and a woman about the same age as Filomena, with bronze skin and her hair tucked into a red turban, who carries herself with a liquid grace. More artists who have stumbled into the haven created by Filomena.

My audience is appreciative, laughing and egging me on. Filomena tells us about the tricks she used to play on her governess, and I can almost see Hero making notes. Instead of being horrified, my uncle laughs the loudest of anyone. Only Ursula seems largely unmoved, her dark eyes watchful as she leans forward, resting her chin on her hand. Occasionally a half smile will tug at her lips, but for the most part she seems almost bored.

"Your turn," I say to Klaus. "Now you know all about me."

"Klaus and Ursula are Austrian," Leo says as he gets to his feet to pour out more drinks. "Filomena met them on her last visit to Vienna."

"Oh." I sit up straight. "I would love to visit Vienna."

"You must," Klaus says. "I shall be your guide. We will go to the Prater and I will win you a goldfish."

"I'd rather go to the university's botanical gardens," I say eagerly. "I expect you've been so many times that the novelty has worn off, but I would find it fascinating. The Empress Maria Theresa had it built in 1754 for the practical study of medicinal plants, but it has grown so much since then, and I believe that the greenhouses hold a particularly interesting collection of carnivorous plants."

Klaus looks startled. "Indeed. I am sure it would be a fascinating experience."

A now-familiar voice joins the conversation. "Of *course* you'd be more interested in the man-eating plants than the amusement park."

Ben. He stands beside the table, one hand in his pocket. I notice that he has not made any effort to smarten up his clothes for dinner—and somehow he makes everyone else look overdressed.

"They're not man-eating," I try to correct him. "They largely eat insects or other arthropods."

But a chorus of delight greets Ben's arrival, swallowing my response. Even Ursula unbends enough to favor him with a slow smile.

"Ben." Her voice is throaty as she holds out a hand to him, which he takes and squeezes in his own before greeting the others.

"He is charming, our Ben, no?" says Klaus, close to my ear.

"So everyone keeps saying."

"It seems you are the only one immune to him." Klaus grins, watching the blond girl move to make room for him, smiling and fluttering at his attention.

"Yes, he was quite keen to assure me of that." I meet Klaus's gaze and roll my eyes.

Klaus chuckles, and Ben's eyes flicker in our direction. "What are you two talking about?" he asks.

"You, of course."

"What could be more interesting?" he says smoothly. He looks to the girl on his left, and for the first time I see his famous charm at work. He turns it on her like a spotlight, laughing at her jokes, teasing her, drawing her out so that soon she is laughing and blushing.

I watch for a while with great interest. It reminds me of the way birds preen and sing during courtship rituals. Ben glances across, and I arch my eyebrows appreciatively, congratulating him on what is, after all, a brilliant performance. He looks startled for a second, and then there's a reciprocal gleam of laughter in his eyes and that devastating, easy smile, the one that reveals his dimples.

"And so, now I have the two lovely cousins to myself," Klaus says, pulling my attention back to him and drawing a giggle from Hero, who has dragged her own chair closer so that Klaus sits between us. He teases us and tells us stories as the sun dips lower and lower and the sky fades from orange to a deep violet blue. I lean comfortably back in my chair, half expecting to hear my mother hissing at me to sit up straight. I realize that hours and hours have passed without any comment on my behavior or my manners. It feels dizzyingly liberating.

We light flickering candles in glass jars, and the lemon drink is followed by earthenware tumblers of red wine, warm and spicy on my tongue. The two older men reach a crescendo in their argument, and the others wade in, while I try to keep up with the flow of words about artists I haven't heard of before. They are so animated, so alive. The argument ends when one man leaps to his feet and utters a stream of furious Italian, stalking away to whoops and cheers from the others. It couldn't be further away from the stilted small talk I am used to.

Klaus laughs and translates some of the conversation for me. I lean forward, eager to hear more. It's hard to explain the feeling of heat in my veins, the way that being around all these noisy people, who talk so passionately about interesting things, makes me feel. It's like when you come inside from the freezing cold and your limbs start to come awake again—an almost painful kind of relief.

Eventually we are interrupted by a jubilant exclamation from Uncle Leo. He greets Rosa, who bustles toward the table with a tray heaped with baskets of warm, cinder-crusted loaves of bread, fat green olives, tissue-paper-thin sheets of tender pink ham, and meltingly soft cheese flecked with bright, green herbs. After several return trips to the kitchen, the table groans under the weight of all the food, and we fall upon it with enthusiasm. I bite into a tomato, so sweet and ripe that you can eat it like an apple; the juice runs down my fingers, leaving me sticky and gleeful as a small child.

By the time we finish eating, the sky is a blanket of stars and I can't shake the feeling that this is all some wonderful dream. Some of this must show in my face, because Filomena's eyes light on me.

"What is it that makes you look like that, Bea?" she asks. "You are like Saint Cecilia in ecstasy."

The others chuckle. I don't understand the reference, but the sentiment is clear enough.

"It's just so beautiful." I try to find the words. "Sitting underneath the bougainvillea and all the stars, eating this food and being with you. It's . . . it's . . . almost too much. If I wasn't seeing it myself, I wouldn't believe such a place was real."

Klaus nods. "I understand," he says. "It is why it is the perfect place to make art. It is a thrill, yes, for all the senses. As if you are seeing everything in brighter colors."

He is right, of course, and for a second I catch a glimpse of what it might be like to be an artist, just a little of what they are doing here. And the feeling is delicious.

CHAPTER TWELVE

◆

In the lull that follows the impassioned argument, where conversation breaks down into quieter, more intimate chat, Leo turns to Ben. "I was going to ask you how the painting was going, my boy," he says. "But I hear it met with a slight mishap."

"I suppose you could call it that," Ben says dryly, his eyes meeting mine.

I give him the slightest grimace.

"I was very sorry to hear about the painting," Filomena commiserates. "I know you were excited about it."

"Such is life," Ben says. I am a little surprised; I had more than half expected him to throw the blame at my feet. He turns to my uncle and Filomena. "I am sorry for the delay, though."

"The painting was for you, Uncle?" I ask.

Leo waves his hand airily. "It's of no matter, my boy," he says. "Take your time."

Ben shakes his head. "I'll finish it within the month." I feel a pang of guilt then. I hadn't realized the painting was a commission.

Filomena has been watching quietly, and I feel her eyes on my face now. "It is our great pleasure to host you, Ben," she says slowly. "We have never needed anything in return."

"Of course not," my uncle puts in briskly, sounding a little offended by the very idea.

"However." Filomena lifts a finger. "There is perhaps a favor you could do for us, if you would be so kind?"

"Anything," Ben says earnestly, leaning forward.

"You could teach Bea to paint." Filomena's expression is demure, but I think I see a glimmer of something—mischief, perhaps—in her eyes.

"Teach *me* to paint?" I exclaim. Of all the things I imagined doing in Italy, it isn't this. I can't quite keep the dismay out of my voice, and Ben looks equally horrified.

"Yes." Filomena claps her hands in delight. "It is a perfect idea. Bea, we promised your parents that we would educate you as a young lady should be—and now we shall."

There's a heavy silence.

"I'm afraid that I would make a very poor student," I say at last, attempting diplomacy.

"On this we are *completely* agreed," Ben says, and Filomena laughs. "Seriously, Fil." His voice rises, entreating.

"This will be a disaster. Ask me anything; command me to the ends of the earth. I will go on the slightest errand to the Antipodes that you can devise. But don't ask me this."

Everyone laughs, but all I can think is that I can't allow my perfect summer to go up in smoke. There are plenty of things I want to do in Italy, and being taught to paint by Ben is not one of them.

"Honestly," I say to Leo, "I really think this is a terrible idea."

"My life is in danger around the girl," Ben adds. "Literally. I rarely escape without some sort of injury." He lifts his fingers to his bruised face, and his blond friend makes a sympathetic mew of distress.

But Uncle Leo is looking at Filomena. "Well, you know, Bea," he muses, "your parents did entrust you to my care, and certainly we've been lax in devising some improving activities for you over the summer." Leo is rewarded by a smile from Filomena.

"I think if you returned home with some skill in watercolors, your parents would be very pleased. Exactly the sort of *ladylike accomplishments* they would appreciate."

"Watercolors?" Ben's groan comes from behind his hands. "Ladylike accomplishments? For *her*?"

Filomena is smiling, and there is something about her expression that is familiar. Suddenly, I realize what it is. It's the same look I've seen in my mother's eyes. Last time, it was the look that led to Cuthbert.

She's matchmaking.

My horrified gaze meets hers and, unbelievably, she winks at me. She's enjoying this.

"Of course"—Filomena sighs heavily now, her expression mournful—"if you can't find the time to do this for us, Ben, then we quite understand." She plays it perfectly, fiddling with the fringe on her shawl and gazing sadly at the ground.

There is a pause. Then Ben says, his expression mutinous, "I'd be delighted, Fil. The least I can do."

Leo laughs. I don't think he has the faintest idea what Filomena is up to, but he's enjoying teasing me.

"And, Bea, we could always ask Hero's governess to give you some lessons," he says. "If you would prefer."

Another pause. "Fine," I grind out. "I'll do it."

"Wonderful!" Filomena is all smiles now, and she lifts her cup in a toast. "And we all wish you every success. To artistic endeavor!"

"To artistic endeavor!" cries the table as one.

As I reluctantly raise my glass, my eyes meet Ben's in the candlelight and he smiles at me wryly.

This is going to be interesting, I think as I close my eyes and drink.

CHAPTER THIRTEEN

◆

My lessons aren't set to begin until next week, so I endeavor to make the most of it. I go on solitary rambles through the hills in the early mornings, returning dusty and delighted by what I've seen, ready to fall on my lunch and then tumble wearily back onto my bed as the hottest part of the day burns itself out.

The heat is a shock to my system: the way it makes my body feel languorous and heavy; the way it takes charge, shaping my days like this. It's like a living, breathing thing whose temperament needs to be considered at all times.

I spend the afternoons reading my book under the shade of a particularly friendly ilex tree, or being driven by my uncle to the nearest village to wander through the market, marveling at the dusty orange buildings jumbled together, at the produce laid out like gifts on display, dipping my fingers into sacks of almonds, cool as pebbles, or inhaling the sharp scent of golden lemons.

In the evenings we all come together again and revel in the cooler temperatures, eating and drinking and listening to records on the gramophone. The ever-changing roster of artists moving through the villa is difficult to keep up with, but only Klaus, Ursula, and Ben are staying on the grounds, and it's them whom I gravitate toward.

Like Ben's painting, Klaus's contain shapes and colors that are unlike anything I've seen before. They're certainly a world away from the paintings we had in Langton Hall before they were all sold. Klaus's and Ben's work is *abstract,* they tell me—they're interested in modernity, energy, movement. I don't really understand the art they are creating, but I understand the restless feeling they describe.

Ursula is a playwright and poet. She talks about a man called Brecht who seems to be something of a mentor to her. I have not heard of him, but when she mentions the man, the others look almost reverent, and from the way they talk, I gather this is a great honor. His name has a kind of solid weightiness about it.

In their midst I feel my own ignorance about the arts very keenly, and I listen, trying to take it in, enjoying as ever the experience of learning about something new. And I must admit this is a very different thing compared to learning from the books in Langton Hall's drafty library. Aside from anything else, our library is hopelessly out of date (apart from my own interventions when it comes to the science books), and the ideas and opinions I hear around my uncle's dinner table feel almost frighteningly new.

"But why is it," I ask them one night as we sit lingering over the remnants of another delicious meal, "that you're painting like this, writing like this, *now*?"

There's a pause as they consider the question.

"I suppose it's partly because of the war," Ben says, swirling his drink around in his glass, staring into it with a frown as though there's an answer there. "Afterward there was what they called the 'return to order,' a sort of need for familiarity after all that trauma, all that . . ." He trails off uncomfortably. We're all too young to remember much of the war, but still it hangs over us, over everyone.

"Return to order," I repeat thoughtfully.

Ben nods. "So, more familiar, you know." He places his glass down on the table, and his hands move animatedly as he talks. "More objective, I suppose. Safer to keep things at a distance."

"But now"—Klaus picks up the thread of Ben's conversation—"artists like Matisse and Picasso are embracing the abstract again. It's as though there's been a falling away of tradition, making space for something new and different, something vital, completely of this moment. . . ."

"Yes, yes," Ben agrees. "Focusing on today, not shackled to the past."

"It's like the metamorphosis of the mayfly," I say thoughtfully. "They spend their whole lives in the water preparing for a single day of dancing in the sun." Everyone looks at me with interest, so I expand. "The Latin name for a mayfly is Ephemeroptera," I say. "It's from the Greek, *epi* and *hemera*, meaning 'to live for a day.'"

"Ephemeral." Ursula's smoky voice joins in. "Something fleeting."

"Exactly," I say.

I have always dismissed painting and writing as being quite frivolous compared to the thrill of scientific discovery, which could change lives. But somehow, listening to these people talk with passion and excitement, I wonder whether I have been missing out on something after all.

"I never expected that I could find art so interesting," I say.

"There's not much in this world that is more of interest, if you ask me." Ben lounges back in his chair with an air of satisfied certainty.

"Well, science," I point out.

"Science?" Ben's eyes glitter in the candlelight. "Cold, impersonal fact gathering." His tone is dismissive.

"Biology is the study of life." I lean forward, gripping the arms of my chair. "It's about finding our place in the universe, unraveling the mysteries of nature. How could something so intricate and beautiful possibly be cold?" I ask. "Science examines what it means to be *alive*."

For a moment my words hang in the air, and Ursula exhales a slow stream of cigarette smoke, a glimmer of something that looks like respect in her eyes.

I'm surprised by her response, by them all—how curious

they are and the attentive way that they listen. In England my scientific interest is treated as something unsuitable, unfeminine, to be squashed down and kept private, not shared or debated. Here it feels, suddenly, as though my knowledge is valued. It leaves me feeling a little giddy.

The conversation moves on, but I glance up and catch Ben still staring at me as though I'm a crossword puzzle he can't quite crack.

The following morning, Filomena awakens me with a surprise. She arrives at my bedroom door, a wide straw hat on her head, dragging a large trunk behind her.

"What's this?" I ask, stepping back to let her in. She dumps the trunk on the bed without ceremony.

"Leo was in town yesterday and he picked up these things for you. I gave him a list and told him where to go and who to speak to—he seems to have done quite well."

I move forward and open the trunk. Inside is a jumble of clothes, a riot of bright colors and textures.

"These are all for me?" I reach out to run a piece of material between my fingers. It is red and silky, as cool as water against my skin.

"Of course." Filomena rummages around. "Ah, here. I think you will like these."

"Trousers!" I exclaim in delight.

I've never been allowed to wear trousers before; despite my protests to the contrary, Mother has always regarded them as something worn by *fast women*. In fact, I have come to realize, all my clothing is quite old-fashioned and more suited to a girl of twelve than one of seventeen. This has become increasingly apparent as I have seen Filomena and Ursula—and even Hero—dressed in outfits that make mine look frumpy and out of place.

I never gave what I wore much thought before. I dressed as all the women I knew dressed—with a sort of shabby respectability. The other women here at the villa dress for pleasure. Their clothes are practical—they keep them cool in the heat—but they're also daring, modern, *pretty*.

I take the trousers from Filomena. They are made of light linen, wide-legged and high-waisted. Filomena pulls out another pair, made of a soft dark-green material.

"These are much more practical for you, Bea," she says. "It is quite wonderful, the way you run around." I feel my heart squeeze at that. The way I run around has always been a problem in the past, not something to be encouraged. Not something to buy appropriate clothing for. It's a small thing, but it feels important, as though my clothes must fit me rather than the other way around.

There are several other pairs of trousers in the trunk, along with two bathing suits and a selection of collared shirts with short sleeves. My clothes from England are all drab pastels—pale, insipid blues, pinks, and lilacs—even more faded with age. The clothes on the bed in front of me are like jewels: emerald, garnet, amethyst.

Encouraged by Filomena, I try things on, a little shyly at

first, but soon I'm spinning around, enjoying the way the silk feels on my skin, the freedom the trousers offer. I stick my hands in the pockets and regard myself in the mirror. I look so grown-up, so different. So free. Somehow the simple cut of the clothing fits me better than any dress ever has.

Filomena pulls the hat off her head and plonks it on mine, laughing at my broad, unstoppable grin. "You like it all, then, Bea?"

"I love it," I say truthfully. "For the first time in my life, I feel like me. Does that make sense?" I shake my head. "I never thought that clothes could do that. It's like magic."

"I think so," Filomena agrees seriously. She glances over me with a critical eye. "It is unusual, these trousers and shirts, but I thought they would work for you, and I was right. You look more of a woman in these masculine clothes." She grins, a wicked grin that makes us into conspirators. "You will turn a few heads, I think," she says, and I flush. "Now that I have finished being the fairy godmother, I must go back to work. If I am in the studio, then the muse knows where to find me."

"Well, the muse can find *me* at the pool. Now that I finally have a bathing suit, I can't wait to swim."

"If you *are* going to go, you'd better go now," Filomena says brightly. "You've got an art lesson this afternoon, remember." She smiles at the reluctant frown on my face. "Oh yes. How do you say? *Time to pay the piper.*"

CHAPTER FOURTEEN

◆

After a glorious swim I return to my room to find a note pinned to my door.

On the terrace at 3

is all it says in an untidy scrawl.

For some reason, I feel odd about spending time alone with Ben; there's the tiniest nervous flutter in my stomach. Why? I wonder if I would feel the same if Klaus was giving me lessons. I test the thought a little, but no, that doesn't seem alarming. Certainly not stomach-fluttering, at any rate.

This is unusual and not precisely welcome. As always, what I need, I decide, are facts, data, information. I have not had a lot of exposure to young men. I will observe Ben closely and try to normalize my response to him. I will be polite, pleasant. I will treat him with cool detachment, as an interesting specimen in a jar.

I wash and change into my new linen trousers and a crisp white shirt with short sleeves. I tuck the shirt into my waistband and turn to look at myself in the mirror, my eyes widening at the unfamiliar sight. I lift one leg and then the other, and I tuck my hands into the pockets. (Pockets! What a delight.) The trousers are light and soft against my legs, and the way they let me move around is genuinely thrilling.

I have to admit that Filomena's taste has proved to be spot-on. The white shirt lies open at my throat, and my slightly sunburned skin loses some of its pinkness, turning more of a tawny gold against the cotton. Instead of looking as though I have been squeezed inside my clothes like an overstuffed sausage, this outfit fits my curves; the masculine cut even emphasizes them in a way that surprises me and leaves me a little bashful. I pull my dark curls into a long braid and reach for the wide-brimmed straw hat to complete my ensemble. I stare at a reflection that is both myself and, at the same time, someone else—a girl who's off to have an adventure.

At ten to three I am sitting out on the terrace, nursing a cup of tea. I take a sip and wince, realizing that I've let it go cold. I think it's the first time since I arrived here that I've had to be anywhere at a specific time. Still, I have put the time to good use, eating at least four of the crumbly almond-scented biscuits that Rosa left out for us.

"Oh, there you are." It's Ben, and the impatience in his

voice implies that he has been searching for me for hours rather than finding me waiting at the exact time and place he told me to. I notice his eyes widen as he takes in my new outfit.

"Here I am." I smile encouragingly.

For a moment neither of us says anything. Ben is looking at me with a slight frown.

"Shall we go?" I ask finally.

"Fine," Ben says. "I've set up in the gardens; follow me."

"It would be my pleasure." I might be laying it on a bit thick now, and certainly the look Ben gives me as we walk along is not friendly.

"Are you making fun of me?"

"Is that something that would make you anxious?" I ask, interested. I wish I had brought a notepad and pen with me to record this sort of information.

Ben comes to a stop and gives me a stern look. "What game are you playing now, Beatrice?"

"No game," I say. "I'm just being pleasant."

"That's what worries me."

"Perhaps you could try it," I am unable to resist muttering under my breath. I know that Ben is as reluctant as I am to do these foolish lessons, but I think he could be a bit more gracious about it.

"Here we are," he says, rather unnecessarily, as we arrive in a small, shaded part of the garden where two easels have been set up. We're in a paved area lined with trees, and the easels face back toward the house. There's a charming view of the villa, its walls glowing rosily, almost pink under the sun. The tumbling red bougainvillea on the pergola is just visible to one side, and splashes of green and yellow from the gardens complete the image. It already looks like a painting.

"So," I say, moving to stand in front of one of the canvases, "how exactly does this work?"

"Well, with painting the general aim is to get the paint on the canvas."

He has set up a small table between the easels, which holds palettes, small tubes of paint, brushes, and jam jars full of water.

"Let's just see what we're working with, shall we? We can start with a landscape. Choose something to use as a subject and begin with that."

"Right," I say. The canvas looks very big and very white all of a sudden. "Right." I pull back my shoulders and pick up a brush, dipping it carefully in the red paint and assessing the scene. The house, the pergola, and the flowers. I can see them all with my eyes. How hard can it be to communicate this vision to my hand?

Ben watches me begin, then goes to his own easel and starts work. Unfortunately, while Ben is soon absorbed, I am not doing terribly well. I can certainly see the view in front of me, and I can sort of see the different lines and shapes that make it up, but something gets very lost in translation as I try to re-create those lines and shapes in my painting. There's a sort of squashed orange cube on my canvas where the house should be, and it's hovering somewhere above the ground.

When I try to fill that in, it looks even more wrong. I push my hair out of my eyes and realize I have smeared paint on my face.

After a while—how long I'm not sure, but it feels like hours—Ben stops working with a murmur of something that sounds like pleasure. He drops his brush into the jar of water and it makes a ringing noise as it bounces from side to side. Ben rolls his shoulders and stretches, blinking as though he has just woken up.

"Well." He turns to me. "How have you been getting on?" His voice is happier, more relaxed now.

"It's not exactly what I had in mind," I mutter, and I can feel myself growing hot with mortification as he comes to stand behind me. The painting on my easel is absolutely horrible, and it's still the best I could do. Being terrible at something in front of him makes me feel vulnerable, and I think that if he makes fun of me now I won't be able to forgive him.

"You've got the perspective wrong." Ben's voice comes from behind me. Much to my relief, he doesn't sound mocking. His voice is measured, and he's standing so close that I can feel the heat from his body on my back. "You need to shorten that line there." He leans forward, pointing at one of my wobbly orange lines, and his arm brushes mine. "And this is closer, you see? So you need to lengthen it." He takes the brush from my hand and makes some quick alterations. It's still a terrible mess, but at least that one corner looks better.

I sigh. "You make that look easy. Why couldn't I see it?"

"You'll get there. It takes practice."

"Which I definitely need," I say glumly.

"Mmm," Ben murmurs, surprisingly diplomatic for once. "It can't hurt. Now you try with this corner here."

Trying to remember his advice, I make some awkward alterations. It's better, but not right.

"Almost," he says, and again he points to the different lines, helping me to see the changes that need making.

A lock of my hair comes loose again, and I swipe irritably at it with paint-stained fingers.

"Here," he says. "Let me get that for you."

As though it's happening in slow motion, I feel his fingers as they skim lightly across my forehead, and then down the side of my neck, and it is as if a trail of sparks follows the path they take, my skin crackling under his touch. My mouth goes dry and my mind empties as I stare up at him, for once lost for words.

Ben's own pupils are wide, and he holds my gaze for a moment before clearing his throat. "You're getting paint all over yourself," he says finally, taking my hand in his own and holding it up in front of me so that I can see.

"Oh," I manage, staring at my hand as though I've never seen it before, completely thrown by my reaction to his touch. His fingers are wrapped around my wrist, his grip gentle, his hand warm.

"We might have to get you some overalls. Don't want to get those new clothes dirty." He releases my wrist and takes a step back, putting some much-needed distance between us, allowing the air to rush back into my lungs. "Especially if you're going to end every lesson looking like you've rolled around in the paints."

"There's no need to talk to me like I'm a child," I say stiffly.

"I wasn't," he says with a grin. "It's simply an observable, objective fact, like the ones you're so fond of."

"Well, if that's the case, I had better go and get changed." I keep my voice deliberately detached. "Thank you for the lesson."

"Do you want to know what I think?" Ben asks slowly.

"Not desperately."

"I think you don't dislike me as much as you would like to believe," he says, using that smooth voice I've heard him use on other girls. The flirtatious eye-twinkling is happening too.

"Oh?" I raise my eyebrows. "Is this the famous charm I've heard so much about?" He looks startled. "I don't dislike you, so you can save the performance, Ben," I say, mildly amused now. "I've already seen it in action, and I'm sure it's very effective on some people, but I don't think it will work on me."

Something that I can't identify flashes in his eyes. "Oh really?" he asks softly.

"Really." I nod.

"What a shame." His voice is low as he moves a little closer, and the tingling feeling of anticipation between us grows again, my heart thumping irregularly in my chest. Soon, we are standing so close that I feel sure he'll be able to hear it himself. I tilt my chin and look up into his so-blue eyes. The exact same blue as the margins of a swallowtail butterfly, I realize.

"Do you want me to kiss you, Bea?" he asks softly.

I take a sharp breath. *Do* I want him to kiss me? My body certainly seems to think so, given that it's currently swaying toward him like a flower toward the sun.

"Absolutely not," I say, relieved to hear that my voice is crisp, steady.

"Well, I won't, then." His voice is still low, intimate. "At least"—the corner of his mouth tugs up—"not until you ask me to. Nicely."

I step smartly back, unable to believe that seconds ago his smirking mouth looked so appealing. "That won't happen," I say firmly, disliking the jangling, nervous feeling in my belly.

"We'll see," he replies with maddening carelessness.

I give him the coolest, calmest smile I can muster, then swing around on my heel and stalk off. His self-satisfied laughter chases after me as I disappear into the tree-lined avenue, determined to put as much space between us as possible.

CHAPTER FIFTEEN

◆

Rounding a corner at some speed, I walk smack into Ursula. She is wearing wide, red silk trousers and a peacock-blue shirt. Large sunglasses with blue frames are perched on her nose and her lips are scarlet. She looks like a particularly glamorous butterfly.

"Oh, sorry," I say, reaching out a hand to steady her.

"Careful!" She springs back, looking at my paint-stained fingers, though they've pretty much dried now. "Why is it," she asks, arching an expressive eyebrow above her sunglasses, "that you are always running about covered in paint?"

"Technically, this is only the second time," I say. I'm still rattled from the strange moment with Ben, and the adrenaline has faded, replaced by a curious, bone-deep tiredness. I'm not sure I'm up to verbal sparring with Ursula. Her moods are mercurial; one moment she's withdrawn and the next she's full of life and enthusiasm.

She watches me for a moment. Then she turns.

"Come with me," she says, heading further down the path we're on before disappearing along a small, rough track that forks off to the right. She doesn't check to see if I follow, but of course I do, surprised by the brisk pace she sets and finding myself stumbling through the trees toward a building I haven't seen before.

It's a small, squat, and rather ramshackle affair made of light timber. A veranda wraps around the outside, and a set of rickety wicker furniture with faded cushions is clustered at the front beside a table full of bottles and dirty glasses.

"Come, come," Ursula calls over her shoulder, and I follow her toward this intriguing building. I thought I had found all the villa's secrets, but this just goes to show that there are still hidden corners waiting to be discovered.

"Where are we?" I ask, looking around at the dappled space, hemmed in by ilex trees. This is obviously a man-made clearing, but it feels a little like the woodcutter's cottage from the fairy tales.

"Leo calls it the summerhouse," Ursula says, coming to a halt on the veranda. "Rather grand, I know. It's a sort of folly he had built a few years ago and then promptly forgot about. It was almost falling down when we arrived. He and Filomena have been letting me use it while I'm here."

As we get closer I see that the building does look a bit

unloved. The roof has been patched up, and the timber veranda is missing several floorboards. From where I'm standing, I can just see through the window to a large, square room with an unmade bed and a small desk pushed to one side. There are hundreds of sheets of paper scattered across the floor.

"There is water around here," Ursula says, gesturing with her hand, and, following her, I see that to the side of the house is an old-fashioned water pump. "You can wash."

Ursula disappears again, leaving me to clean up. The water that comes up from the earth is freezing cold, and as I wash my hands, removing the smears of paint that reach up almost to my elbows, I am left breathless by its icy touch. There's a bar of Italian soap next to the pump, and it leaves a lingering scent of mint and verbena on my skin, a clean, sweet smell that lifts my spirits. I wash my face as well and notice that while there is paint on my shirt, my trousers seem to have escaped unscathed. I scrape my hair back from my face and tie it into a knot, feeling as presentable as I think I'm going to without a change of clothes.

When I make my way back around the veranda, I find Ursula mixing drinks at a small trolley, her sunglasses pushed back onto the top of her head, an unlit cigarette clamped between her lips. "Ah," she says, from the side of her mouth. "Here. Take this."

She holds out a glass with a healthy splash of some dark, coffee-colored liquid in it, and I take it from her. She reaches into her pocket with her free hand and pulls out a lighter, lighting her cigarette and inhaling deeply before gesturing toward one of the low wicker seats.

"Please, sit," she says, exhaling a thin stream of smoke from between her lips. "Would you like a cigarette?"

"No, thank you." I shake my head, somewhat thrown by all this hospitality. The chair is wide enough that I can pull my feet up, so I kick my shoes off and curl in properly. I take a thirsty swallow of my drink and gasp as the rough flame of it slips down my throat and settles in my chest. Ursula smirks, and I try to look unmoved as she drops into the seat across from me, mirroring my pose.

"What is it?" I ask, nodding at my drink.

"Nocino," Ursula says. "It's made from walnuts. I get mine from a woman in the village. She swears her family has the best recipe."

We sit quietly for a while; the only sounds are from the orchestra of birds and crickets, whose music carries through on the tiniest whisper of a breeze. After the initial burn of the drink I do not find the taste unpleasant, and I sip more cautiously this time, feeling my limbs relax. The cool of the shade here is a welcome relief from the heavy heat.

"So, you have had your art lesson with Ben," Ursula says, finally breaking the silence.

"Yes," I say as she watches me keenly over the top of her glass.

"And did you find the experience instructive?" she asks.

"Not really," I say, ignoring her suggestive tone. "I'm afraid all it did was confirm my belief that there's not an artistic bone in my body."

"Hmmm," Ursula murmurs, taking another drag on her cigarette and half closing her eyes in a curiously feline expression. "I was wondering whether you learned about more than art with Ben."

I take another swallow of my drink. "Nope. In fact, we barely spoke about anything. I'm not sure if we like one another very much."

Ursula gives a small, unwilling laugh. "I cannot tell if you really believe that or not," she says.

"Of course I believe it," I say, pushing down my doubt. I hesitate. "We did have a bit of a strange moment just now." I decide I need to share it with someone, and that someone might as well be Ursula. "He asked if he could kiss me and I said no. But that was the end of it."

Ursula stubs the cigarette out in the chipped china saucer on the table beside her and shrugs again, a shrug that shimmers through her whole body. "I just think that perhaps someone should warn you about him."

"*Warn* me?" I ask, startled.

She settles back in her chair. "Yes, warn you." She reaches for her cigarette packet and toys with another cigarette before leaving it untouched. "Ben *is* charming." She pauses at my snort of derision here. "Or at least he can be," she concedes, "but he's not the sort to settle down, Bea." Her voice is surprisingly gentle now. "He is kind, yes, he really is—but ultimately he is selfish. In short . . ." This time she does pull the cigarette loose from the packet and lift it to her mouth. "He is not for you." She says this with finality, and she turns away to light the cigarette.

"Well, I don't want him," I say, irritated suddenly. "So your point is irrelevant. And," I add, making some quick deductions, "I think perhaps *you're* the one who wants something more from him."

She glances up at me. "I do like you, Bea," she says, smiling suddenly. "I didn't think I would. But I do."

I eye her warily, but in her gaze I see nothing but a blunt forthrightness.

"Perhaps I did hope for more from Ben at one time," she says slowly. "But now we are good friends. That is why I am well qualified to pass on this warning. You have obviously never been in love before. . . . Believe me when I tell you that Ben is not a sensible place to start, unless you wish to be nursing a broken heart." She exhales another stream of smoke. "I have given you my advice. What you do with it is up to you."

I sit for a moment, absorbing what Ursula has said. "Look," I say finally, "you don't need to tell me that Ben doesn't want to settle down. What I don't understand is why you would think that's something I want either."

"Because you are the typical English young lady. You're Leo's niece, so you must come from a good family, and isn't that what you all do? Coming-out parties and good social matches and all that?" She wrinkles her nose distastefully.

"That's what my parents would like for me, but believe

me when I tell you that I'm *very* glad to get away from it," I say shortly. "I am certainly not out here husband-hunting, if that's what you're getting at. My goodness, I'm only seventeen. I haven't actually done any *living* yet." Even I can hear the frustration in my voice.

Ursula smiles at that. "I understand. Where Klaus and I come from, they are very traditional too. We did not have a happy time there, but we had each other." She pauses for a second. "We left as soon as we could. Then we were in Berlin for a while before we came to Italy, and it felt so wonderful, so free. There was so much happening there creatively." Her voice is ardent now, her eyes huge and dancing as though she is being lit from within, before the light drops away to be replaced by something haunting. "I would like to return there after the summer, but I think it will not be possible."

"Why?" I ask.

"The situation is becoming dangerous in Germany. Particularly for people like Klaus and me, who have enough Jewish blood to be considered . . . *problematic.* If things continue as they are, I think that people like us will soon find it difficult to remain. So many are leaving already."

I shiver. It is one thing reading the sober newspaper stories coming out of Germany, but they are hints only. This makes it feel very real.

"I'm sorry," I say inadequately, and she shakes her head.

"Let us speak of Ben instead. If you want a fling, then that's different," she says, apparently happy to change the subject. "But even so—you do not have the experience needed to fence with a seasoned seducer like Ben."

"I think I can hold my own against Ben, thank you very much," I say firmly. "He's neither as clever nor as charming as he thinks he is. Although . . ." I hesitate. "Although you *are* right that I don't have a huge amount of experience with . . . with seduction."

That is an understatement.

"Oh, well, darling." Another sort of smile curls on Ursula's lips, and her voice is a purr. "If you need advice in *that* department, you've come to the right person."

CHAPTER SIXTEEN

◆

What follows is quite enlightening. My glass is topped up a couple more times over the next lazy hour, and Ursula and I talk.

Or, rather, she does. She spins stories of the various romantic liaisons she's had, and each one is more scandalous than the last. I'm fairly sure she's trying to make me blush, but there's nothing new under the sun, as they say, and if one has observed the natural world as closely as I have . . . well, let's just say it's a lot harder to shock me than she might think.

"The honeybee mates in mid-flight, you know," I say at one point. "But the male bee dies shortly afterward, as his reproductive organ is ripped from his body during coitus." I take a thoughtful sip of my drink. "I wonder if it's worth it."

Ursula's eyebrows shoot up, and she looks as though I've

rather taken the wind out of her sails. "I suppose you'd have to ask the bee," she murmurs finally. She rises and stretches, then holds out her hand to me.

"Come on," she says. "Let me give you the tour."

She shows me around the rest of the summerhouse—not that there is a lot to it—and it turns out that what I saw spread across the floor in her room are the pages of her current manuscript, all written in a cramped, spiky hand. She writes outside, she says, then types the handwritten work up on the rusting typewriter on her desk.

"I can't exactly lug that thing around," she says, gesturing at the lumbering typewriter. "And there's something in the air here . . . I'm getting so much work done. It's not just the place either; it's the people. Filomena has made something special. The ideas, the arguments . . ." She trails off here, but I am already nodding in agreement. I understand the feeling she's describing. It's one I feel too.

Eventually I decide to leave Ursula to her work and head back. I find I am slightly unsteady on my legs as I make my way through the grounds. On the terrace, I see Filomena deep in conversation with Ben. It's strange seeing him so soon after this afternoon and then my conversation with Ursula.

"Bea!" Filomena calls. "Just the person I wanted to see." Filomena looks calm as always, but Ben's expression is unusually preoccupied. "Are you all right?" she asks, looking closely at my face. "You look flushed."

"A bit too much sun," I murmur.

"Ah." She smiles. "Perhaps a rest before dinner?"

I nod in agreement, trying not to sway. "Absolutely."

"We have more guests arriving to stay in the next couple of hours," Filomena continues, "so I'd better get on." With a wave that sets her golden bangles jangling, she whirls into the house, calling for Leo in her musical voice.

"How are you feeling?" Ben asks.

"Fine," I say, smiling at him generously. "Completely and absolutely fine."

A Cheshire cat grin stretches across his face. "You're drunk!" he exclaims delightedly.

"*You're* drunk!" I say, unthinking. "I mean, I am *not* drunk." I shake my head again, trying to get a grip on the conversational thread, which seems to be slipping through my fingers. "I have *had a drink*. But I am *not* drunk." Though, truthfully, the world does seem to have taken on a rather smudgy, fuzzy-edged appearance.

The annoying smile remains in place, and it makes me unreasonably angry that he seems so sure of himself. I squint at him, suddenly furious that his face is so perfect. Why does anyone need to have a face like that? It's no wonder it leaves a girl feeling confused and off balance.

"Why are you looking at me like that?" he asks.

"Your face," I say, pointing an accusing finger at him, "is bothering me."

Before he can say anything else, I go inside and head up to my room. My head is spinning. One thing is certain, I decide—nocino is not my friend.

Back in my room I pour a big glass of water from the pitcher on the nightstand, then lie on my bed for a while, waiting for the walls to stop wavering around me. I curse Ursula and her drinks trolley to a dark place. A dull headache is starting to pound behind my eyes, and my limbs feel tired and heavy. An image comes unbidden into my mind—Ben's face right before he asked if he could kiss me. I close my eyes tightly.

When I open them again, the room is dark and I am disorientated for a moment. My stomach rumbles angrily. It must be dinnertime.

I lift myself on my elbows and give my head a tentative shake. It aches a little, but the fuzzy feeling is gone. After a quick, cold shower I am feeling much better, and I throw on a clean shirt.

It's only then that I notice the envelope propped up on my nightstand. I recognize the slightly florid handwriting immediately—it belongs to my mother.

Sitting down on the bed, I tear open the envelope and pull out the lavender-scented pages, running my eyes over the lines. There is the usual local gossip, an update on her social calendar, news of her friends' much more well-behaved daughters and their achievements, which seem largely matrimonial. Finally, there's a paragraph that sends a shiver down my spine.

Your father and I passed a very enjoyable evening with the Astleys on Thursday. I think that we have managed to smooth over much of the unpleasantness from the horrible scene last month. By the end of the evening Cuthbert even admitted to finding your spirited nature rather charming! I believe there may still be hope there if you could learn to curb your wildness, Beatrice. Indeed, Philip made it clear that he would look very kindly on the match. Well, absence, as they say, makes the heart grow fonder; now let us hope the expression proves true for young Cuthbert! Really, Beatrice, eligible young men do not grow on trees, and we need to begin approaching your future with far more seriousness.

The rest of the page blurs before my eyes, and I crush the paper between fingers that are shaking slightly. A familiar hollow feeling settles in my chest. It brings home the truth: that my visit here really is only a temporary reprieve from my parents' machinations.

Well, I think, dropping the letter calmly onto the floor and kicking it under the bed and out of sight, *if that's the case, then I'd better make the most of it.*

CHAPTER SEVENTEEN

◆

"There you are!"

I look up to see Hero in the doorway. "Are you coming out to the garden?" she asks. "The people here tonight won't stop talking politics, and I'm fed up."

I force a smile, pushing Mother's letter to the back of my mind. "As long as there's plenty of food," I say. "I'm starving."

We arrive at the dinner table to discover that of course there *is* plenty of food and that Hero is quite right: politics has taken over the conversation.

"Italy is the home of art, of culture, of civilization!" one man is shouting, waving his cigarette to punctuate his sentences. "We are the children of the Roman Empire!"

"So you think it's your history that makes you superior now, do you?" another man asks.

"He's got a point, darling," a woman puts in. "I hadn't realized you'd been around so long that you could personally take credit for the Battle of Carthage."

The first man's face turns a mottled red. "Our history is our blood, our birthright. Mussolini understands this. . . ."

I pick up a plate and pile it high with smoky grilled fish and sweet peppers, listening all the while. Most of what I know about Mussolini comes from the film reels, enthusiastic in their approval of his efforts to regenerate the country, his emphasis on everything running like clockwork. I have also seen the silent footage of young, strong troops marching in perfectly ordered lines. The cold, mechanical quality of it left me feeling more disturbed than impressed. While I may not know much about Mussolini and Italy, I do know a little about Mosley's new British Union of Fascists, and what I see frightens me.

"But look at Germany," another voice breaks in. "Look at what is happening there. That's the danger. Don't think it can't happen here."

"You can't deny that under Mussolini things are improving," Uncle Leo says, taking a sip of wine. He is not alone—others are nodding.

"What about the Blackshirts?" I ask then.

"Not you too," Hero groans under her breath. "I give up." She turns on her heel and stomps back toward the house.

"What do you know about the Blackshirts?" Leo's smile is indulgent.

"That some of their methods are less than pleasant," I say

calmly. "And that, historically speaking, fanatical national-ism doesn't usually end well."

There's a brief silence while Leo looks at me with sur-prise in his eyes.

"Well, when I met him, I thought Il Duce was rather charming," a languid redhead says, before flashing a dazzling smile at Ben, who has just appeared on the terrace. The hum of debate picks up again. I take the opportunity to bite into a good chunk of warm bread, briefly closing my eyes in ap-preciation of Rosa's genius.

"Good to see you again, Simone," Ben murmurs, wrap-ping his fingers around the woman's hand and smiling down into her wide green eyes. There's something lingering in the look they share, and I wonder suddenly if they have been to bed together. Then I push the thought away. It's none of my business, after all.

"Ah, Benedick." She sighs. "How nice to see you."

"*Benedick?*" I choke on a giggle, and he shoots me a warning glare. Simone's wide eyes shift and sweep over me in a leisurely fashion, taking it all in, from the top of my head to the tips of my toes. The slight wrinkling of her nose and the way her mouth tightens into a brief pucker of disdain tells me that she has found me lacking in every way. For some reason, I find it amusing rather than insulting.

"Come and sit beside me." She returns her limpid gaze to Ben, gesturing to a chair. "We have so much to catch up on." Her voice is a purr. It's all such a cliché and the sort of scene I've seen Ben act out often enough now to find quite funny.

When I look up, though, I see that Ben isn't looking at her—he's looking at me, and there is something odd in his expression. I wonder if he caught her disdainful glance.

Ben hesitates.

"Oh, don't mind me, *Benedick,*" I say cheerfully. "I'm just here for the food."

He gives me a glare that tells me he knows I'm laughing at him and he doesn't appreciate it. But before he can respond, Klaus appears at my elbow.

"There you are!" he exclaims, leaning in close. "Ursula and I had to get away from this lot. Fil's guests this evening leave a little to be desired." His eyes linger distastefully for a moment on Simone.

"What do you suggest?" I ask.

"Join us for a picnic, of course," Klaus responds promptly, flashing me a grin that shows off his white teeth to their best advantage. "We're down by the fountain. Ursula sent me for wine and to fetch you."

"In that order, I expect," I say, and it's Klaus's turn to laugh.

His lips are close to my ear. "Your only mission is to find dessert."

"You have come to the right woman for the job," I reply. "Rosa won't have let us down, I'm sure. Take this for me, will you?" I hand him my laden plate, and he bows slightly.

"I am, as always, at your service, Bea," he drawls.

"So chivalrous," I call over my shoulder, already making my way back to the kitchen.

Once inside, I find that I have not misjudged the situation. Though she is nowhere to be seen, Rosa has left neat rows of homemade cannoli laid out on the side. The shells of fried pastry are as pretty as a picture, stuffed with sweet, creamy ricotta, their ends dipped in dark chocolate and delicate green pistachios. I take a plate and begin filling it.

"What are you doing?" Ben's voice makes me jump and I swing round.

"I'm getting some dessert," I say.

"For you and Klaus?" Ben asks casually, strolling over and swiping a cannolo from my plate.

"Yes," I reply. "What are you doing here? Shouldn't you be practicing the art of seduction out in the garden?"

He leans back against the counter, his arms folded. "What do you mean?"

"Oh, you know," I murmur, turning my attention back to the pastries. "Staring into her eyes for a fraction of a second too long, leaning in closer, brushing your arm against hers as if it's an accident, whispering something seductive in her ear . . . Well, you hardly need me to tell you, do you?"

Ben looks torn between anger and amusement. "You certainly seem to be paying attention," he says dryly. "Are you studying me like one of your glowworms?"

"Young men, you mean?" I laugh, caught in the act. "You and Klaus are certainly interesting subjects," I say.

"Oh, I'm sure Klaus will be *delighted* to help in any way that he can." Ben rolls his eyes.

"I should think so," I agree. "Overall I have found him to be much more amenable than you."

"Well, he would be, wouldn't he?" Ben says, his voice not quite as easy as usual. "He's had his eye on you since the moment you arrived."

"Has he really?" I ask, surprised. "I assume by that you mean he considers me a potential sexual partner?"

Ben stares at me for a moment. "Strange sort of sheltered upbringing you've had," he manages finally.

"I've never understood why we can't talk about sex." I shake my head. "I mean, for goodness' sake—without it none of us would be here. It's hardly a great mystery, is it?"

"Yes, yes," Ben says, "but it's not typically something one discusses with . . ."

"Young women?" I sigh. "I know, and it's such a shame. Ursula and I had a good chat about it all this afternoon, and I really think there's a lot to be said for modern attitudes." I'm warming to my theme now. "And, after all, Ben, it's clear that you're hardly living a chaste existence. Look at you and Simone, for example."

"What Simone and I do"—Ben flounders—"or . . . did, is none of your business."

"Just as, say, what Klaus or I do is none of yours."

"What are you and Klaus going to do?" Ben's frown is back.

"It was just an example. You're the one who brought it up."

"You're the one talking about potential sexual partners,"

Ben puts in stubbornly. "And I think you'll discover there's a big difference between theory and reality in that department. It's a lot more complicated than you think."

I fall silent at that. It's true that I have very little actual experience with romance. And he's not wrong—there's a huge difference between reading something in a book and experiencing it. It's theory versus practice.

"You're right," I say finally.

"Good," Ben says automatically. Then: "Wait . . . right about what?"

"About my lack of experience." I give Ben a look that my mother could warn him means mischief. "I should do some more research," I continue, keeping my tone deliberately thoughtful. "In fact, perhaps I should take a lover."

And with that, I waltz past him and out the door.

CHAPTER EIGHTEEN

◆

Ben trails after me, spluttering and slightly incoherent.

"'Take a lover'!" I hear him mutter under his breath, and I repress the urge to laugh. I'm surprised that shocking him was so easy. I thought he was made of sterner stuff than my parents' dinner-party guests.

"You're abandoning Simone," I point out as we make our way deeper into the gardens. "I think you were doing quite well there."

He doesn't dignify that with a response.

We find Ursula and Klaus sprawled on an old red blanket in front of the fountain. There are candles in a rather Gothic-looking brass candelabra in the middle, casting the pair in a warm, flickering glow. More candles are arranged in glass jars along the edge of the fountain itself, and a makeshift feast has been laid out, along with two bottles of wine.

"What kept you?" Ursula greets me, holding out her hands to receive the pastries with all the reverence they deserve.

"We were just talking," Ben says, his usual easy charm restored.

"I don't know what you can have been talking about to have taken so long," Klaus complains, handing me my plate. "And why it has kept my dessert from me."

"Ben was suggesting I take a lover," I say, applying myself to my dinner.

Klaus chokes on his wine; Ben drops his head into his hands and groans. Ursula's eyes meet mine with a glimmer of appreciation. "What an excellent thought," she says. "Did Ben, ah, have anyone in mind?"

"Well—" I begin.

"No, he didn't." Ben's voice is weary. "And I'll thank you not to credit me with the idea."

"In which case . . ." Klaus's voice holds a slight quaver of laughter. "I wonder what inspired such a suggestion?"

He holds out a glass of wine and I take it.

"Ben simply pointed out that there is a big difference between theory and practical experience," I say. "The logical thing to do if I wish to truly understand that difference is to take a lover. An experiment, of sorts."

Klaus is laughing openly now. "An experiment?" he says.

"Again," Ben cuts in, "I want to be very clear that this was not my suggestion. This is just Bea's idea of a hilarious joke."

"Well, you made it easy. I didn't expect you to be so

puritanical about it," I say over the top of my glass, enjoying watching him squirm.

"Why does it have to be a joke?" Ursula asks. "I think it's a wonderful idea."

"Me too," Klaus chimes in. "I'm sure finding a suitable candidate would be easy enough."

"Don't encourage her!" Ben groans. "The idea is ridiculous."

I feel my spine stiffen at that. Is the idea of romance with me really *so* absurd?

"Actually," I say, a little more forcefully than I intended, "it could be just what I need."

"A romantic experiment?" Ben shakes his head. "What happened to, I don't know . . . hearts and poetry and love in a gardenia-scented garden? Aren't women supposed to care about those things?"

"I don't think gardenias would do very well here," I say doubtfully, taking a bite of food. "They might struggle with the heat and dryness. They can be very temperamental."

"The gardenias are irrelevant!" Ben exclaims in tones of exasperation.

"Well, you brought them up." I look at him. "Is that what *you* want, then?" I ask, curious. "Hearts and poetry and gardenias?"

Ursula laughs into the wineglass at her lips.

"Me?" Ben looks stricken. "God, no. That's the *last* thing I'm looking for." He shifts awkwardly. "But that's what women want, isn't it?"

I shrug. "I wouldn't know."

"If you've never been the subject of romantic attentions in England, then all I can say is the Englishmen must be a very cold breed," says Klaus gallantly.

I hesitate. "I wouldn't say that, exactly. But, well . . . you'd understand if you'd met Cuthbert."

"Who's Cuthbert?" Ursula asks, leaning back as she lights a cigarette.

I tell them the whole story of our brief "courtship," including the disastrous dinner party, and by the time I finish, they're all laughing. Ursula, more animated than I have ever seen her, wipes tears from her eyes.

"You lectured the vicar on the mating habits of glow-worms?" Ben asks weakly. "Of course you did."

"I wish I had seen it," Ursula manages. "So that's the plan, is it?" she continues more thoughtfully now. "Your parents want to marry you off to a weak-chinned aristocrat and move him into the family manor?"

"That's about the size of it." I feel a pang as I remember my mother's letter, shoved out of sight in my room. "They're not doing it to be cruel," I add quickly. "I know they genuinely think it's what's best for me. They just can't conceive of the kind of life I want for myself."

"And you're going to let them do it?" Ben asks, his eyes on mine. "You'll let them marry you off to the poor sap?"

"I don't know. I think they've always thought I'd change," I say. I look at my hands in my lap. "The thing is," I add, and my voice is low now, "I almost wish I could change too. Be someone else: the daughter they want. Despite everything, I do want to make them happy. I suppose settling down and marrying a Cuthbert type is what I'll do in the end. I don't really have a lot of options, do I? I can't just hang around the house forever. And"—I try to sound a bit more cheerful—"I suppose marriage would bring a sort of freedom . . . from my parents' rules, at least."

There's a long silence after this, and I'm quite glad that no one says anything. I probably couldn't have said all that in the daylight, but here, in the quiet, under a blanket of stars, it feels like there's space for whispered secrets.

"Well," Klaus says, breaking the silence. "Under these circumstances a summer romance would appear to be just the thing."

"Yes," Ursula says. "*Exactly* the thing. One summer of dalliance—kisses and romantic gestures—but with no expectations for the future."

I snort. "Romantic gestures? You're as bad as Ben."

"Well," Ursula smirks. "He is, after all, the most notorious flirt for miles around."

I crunch into one of Rosa's cannoli, briefly closing my eyes with pleasure. "I have actually been observing Ben's efforts at flirtation for a while," I say, licking cream from my fingers. "And I must say I find the dynamic quite fascinating. Although I doubt that those particular charms would have much effect on me."

Ben is unruffled. "I think you'll find that if I wanted to win you over, I could do it fairly easily."

"Why not put it to the test?" Ursula asks.

Ben leans forward and takes a pastry. "What do you mean?"

"Well," Ursula says slowly. "On the one hand we have Bea, who has no experience of romance, and on the other we have Ben, seasoned womanizer and expert in the art of romance, who claims he could win the heart of any lady." She smiles, and I now see her expression for what it is: pure mischief. "I think the solution is obvious."

There's a choking sound as Ben inhales a little of his cannolo.

"But—but that's a terrible idea," I say, once I can speak.

Ursula smiles. "Why?" she asks. "Are you afraid?"

"No!" I exclaim. "Absolutely not. It's just—it's completely ridiculous."

"Of course it is," Ben puts in, and although he's agreeing with me, something rankles.

"Well, if you're saying no, Ben," Klaus cuts in smoothly, "then I would be delighted to assist Bea in her experiment."

Ben frowns. "I'm not saying *no*."

"Wait. You're not?" I ask, thrown.

His eyes meet mine. "No," he says. "I'm not saying no."

"Oh." For once I don't know what to say.

"Unless you are?" Ben's words are a challenge.

"Bea would not be such a coward," Ursula insists. "She is not stuffy, like her parents." She grins. "Or is she?"

I look at her for a moment.

"Fine," I say. "I'll do it. If Ben wants to."

There is a short pause. "I do," he says, his face giving nothing away. I feel my heart thump.

Ursula claps her hands.

"There would have to be rules, of course," Klaus muses.

"Good idea," Ursula agrees, getting down to business. "Number one—time frame."

"That's fairly easy," Klaus says. "Bea is here till the end of August."

I feel my heart thump, but I try to keep my expression just as impassive. "That's correct."

"So, six weeks, then," Ursula says. "The perfect amount of time for a romance." I wonder if that's scientifically accurate, but then I suppose we'll find out.

"Number two. We must be the only four who know about it," she continues, and Klaus nods seriously.

"Yes, a secret between us. The others may not approve. After all"—here Ursula grins mischievously—"Bea is supposed to be under the strict supervision of her uncle. We wouldn't want to give Leo anything to write home about."

I glance over at Ben and he rolls his eyes. It's as though the two of us might as well not be here.

"And number three. Ben must treat Bea to the full romantic experience," Klaus says. "He has to woo her properly, win her favor. Everything must be on her terms." He glances slyly at Ben. "If you think you can handle that."

"I think I'm up to the challenge," Ben says with a put-upon sigh. "I was right all along, then—it's going to be love in a gardenia-scented garden."

"The gardenias are not a possibility," I remind him. "The soil around here—"

Ben waves a hand. "Details, details," he says airily. "I think I can woo Beatrice to her satisfaction." He stretches lazily. "It means that I can unleash my inner romantic."

"*Unleash* him?" I raise my eyebrows. That sounds rather . . . alarming.

Ben smiles wolfishly. "Typically, I have to show some restraint. Don't want to leave a string of broken hearts around the place, you know."

I hesitate, thinking of our past interactions. "I'm just not sure how this is going to work. We argue a lot, for people who hardly know each other."

"That's what will make it interesting," he says, and his eyes meet mine again. This time I find myself flushing.

"Then it's settled," Ursula says swiftly. "Klaus and I will act as witnesses to the pact."

"There is one rule we haven't mentioned." Ben lifts a finger in the air, and I wonder what he's going to say. There is an expectant pause. "You must not, *under any circumstances whatsoever*, fall in love with me."

That surprises a laugh out of me. "That certainly won't be a problem," I say, when I can speak. "And *you* must promise not to fall in love with *me*."

The derisive noise Ben makes is actually quite insulting.

"It's a deal, then?" asks Klaus.

I look at Ben, daring him to say no. His gaze is steady and, slowly, he nods.

"I look forward to working together." I hold out my hand, and Ben reaches out to shake it. "I just don't want you to feel bad if your technique doesn't work."

"Oh," Ben says, a dangerous gleam in his eyes. "You asked for romance, and you're going to get it."

I try not to worry that it sounds like a threat.

PART THREE

Villa di Stelle
July 1933

Thou and I are too wise to woo peaceably.

—*Much Ado About Nothing*, act V, scene 2

CHAPTER NINETEEN

◆

It's around noon on the following day when an envelope appears under my door. Inside is a note written in a slightly more careful hand than the one summoning me to my art class.

Bea,

This is a romantic letter.
> *You don't yet realize it's romantic because you are new to this, but I wanted to give you a very clear warning so that you could prepare yourself. Are you ready?*
> *Meet me, my raven-haired angel, on the terrace at 3 p.m. for a romantic rendezvous. My heart aches for you and I count the moments until we are together again.*

—B

Raven-haired angel is the phrase that tips me over the edge into hysteria, and I end up in a stomach-aching fit of laughter. Not, I imagine, Ben's desired result. I try to picture myself in the role of romantic heroine and fail spectacularly. Perhaps I'm not suited to this romance business after all. What if Ben tries this sort of flowery romance in person and I laugh in his face? I'm fairly certain that won't go over well.

Still, I decide that if Ben is making the effort, then I will too. What, I wonder, stepping over to my wardrobe, does a romantic heroine wear?

For a moment my eyes drift toward my old dresses. I shake myself. Not those. Those are for a different me. Certainly not a me who is being swept into a romantic dare.

Instead, I pick a pair of mossy green trousers that are high at the waist, and a crisp white shirt with the sleeves rolled back to my elbows. I put my hair up as best as I can, jabbing pins into the most unruly curls in an effort to look neat.

I take a step back and look at myself in the mirror. I'm not sure if I look like a romantic heroine, but I look like me, and that feels more important.

I glance at my watch and decide I will call in and see Ursula. There is plenty of time before my assignation with Ben, and I'm quite looking forward to talking over the events of the night before with another woman.

I arrive at the summerhouse to find Ursula trying to set her typewriter on fire.

"You'll need a lot more kindling if you're going to get that to work," I observe as she flicks another stuttering match at the smoldering embers underneath the bulky machine.

"I hate it," Ursula storms, tossing down the matches and delivering a swift kick to the machine. This achieves little except causing a stream of expressive German as Ursula hops about, clutching her toes.

"The work's not going well, then?" I ask mildly.

Ursula glowers at me. "Do tell me, Sherlock Holmes— whatever gave you that impression?"

Turning her back on the typewriter with another muttered string of words I don't understand, but that I'd be willing to bet my life are quite colorful expletives, she storms back to the rickety porch and pours herself a drink.

"The work is dead," she cries dramatically.

"Oh dear," I say.

"Oh dear," Ursula mimics me sourly. "You English, always so cold and passionless."

"I suppose we are."

"Although . . ." A gleam flickers in her eyes, and she takes a sip of her drink. "This experiment should take care of that, eh?"

I flush and she smiles.

"Don't leave me up here drinking alone," she says.

I make my way onto the veranda and accept the glass she pours me. Ursula settles herself in a chair and grabs a packet from the table beside her, taps out a cigarette, and places it between her lips.

"I thought you were against the whole idea of me having

a romance with Ben," I say. I hesitate. "Won't it be painful for you? Because I would never—"

"Oh God," Ursula says from around the unlit cigarette, "not that, I beg you." She lights the cigarette with a flourish and inhales deeply. "I can't bear one of those disgusting weeping scenes where we pledge not to let a man divide us." She waves her hand in the air, leaving a thin line of smoke trailing behind.

"Well, I certainly wasn't planning on weeping," I say. "Were you?"

Ursula gives a reluctant bark of laughter. "No," she says. "There will be no weeping on my part."

"Good." I smooth my hands over my trousers. "So, would you like to tell me why you suggested this scheme?"

Ursula continues to smoke in silence for a moment, her eyes half closed as though she is considering her answer. "I think it will be entertaining," she says finally.

"Entertaining?" I repeat in surprise.

She gives me a thoughtful look. "I underestimated you, Bea," she says. "I thought at first that you were just another of those upper-class English girls. Simple, sheltered."

"I *am* sheltered," I say. "I've lived almost all of my life within about a five-mile radius."

"But not up here." Ursula touches a finger to her forehead. "You're sharp, Bea." She pauses again. "I think you could be good for Ben. And," she says slowly, tapping her cigarette so that the ash falls, "I think he could be good for you."

"Good for me?" I ask. "How?"

"Ben likes you, I can tell. And I believe he will prove to be a satisfactory lover." Her eyes meet mine and she smiles. "However"—her tone changes, becomes more brisk—"I do not believe it will be a lasting affair. He is not a lasting-affair sort of person, and that will suit you perfectly. What you need, Bea, is an adventure."

I consider this. "Well, I certainly agree with that," I say. "But why do you think I will be good for Ben?"

Ursula smiles, a smile that shows off all her teeth. "Because Ben's ego needs puncturing, and you, my dear, are a perfectly sharpened pin."

"Thank you," I say wryly. "That's one of the nicest things anyone has ever said to me."

We sit quietly, as I try to arrange my thoughts. Finally, I decide to share something that's been worrying me.

"The way I . . . react to Ben," I say carefully, "when he stands near me, or when he touches me . . ." I pause. "It's strange. It feels . . . unpredictable, like it's outside of my control." I risk meeting her eyes. "I'm not sure if I like that."

Ursula sighs again, more lustily this time. "Beatrice, my sweet innocent. What you describe is the beginning of any love affair. Don't you understand that?" She shakes her head. "No, you don't, but you will. You say you wish to live, Bea. Well, then you must take risks. You must make yourself vulnerable. You can shut yourself away in a cold, lonely house in England and keep your heart perfectly intact—but you will live only half a life."

I think about this for a moment. Ursula is right, I decide.

I may rail against my parents, against Langton, but all the same I have been afraid of what is waiting for me beyond those walls in a world that is messy and unpredictable, a world that doesn't follow the careful rules I apply to my studies.

"You're only two years older than me, Ursula," I say. "How did you get to know so much?"

"I lived, darling." She takes another drag on her cigarette and gives me a sad smile. "I lived."

CHAPTER TWENTY

◆

As I make my way through the gardens back toward the terrace and my appointment with Ben, I have to confess to feeling a little nervous. It's silly, I tell myself; after all, it's only Ben, and it's not like any of this is *real*—it's an experiment, a dare, an arrangement. Call it what you like, there's no reason for my heart to be thumping the way it is.

I have just convinced myself of this when I spot Ben. In my current mental state his handsomeness feels like an attack. His tall, muscular frame is sprawled in one of the chairs, and the sun catches his golden hair and falls across his perfect face.

"You're late," he barks when he sees me.

I come to a halt. "I think you'll find I'm extremely punctual."

With perfect timing, the faint but carrying sound of the grandfather clock in the living room begins to chime three.

He looks a little sheepish then. "That clock is slow." There's a pause. "I thought maybe you'd changed your mind."

"Oh no," I say lightly. "I intend to follow this through."

"In the spirit of scientific inquiry?" he asks, and smiles. "On that note, here. You look lovely, by the way."

He hands me a small bouquet of flowers, tied with a blue ribbon.

"Thank you." I bury my face in them to hide the slight flush on my cheeks, inhaling their sweet scent.

"All part of the service." He stands. "Since you're always to be found outdoors, I thought that we might have a picnic."

I notice a wicker basket at his feet. "That sounds perfect."

"Let's go, then."

The spot he has chosen is deep into the grounds and up a hillside. There's a bit of clambering to get there, and I am once again grateful for my trousers, which allow me to stride and scramble about just as easily as Ben does. I stop occasionally to catch my breath, and to enjoy the changing scenery: the orderly rows of vines and the cypress trees with their military bearing set against the gently undulating rise and fall of the hills.

"Here we are," he says at last.

We're in a meadow high on top of one of the hills, with far-reaching views. He lays the blanket down in the shade of a very ancient-looking oak tree and begins unpacking the parcels of food from the hamper.

I take a moment to enjoy the view laid out before us, and the gentle tickle of a cool breeze on my neck, before I sit, pulling my knees up to my chest. "It's beautiful," I say.

Ben's dimples appear. "I thought you'd like it. I come up here to paint sometimes."

"I can see why," I say. A flash of yellow has me turning my head. "Oh!" I exclaim. "Ben, look!"

Perched on a branch beside us is a butterfly the color of sun-kissed Italian lemons. On its forewings is a perfect orange blaze that looks almost like a setting sun.

"*Gonepteryx cleopatra,*" I breathe, getting silently to my feet and edging over.

"I don't know what you just said," says Ben, following my gaze. "But the colors are incredible." He comes over to join me.

"It's a Cleopatra butterfly, a male," I explain in a low voice. "You can tell because of his coloring. The males are much flashier than the females."

Ben chuckles at that. With a faint trembling of its wings the butterfly takes to the sky again, drifting quickly out of view, like a dream. When I straighten up I realize that Ben and I are standing very close together. I can feel the warmth from his arm against my own.

"Hungry?" Ben asks, holding my gaze for a long moment.

"Starving," I agree firmly, dropping back down onto the

blanket, where Ben joins me. He reaches into the picnic basket and passes me a wax-paper-wrapped parcel. Our hands touch, and I feel a zing of awareness run up my arm; my cheeks flush with heat.

These involuntary physical responses that I have around him are really very interesting, I tell myself, trying to steady my breathing.

"What are you thinking about?" Ben asks, his voice a little husky.

"I was thinking that the physiological and psychological causes of blushing are deeply fascinating," I say, wrestling with the wax paper around my sandwich.

"Of course you were." Ben sighs, leaning back on his elbows.

"Charles Darwin called it the most peculiar and most human of expressions," I say, biting into bread filled with sweet roasted peppers and cured ham. I make a sound of deep approval. "This is amazing."

"I know," Ben says, turning his attention to his own lunch. "I think it is Rosa I will miss most of all when the summer is over."

My mouth is suddenly dry. "Don't even speak of it," I say. "It seems impossible that it can all come to an end."

Ben must be able to read some of the sadness on my face. "What will you do, do you think?" he asks lightly. "When you are home again?"

"Do?" I repeat, my voice dull. "Nothing really. Nothing at all."

"What a waste." Ben dips his fingers into a jar of black olives that shine like slick chips of magnetite.

I force a smile. "I don't have a huge amount of choice in the matter."

"Rubbish," Ben says succinctly. "For someone who's such a loudmouthed, antagonistic troublemaker, you come over all meek and mild-mannered when you talk about going home."

"Thanks a lot," I say.

"It was actually supposed to be a compliment," Ben replies. "I just don't understand why you're trying to make yourself all . . . all *small* and docile, when that's not who you are at all."

"That," I say, "is because you have the privilege of being a man and because you obviously don't have parents like mine." Suddenly the words are spilling out of me. "If *you'd* spent seventeen years being told to make yourself smaller and to stay quiet and out of the way, that everything you loved and enjoyed was wrong and unladylike, if *you'd* been greeted by recriminations and angry words and floods of tears every time you failed to meet the standards that were set, which you did over and over again despite all your best efforts, your endless good intentions, and your desperate longing to make them happy, to win some crumb of approval . . . well, then you'd realize it takes more than a couple of weeks in the sun to change the way you see yourself."

There is silence as I get to the end of this little speech. I can feel the heat in my face, the judder of my unsteady pulse.

I am trembling, as though I've unleashed something that I have been holding in check for as long as I can remember.

Ben is frozen, his hand still in the jar of olives and a look of surprise on his face.

"Feel better?" he asks at last.

"A bit," I admit with a shaky laugh. I do, but I also feel an immediate pang of disloyalty, as if even that outburst is just another way that I've failed my parents.

"I don't want to think about the summer ending already," I say quietly. "Not when it's only just begun."

Silence stretches out between us and I pluck at a piece of grass.

Ben is quiet for a moment.

"You're right that I don't have parents like yours," he says. "But I know what you mean, at least a little bit, about feeling in the way. I—well, I took matters into my own hands, I suppose. I ran away from home when I was fourteen."

"Fourteen is very young to be on your own."

"It is," he agrees, and one side of his mouth lifts in a humorless smile.

"Only the same age as Hero."

"Oh, but I was much more of a tearaway than Hero." Ben grins. "Just ask Filomena."

"You knew Filomena back then?" I am startled. I hadn't really given much thought to how she and Ben knew each other. I suppose it always seemed that Filomena picked up interesting people in the same careless way one might collect shells on a beach.

Ben nods, his gaze inscrutable. "Yes, I knew her," he says.

I'm distracted after a moment by a buzzing in my ear. I brush something away with my hand and notice it's a flying ant.

"So," Ben says, his voice suddenly brisk. "Back to romance."

"I'm ready." I try to match his tone. "I am actually very intrigued to hear your outlined suggestions about the parameters of the experiment and its projected outcomes." Another ant flies past my face.

Ben stares at me. "We don't need an outline," he says gently, but with some exasperation in his voice. "This is a romantic picnic, Bea. Parameters and projected outcomes are not romantic."

"Right," I say, distracted by another ant. It occurs to me then that we have a more pressing problem. "Actually, Ben—"

"No, Bea," he says, holding up a hand to stop me. "I know you think you can handle this like any of your other experiments, but in this instance, you have to admit that I know a little more than you—"

"Fine. But the thing is, Ben—" I try again, flicking my hand as yet another ant buzzes in front of my face.

"Bea," he exclaims, "if you're going to keep interrupting me, then how am I supposed to concentrate? You're the one who said you wanted romantic gestures, and I've actually got several ideas." He takes out a slim volume. "I thought perhaps some poetry," he says. "I know you said it was a waste of time, but *this*—well, this will change your mind."

I look up at the sky while he begins to read aloud from the book. Several crows wheel high above us, snapping at the air. I debate whether or not to try to point this out to him, but decide instead to simply sit back and let events unfold as they may.

"But thy eternal summer . . ." Ben breaks off, batting at his face.

"Yes?" I ask mildly.

"Thy eternal summer . . ." Ben tries again and stops, his hand flicking near his ear. "Oh, buzz off, you bloody things," he mutters as several more insects join the first. "What the hell is going on?"

"Well," I say. "As I was trying to tell you, I believe we might have disturbed a nest of *Lasius niger* during their nuptial flight."

Ben looks at me as though I have sprouted an extra head. "And in English, please?"

"Flying ants," I reply.

"Of course," he grumbles, snatching up the remains of the picnic and stuffing them hastily back in the basket as the cloud of ants grows in the sky overhead. "Try and take you anywhere and suddenly it's swarms of flying locusts."

"Locusts?" I chuckle, folding the blanket. "Oh, Ben, you couldn't be more wrong. A locust is part of the order of Orthoptera, while an ant belongs to the order of Hymenoptera along with wasps and bees."

"Very interesting," Ben says frostily.

"It is, actually." I pause to observe the ant that has just

landed on the back of my hand. "The nuptial flight is when the young queens all leave the nest to strike out on their own and start new colonies. They mate with the smaller male ants in the air." I look up at the throng. "The male ants live for just a day or two after the flight—their only job is to mate with the new queens." I smile at him. "As with so much of nature, it all comes down to sex."

Ben grabs my hand, dragging me away from the swarm and in the direction of the villa.

"Maybe we should stay and watch," I say. "It only happens one day a year."

"Being attacked by a horde of Hymenopteras was *not* high on my list of romantic activities," he grumbles.

"You are using that word wrong," I point out.

"This experiment is going to be a disaster if you won't take it seriously," Ben says crossly. "You've got the romantic soul of a . . . a . . . plank."

"That is very unfair!" We are a safe distance from the ants, and I pull my arm out of his grip. "And," I add, "if you think that poetry is going to work on me, then you're wrong. Why were you waving your arms around like that?"

"It's called emotion," Ben says, giving me a dark look. "It's *usually* something that women appreciate."

By the time we arrive back at the villa we have settled into silence. We are greeted on the terrace by Filomena and Hero.

"Ah," Filomena exclaims. "There you are! Your uncle was

looking for you, Bea. I'm afraid he has had to go to Milan for a short time on business. He wanted to say goodbye, but we couldn't find you."

Although we haven't been doing anything wrong, I notice with interest that Ben flushes a little at this.

"We went for a picnic," I say, at the same time that Ben says, "We were having an art lesson."

Filomena's amused glance takes in both of us. "I see."

"At least you managed to avoid getting covered in paint this time, Bea," Hero says. "You must be improving. Not a speck of paint anywhere, in fact."

There's a pause.

"I think I'm getting better," I agree at last.

"She's certainly . . . trying," Ben says. *"In every sense of the word,"* he adds quietly, so that only I can hear him.

I choose to ignore this. "How were *your* lessons, Hero?" I ask. I immediately realize this was a mistake, as my cousin unleashes a rather disjointed rant about Signora Giuliani and her various shortcomings both as an instructor and as a human being. From the pained look in Filomena's eyes, I suspect that she has heard this already.

"She's just so awful!" Hero finishes. "Awful!"

"I know, I know," Filomena says soothingly. "But we must respect your father's wishes, my dear."

Hero's mouth sets in a straight line. "I don't see why, if he's not even going to be around!" she exclaims, and then she turns and stomps into the house. With a heavy sigh, Filomena follows.

"Hero!" she calls. "Hero! Wait!"

Ben and I are left standing on the steps. We don't look at each other.

"Well," I manage at last, clearing my throat. "It looks as though our romantic rendezvous was a bit of a disaster, doesn't it?"

"Not at all," Ben replies quickly. "I think it just means that I need to increase my efforts."

"The picnic was a nice idea, though," I say encouragingly.

"Next time I'll try and keep the swarming insects to a minimum."

"Don't bother on my account," I respond cheerfully. "I would have been very happy to stay and watch."

"You really would, wouldn't you?" Ben rubs his neck ruefully. "I can see I'm going to need to rethink my tactics."

"I don't think it's supposed to be a military operation."

"Oh no?" He raises an eyebrow. "Well, it's a challenge, at least, and one I mean to win." There's a glint in his eye as he says it, one that sends a prickle of awareness down my spine. There's also a swagger in his step as he turns and walks away.

I watch his retreating back until he disappears around a corner, and then I sit on the steps with a sigh.

It seems that young men are going to prove even more interesting than glowworms.

CHAPTER TWENTY-ONE

◆

Although I would have sworn that my time in Italy could not possibly become more relaxed, it seems I was wrong. My uncle's absence has a curious and unexpected effect on the atmosphere at the villa. Everyone seems to breathe out a little. As the days pass, melting seamlessly into one another, our tenuous grip on routine is lost completely.

"What time is it?" I ask one morning from the lounger where I am sprawled, my wide-brimmed hat pulled down low on my face. A battered copy of *Lady Chatterley's Lover* dangles from my fingers. Ursula gave it to me to read, saying that if I was going to take my romantic education seriously, then this was the proper place to start. So far it has been quite illuminating.

"I have no idea," Ursula murmurs from the lounger beside

me. "You're the scientist. Can't you work it out from the position of the sun or something?"

"I can't believe it's so hot," I moan, ignoring this. "How can it keep getting hotter?"

A trickle of perspiration runs down my chest, and I fan myself wearily with the book. We have been enduring a heat wave over the last few days, temperatures spiking so high that it's impossible to escape the stifling, smothering feeling. The heat is something else: heavy and pulsing, wrapped suffocatingly around us all and leaving oil-slick shimmers in the air. The villa is unusually quiet, with just Klaus, Ursula, and Ben still here with Filomena, Hero, and me. There have been no other visitors for days.

"I'm going to swim," Klaus croaks from the chair he has pulled into the shade. "In a moment, when I can move, I'm going to swim." He is wearing only bathing shorts, his head flung back, his arms limp by his sides. These days we all wear as little as possible, and I'm a bit surprised by how quickly I've grown used to it.

Well, almost. I still think it's rather daring that I lie out in my bathing suit, but that article of clothing is positively puritanical compared to the two-piece costume that Ursula wears. When I first saw it my eyes nearly popped out of my head, and Ursula laughed, calling me the "little Victorian."

"Swimming won't help," I groan. "The pool is warm. Everything is warm. I'll never be cold again."

"I need water," Klaus says hoarsely.

"Yes," Ursula says longingly, "in a tall glass with ice."

"Ohhh," I whimper.

"Go on, then." Ursula kicks her leg halfheartedly in my direction. "You go."

"I can't move. You go."

"Did someone call for drinks?" Ben appears, a tray in his hands.

"Is that . . . cold lemonade?" Ursula rallies slightly, lifting the sunglasses up from her eyes to squint at Ben. "Are you a vision? An angel?"

"Lucifer, possibly," I say, smiling up at him.

"Do you want a drink or not?" Ben asks sweetly.

"Yes, please." I take the glass he hands me, draining the lemonade inside in one long, thirsty draft. It is icy sweet and lip-tinglingly sour at the same time, and utterly delicious.

"Where have you been?" Ursula asks Ben. Revived by her drink, she pulls herself into a sitting position, admiring the biscuity tan on her legs.

"Working," Ben says, taking a sip and wiping his mouth with the back of his hand. My eyes catch there on his lips for a moment. "Like the rest of you should be."

"Not me," I point out over Ursula's and Klaus's groans. "I'm on holiday. Or enforced exile, I suppose. Reflecting on my bad behavior."

"Well, I should think that's plenty to keep you occupied." Ben sits, lowering his feet over the edge into the pool. "It's like bathwater!" he exclaims.

"This heat is unnatural," Ursula says. "I remember what

it was to be cold once." Her voice takes on a wistful quality. "To have to wrap up in coats and scarves against the biting wind." She sighs. "I'm actually starting to miss Vienna."

"Don't be foolish," Klaus says, finally dragging himself to his feet. "This place is heaven and you know it."

"Klaus is right," I say drowsily. "I can't think of anywhere I'd rather be."

Klaus smiles sweetly at me and I smile back, lowering my eyelashes in what I hope is a flirtatious gesture. There seems to be a lot of fluttering eyelashes in the business of flirtation, and I am supposed to be learning about romance, after all.

"Have you got something in your eye?" Ben asks sourly.

"Let me check that for you," Klaus says smoothly, and he bends down so that his face is close to mine, one hand cupping my chin.

"Hmmm," he murmurs, his breath fanning warm against my skin. "I don't see anything."

"Are you sure?" I ask softly. This is going marvelously. Full marks for flirtation; it seems I am a natural after all.

"He's sure," Ben says. "Short of climbing inside your eye, he couldn't be looking more closely."

Klaus releases my chin and steps back, his eyes laughing. "I think that the heat has got you on edge, my friend."

"Is it perhaps that our little experiment is not going to plan?" Ursula murmurs. "Perhaps Bea is not as susceptible to your charms as others, Benedick."

Ben grins, a flash of white teeth in his tanned face. "I think that Bea just needs more exposure to them." He gets to his feet and holds out a hand to me. "In fact, that is precisely what I came to discuss with you, Bea, if you don't mind a word in private." He glances over at Ursula and Klaus, who are watching avidly. "It's a bit much to ask a man to do all his wooing with an audience."

"Of course," I say. "Let's talk." I place my hands in his and let him pull me up; then I pick up the trousers pooled by my sun lounger, stepping into them before slipping my feet into my sandals.

Ben leads me around to the other side of a tall laurel hedge before turning to face me. He is, I notice, still holding lightly on to my hand, his fingers tangled through my own.

I look up at him, waiting for him to speak, struck again by how blue his eyes are.

"You're flirting with Klaus," he says.

"Oh, am I?" I say, pleased. "That is good. I wasn't totally sure I was doing it right."

Ben looks torn between irritation and amusement again. "Oh, you're doing it right," he says, his fingers toying gently with mine. "I suppose I just hoped that if there was going to be any flirting it was going to be . . . well, with me."

"Oh," I say.

"I know the picnic didn't go to plan," he says, "but I think we need to give it another chance."

I consider this for a moment. "A good experiment should always leave a margin for error."

"So we can try again?" I think the smile Ben gives me is actually a little relieved.

"All right," I say. "We can shake on it again if you like."

Ben tugs a little at my hand, and we're standing very close together now. I pull back to look at his face, finding my eyes are on a level with his mouth. My brain empties and, for a second, something electric snaps in the air around us; what little distance there was between us seems to be fast disappearing, and I feel Ben's arm close around my waist.

"Oh, I think we can do better than that," he murmurs.

There's a breathless beat as he bends his head toward mine. An outbreak of voices and laughter comes suddenly from the pool and breaks the tension. I pull away from Ben, surprised to find my breathing slightly ragged.

"Let's go back," I say.

"As you wish." He is, I notice, also a little flushed, but he holds out his hand to me, and as we walk back, his easy charm slips seamlessly back into place.

We reach the pool to find that Hero and Filomena have joined the others. Filomena is dressed in paint-and plaster-spattered overalls; Hero is pink-faced and frowning.

"Look at you all having a lovely time," Hero complains, "while I'm stuck inside with Signora Giuliani, conjugating verbs."

"Your father would not be pleased if I allowed you to abandon your schoolwork," Filomena points out gently.

"I still don't think it's fair," Hero says.

It's difficult for her, I think—the three-year age gap between us can feel so big, and I know she sometimes feels excluded from our group.

"It's much too hot to be studying." She sighs. "I wish it would rain."

"Rain," Ursula repeats dreamily. "I remember rain."

"It's boring and hot," says Hero again. "Oh, I wish that something would happen."

Filomena is watching Hero, and her expression is understanding. "Well, then, there is nothing else for it," she says, squeezing the girl's arm. "Tonight we must have a feast for Jupiter, god of thunderstorms, in the hope that we appease him and bring rain."

Hero gasps.

"Truly, Filomena?" she says, her eyes bright. "A feast for Jupiter? Will there be a ritual? A blood sacrifice?"

Filomena chuckles. "No blood sacrifice," she says, and Hero's face drops so dramatically that Ben snorts with laughter. "But a ritual, certainly," Filomena continues, and Hero hops delightedly from foot to foot. "We will honor our ancient Roman ancestors properly." She glances around at the rest of us. "I hope you will all be there."

"If it means rain, then I'm all for it," Ursula says.

"Me too," Klaus says.

"What do we have to do?" I ask suspiciously.

"Leave it to me." Filomena is enigmatic. "You may await my instructions." She turns. "Come, Hero; we have much to organize."

"Why does that sound ominous?" Ben asks as we all watch Hero hurrying off after her future stepmother.

CHAPTER TWENTY-TWO

◆

Later that night I am sitting in front of the mirror. I can't stop thinking about the moment I shared with Ben in the garden. What would have happened, I wonder, if Hero and Filomena hadn't interrupted us? Would Ben have kissed me?

The reflection before me shows my eyes wide and shining, and I can't seem to stay still.

My thoughts are interrupted by a knock on my door, and I open it to find Hero, beaming and clutching a pile of bed linen to her chest.

"What have you got there?" I ask.

"It's your costume, of course," she says, stepping over the threshold.

"My what?"

Hero drops the sheets onto the bed, and I realize that she is wearing what can only be described as a white toga.

"Oh no," I say quickly, holding my hands up in front of me. "I'm not wearing one of those."

"You don't have any choice," Hero says, giggling evilly. "It's all part of the ritual." I eye the sheets uneasily. "I'll dress you—Filomena taught me how to do it," she insists. "I think you'll look lovely, Bea, like a Roman goddess. Please let me; everyone else is."

"This is ridiculous." I sigh, but I'm no match for Hero's pleading face. "Go on, then," I say reluctantly.

"Take off your clothes," Hero orders as she snatches up a large white sheet victoriously.

I stand in my underwear and let Hero wind the sheet around me, moving the white cotton this way and that, her face screwed up in concentration.

"Ow!" I exclaim as she jabs me with a pin.

"Sorry, sorry," she mutters. "It looked much easier when Filomena did it."

"I can't believe I'm letting you get away with this," I say. "And I can't believe Ursula did either."

"Not just Ursula." Hero smirks. "Klaus looks *very* fetching in a sheet."

"Don't tell me Fil's got the boys to agree to this as well?"

"Mm-hmm." Hero nods, a frown of concentration on her face as she fiddles with the sheet at my shoulder. "Okay." She smiles, standing back and looking at me proudly. "All done."

I turn to look in the mirror and it is, unfortunately, not a transformative moment.

Far from resembling a Roman goddess, I look exactly like I've been wound up in two long white sheets, one around my waist and one around my torso, which is tied together on one shoulder. The outfit is finished off with a white-and-gold braid, which I recognize as being a curtain tie from Leo's study, cinching me in at the waist.

Still, Hero looks happy, so I murmur something about it being surprisingly comfortable. (That part at least is true, even if I do look like a badly prepared mummy.)

"Let me do your hair now," Hero commands, gesturing imperiously to the chair in front of the mirror. I sit, and she spends the next few minutes carefully plaiting and coiling my hair into a glossy dark knot on top of my head, which she pins in place. This part of the costume, I must admit, is rather flattering, and I tip my face from side to side, enjoying her work.

"You are clever, Hero," I say.

"Filomena taught me," she says. "I suppose Mother might have shown me how to do it one day. . . ." She trails off, her hand resting lightly on my shoulder. I reach up and squeeze her fingers.

"I suppose she might have," I agree, even though I find it hard to imagine Aunt Thea having anything at all to do with tonight's festivities. "Are you happy, Hero?" I ask. "About Uncle Leo and Filomena, I mean?"

"Oh yes," Hero says, just a shade too brightly. "I think Filomena is wonderful. I suppose it is a bit strange imagining them actually being married."

I know what she means. *Marriage* sounds so respectable and ordinary that it is difficult to imagine Filomena doing it. Perhaps that is the reason for the slight reserve I have noticed on her side, I think, and the fact that no one ever mentions a wedding date. Maybe it isn't what she really wants.

I bite my lip and look up at Hero's reflection. She is playing with a loose curl that she has left out of my elaborate hairstyle, toying with it so that it brushes my bare shoulder, her face a mask of concentration. I hope that if Filomena changes her mind about the wedding, Hero will not be too upset.

"Right," she says, clapping her hands together. "Are you ready?"

"As I'll ever be," I say, getting to my feet.

"Then let's go."

Hero leads me through the house and outside. I'm surprised when we pass by the empty terrace and keep going through the grounds, heading for the dense tree line that borders the edge of the villa's property.

It is twilight, and the night is perfectly clear, not a rain cloud in sight. The stars are just beginning to show themselves, winking against the bruised blue-black sky, and I know that soon there will be thousands of them, scattered as carelessly as glitter across the darkness. I know this because it happens every night, but it still feels like a gift.

The balmy air is warm against my skin, and the humidity is high. I suppose that going out dressed in a thin bedsheet has its advantages. As we push further into the forest of ilex trees, the carefully executed scene comes dramatically into view.

There's an abrupt opening in the woods—a glade, I suppose—and it's exactly the sort of place one might expect to trip over a cast of Roman gods. In the middle of the space is a fire pit circled in large white stones, and the beginnings of the fire are already kindling there, orange flames licking over the tall pyramid of crackling dry branches, casting the scene with a strange, feverish glow.

Brightly colored picnic blankets are spread on the ground around the fire, and there are dark stone dishes dotted about, piled high with cold roast chicken, bread, cheese, and deep purple grapes. These are interspersed with flat silver platters holding clusters of tall pillar candles. The heat from the fire adds to the otherworldly effect of the scene, and it sends shadows leaping around us as if we find ourselves standing in the middle of a magic lantern.

"Beatrice," Filomena cries, her voice throaty as she strides toward me. The fire behind her highlights the curves of her silhouette, though I notice that her toga, unlike mine and Hero's, is blood-red, and she wears a circle of fat red roses in her hair. "This is for you," she says, holding a crown of laurel leaves tied with a white ribbon, which she sets gently on my head.

"Um, thank you," I say, trying to inject my voice with solemnity, and I hear a muffled snort of laughter. I notice

Ursula stretched out on one of the blankets like a cat, half in darkness. Only the cigarette in her hand and the familiar flash of scarlet lipstick betray the fact that she isn't an ancient goddess fallen out of time. I can't help but observe that the white toga looks far more convincing on her.

"Come and sit with me, Goddess Beatrice," she murmurs. "You might enjoy the view."

I move to sit beside her, the heat from the fire flaring across my skin. Then I see what she means. Walking toward us are Ben and Klaus.

Ben gives me a courtly wave and I smile.

"I take it the experiment is progressing well?" Ursula says.

"I think so."

"Your flirting is already more accomplished." She raises an eyebrow at me. "Careful you don't have my brother falling all over you as well."

I laugh. "Ben was rather put out by my success there."

"Men, darling." She sighs. "So insecure."

As the boys reach us, Ursula and I cheer and whistle.

Klaus smooths down his toga. "This is far less restrictive than usual evening dress," he says. "I could get used to it."

"I can't believe I let Filomena talk me into this nonsense," Ben says, though his grin belies his words.

"Oh, don't," I say. "Look how happy Hero is." We all look over to see Hero laugh as Filomena straightens the laurel crown on her head. Ben's face softens.

"She does look happy," he says.

"And I think you both look very handsome," I add.

"I have to say, I agree," he says, glancing down at the makeshift toga, which I must admit is showing off his muscular arms and shoulders to their best advantage.

"*Both* of you," I stress.

"But me in particular, I expect." Ben preens and I groan. Hero dances over with laurel wreaths for the boys.

"Please, be seated," Hero says solemnly. "It is time to begin the sacred ceremony."

Ben rolls his eyes but drops down good-naturedly beside me on the blanket, reaching across to pluck one of the purple grapes from the bunch and popping it into his mouth.

"Don't start the feast yet!" Hero cries, making Ben jump. "There's an order to things that must be observed," she says seriously.

"Hero is right." Filomena stands beside her now, the light from the fire dancing across her face. "Tonight we come to make a bargain with the gods. We shall feast, celebrate, dance, and we will do so to honor the ancient ways." She pours red liquid from a glass bottle into a large earthenware bowl. I think I recognize it as the fruit bowl from the kitchen. "We begin with the ceremonial wine."

"Ceremonial wine is just what I need to get through this," Ben says, but when I catch his eye he composes himself and sits straight.

Hero takes the bowl from Filomena and insinuates herself into the circle, standing between me and Ursula.

"Oh, Jupiter," she intones. "We come tonight to ask for rain, that the scorched earth may feel your tears once more upon her lovely face." She lifts the bowl up high and then brings it to her lips, taking a sip before passing it to Ursula.

"That was excellent," I whisper as she takes a seat beside me. "Very dramatic."

"I wanted to say it in Latin, but I couldn't remember my declensions and I didn't want to mess it up," she murmurs, her face intent. "I wouldn't want to do anything to anger the gods."

"I thought it was a very effective toast. Poetic, even," I reassure Hero before turning to Ben, who is holding the bowl out to me. I take it from him, lift it to my mouth, and take a sip before handing it back to Hero.

"And now . . ." Hero pauses dramatically. "The feast BEGINS!" And with that she hurls the bowl into the fire, where it cracks in two.

Her audience cheers loudly, though I can't help but think it was a waste of a perfectly nice fruit bowl. Still, I suppose it all adds to the drama.

Great platters of chicken are passed around, and we fall on the food, laughing and throwing the chicken bones into the flames as further evidence of our sacrifice.

When we have finished, Filomena stands and recites a poem in Latin. She's much more convincing than Ben, when it comes to the drama; her voice is low but compelling, and I can just about understand the words.

Da mi basia mille, deinde centum,
dein mille altera, dein secunda centum,
deinde usque altera mille, deinde centum;
dein, cum milia multa fecerimus,
conturbabimus, illa ne sciamus . . .

"What is she saying?" Ben whispers, his voice warm on my neck.

" 'Give me a thousand kisses, then a hundred,' " I begin, and then I turn to see him looking at me, the flames from the fire dancing in his eyes, and my mouth goes dry. I shake my head. "I—I'm not sure about the rest," I finish weakly. The truth is that the parts that I do understand are so achingly romantic that I can't bear to say them out loud, particularly to him.

The wine flows. They have brought out the wind-up gramophone, and Hero puts on a record. The music sounds wilder out here, all shrieking brass and jangling piano. The crackle of the needle over the record echoes the sound of the flames, as though the music itself is burning. We dance barefoot around the fire, happy and dusty and raising our glasses over and over again to the god of thunderstorms. It feels a bit magical, this, a little like we really are in touch with the elements. As if anything could happen.

The flames twist higher and higher, sparks flashing in the air like pieces of copper foil falling around us. Klaus grasps my hands between his own and reels me around and around until I am doubled over, laughing and breathless. It's feverishly hot now; the air is smothering, thick with the taste of smoke, and the stars have begun to disappear as clouds roll in across the sky.

A hand grabs mine, and I spin around to find myself looking up at Ben. He takes me in his arms and the music slows down, a dreamy melody with a man singing about lovers and starlight. Ben's hand is tight on my waist, and as I put my palm on his chest I can feel his heart beating as fast as my own. We come to a halt, and when I look up, I see his eyes are on mine.

"It's working, it's working!" Hero cries as a rumble of thunder groans and the air around us trembles. I pull away from Ben as the first drops of rain start to fall. With a crack of lightning scissoring through the sky in the distance, the heavens finally open.

"Yarooooo!" the cry goes up, and the others dance, laughing, half running back toward the house, their arms in the air and their delighted screams echoing around us.

I go to follow them, but Ben stops me, putting a hand on my arm.

"What is it?" I ask, looking up at him. A nervous feeling shivers through me.

"It's about the experiment," he says, drawing me closer. "I think there's something that Ursula mentioned that we haven't tried yet." The briefest glimpse of uncertainty flashes in his eyes. "If you're interested, I mean."

Suddenly I'm not afraid at all. I feel utterly, uncontrollably alive. Rain drips from his curling gold hair, and an unstoppable grin spreads over my face.

"You look pleased with yourself," he murmurs.

I lean toward him, my hand going to his cheek to pull him toward me, my lips against his ear. "Do you want me to kiss you, Ben?" I whisper softly, and I feel him freeze. "You only need to ask." I fight the laughter rising inside me; the joy of turning the tables is so complete. "Nicely."

There is a pause, half a second that feels like forever.

"Yes," he replies. "Please."

CHAPTER TWENTY-THREE

◆

There's a split second where I can't believe it's really going to happen, and then, just like that, it does. I am kissing Ben, and it turns out that kissing Ben is magic.

His mouth brushes against mine, soft at first, and my arms twine around his neck seemingly of their own accord. I lean toward him with a little sigh and feel his smile against my lips. I pull him closer to me, my eyes fluttering closed as I enjoy the sensation of being so near. He tastes of wine and something sweet and spicy, like cinnamon.

The rain hammers around us, and the kiss deepens into something hungry, as if my body is starving for something that I don't even understand, a need pooling in my belly. His hand tangles in my hair, all of Hero's carefully placed pins tumble to the ground, and it feels as though electric currents pass between us, as though everywhere he touches me sparks and shivers. It's greedy and urgent and it leaves me trembling.

After a moment that feels both fleeting and endless, I seem to come to myself again. I pull away and blink, the world coming slowly back into focus. The others have completely disappeared. Ben and I stand in the rain staring at each other. His pupils are wildly dilated, and we are both breathing heavily.

I try to remember the experiment, to think of this kiss as an intriguing result that needs recording, but all my usual poise has deserted me. All I can do is look at Ben, and the only relief I can find is that his expression is as stunned as mine must be.

Another crack of lightning slices through the sky, and that finally jolts me out of my stupor. I am, I realize, standing in the middle of a forest during a thunderstorm, kissing a man in a bedsheet. I choke on a giggle that contains more than an edge of hysteria.

"I can't believe it really rained," Ben says, looking around him.

"The significant increase in humidity today made it likely," I reply automatically.

"Or the god of thunderstorms has been appeased." Ben's dimples flash, and just like that I'm thinking about kissing him again. His eyes drop to my mouth and I know the feeling is mutual; we lean in toward each other again, like magnets irresistibly drawn together. I can feel the warmth of his breath against my wet cheek.

"We have to go," I manage, my voice hoarse as I take a firm grip on myself.

"Absolutely," says Ben, blinking. "Yes."

I swing around, wrenching myself away from him, my legs still unsteady as I march back to the house. I don't turn to see if Ben is following me. Impossible as it seems, we arrive back at the villa only a couple of minutes after the others, who are still shrieking and shaking the rain from themselves. Only Ursula seems to notice our brief absence, and the look she gives me is enigmatic.

I am shivering, a fact that I put down to the chill as the water evaporates from my skin. Filomena is already handing out towels, and I wrap one around myself, welcoming the rough warmth.

"We did it! We did it!" Hero exclaims as she skips about the kitchen. She throws her arms around Ben in excitement. His eyes meet mine over the top of her head, and my stomach feels as though I'm suddenly falling from a great height. What on earth is the matter with me? Perhaps I'm ill. I touch my fingers to my wrist, and my pulse is certainly a little faster than usual.

"I'm going to go and get changed," I say, longing for a moment alone to sort through my disordered thoughts and feelings.

"Yes, yes," Filomena says, waving a hand. "Go and change into dry clothes and then we will have hot tea in the kitchen.

I will not have everyone succumbing to influenza while Leo is away. I know how delicate you English are—I have read my Jane Austen."

Closing the door of my room behind me, I lean back against the solid oak for a moment, catching my breath. My heart is still skittering. I glance at the mirror, and looking back at me is a wide-eyed, bedraggled, drowned wreck of a girl. My hair stands out around my head in a sodden tangle; my face is a pale moon. My makeshift toga is soaking, but, thanks to Hero's enthusiastic wrapping, at least it is not transparent.

"It was just a kiss." I surprise myself by saying the words aloud into the empty room. They seem to linger in the air. My voice is firm, convincing.

Still. I raise my fingers to my lips again, and the pale girl in the mirror does the same. That kiss. It was as if all that strange crackling tension between Ben and me was the gunpowder leading to that inevitable explosion. I had no idea, *no idea* that it would be, could be, like that. I wonder if it always is. I wonder if Ben is as startled as I am or whether that was just another kiss for him with just another girl.

Mechanically I begin to undress and change into my nightgown. I towel my hair and do my best to untangle it, scraping it up and away from my face; then I get into bed and hide under the covers like a child.

I can't go back down there tonight. I'm too full of it all. I think if I see Ben now, then I might burst. When Hero calls softly through my door, I pretend to be asleep.

In the distance I can hear the revelry continuing in the kitchen, the odd squawk of laughter or shout of excitement. The rain is still drumming outside, against the earth, against the pine needles. There's a music to it that sings through the window, and I listen to it for a long, long time before I finally fall asleep.

CHAPTER TWENTY-FOUR

◆

The next morning, I wake feeling groggy. When I throw open the shutters, I am greeted by another perfect sunny day, and it's almost hard to believe that the rain really came last night.

Almost, but not quite, because the air has that sweet, stripped-clean feeling about it, that freshness that only comes after a storm. I take a deep breath of it, enjoying the green smell of the hills. I stand for a moment, looking unseeingly at the view, thinking again of Ben's lips on mine. I am only brought back to my senses when the sound of birdsong sends me lurching for my binoculars. I am relieved to see that the kiss hasn't completely scrambled my brain. Again I fail to catch a glimpse of the bird that's been eluding me.

After a quick wash I pull on my trusty trousers and a soft shirt the color of the bluebells that carpet the woods near Langton each spring. I grab my hat and go downstairs.

Everything is quiet and there is no sight of the others. Without really knowing where I am heading, I begin to wind through the gardens, following the paths that cut between the yew hedges until I reach the stone fountain in the center.

I suppose part of me knew that I would find him there. He is sitting on the broad stone ledge that borders the fountain, a book in his hand. He looks relaxed, rumpled, his long legs stretched out in front of him and crossed at the ankles. I clear my throat and he glances up.

"Hello," I say. He lays down his book and gets to his feet. I recognize the book as a mystery story full of sensational twists and turns—I have read it myself, picked it up from behind Mother's plant pots, in fact.

"I didn't have you down for a mystery reader," I say.

"It's one of her best," he says easily. His voice is warm. It feels intimate, as if the way he speaks to me is different now.

He drops back onto the stone seat, patting the space beside him companionably, but I remain standing, looking down at him, my hands clasped behind my back so that he can't see me twisting them anxiously. "About last night . . ."

"Ah yes," he says. "It's been on my mind as well."

"It has?"

"I've thought of nothing else." The corner of his mouth tugs up. "Klaus really does not have the build to be wearing a toga in public."

I bite back a laugh. "I was talking about the kiss."

"Mmmmm," Ben murmurs, his eyes moving to my mouth. "Now, *that* was quite the revelation." He stretches, looking pleased with himself. "A good introduction to kisses, I'm sure you'll agree."

I feel a flicker of annoyance. After all, I had something to do with it too.

"Well, yes," I say briskly. "It was adequate."

"Adequate?" His mouth drops open.

"Yes." I wave my hand. "I'm sure that next time it will be more . . ." I pause, pursing my lips, schooling my features into something thoughtful.

"More *what*?" he demands icily.

"I don't know," I muse, "just . . . well, *more*."

He surges to his feet, laughter and outrage writ large on his face, and I enjoy a moment of victory before I find myself kissing him. Again.

I don't know who kisses who first this time, but it's as if there was no gap between this kiss and the one last night. His hands cradle my face and, just like that, all of the want, all of the blissful, delicious sensation of last night surges instantly through my body at his touch, like a fuse immediately alight.

When we finally break apart, Ben eyes me with something like reproach. "Adequate, indeed," he says.

"I'm sorry," I say, with a breathless laugh, "but you looked so horribly smug, Ben. I couldn't resist."

He resumes his seat, and I sit beside him, pulling my legs up so that I can cross them. For some reason this second kiss seems to have broken through my nerves. I don't really understand why, because, if anything, the ferocity of it should have been unsettling. Instead, it is as though the ice has been broken. Well, less broken and more completely and utterly melted.

"A successful result," I say. "The first time could have been an anomaly, but it seems not."

"That's one way of putting it," Ben says, looking at me as though he's not quite sure what I'm going to say next.

"I'm glad," I say, pulling a notebook from my pocket and opening it. I pick up his abandoned book to rest it on. "Because I have quite a few questions."

Ben looks startled. "Questions?"

I regard him through narrowed eyes. "You've obviously never taken part in an experiment before," I say. "Collating accurate information is very important."

"I can think of more important things," he says huskily, his hand on my knee.

"Oh, really?" I ask, producing a pencil from my pocket and holding it over the paper. "And what might they be?"

There's a pause and Ben shakes his head in exasperation, removing his hand.

"Why don't we just start with your questions?" he says finally, his tone resigned.

"All right," I agree. "First of all. The kiss. We have established that it was somewhat above adequate. . . ."

"We have."

"But it would be helpful if you could provide more detail about your response."

"Such as?" Ben raises his eyebrows.

"Well, you have a much larger sample for comparison. I

have only been kissed once before and it was not terribly successful. Our teeth seemed to knock together too much, and it was a bit . . . wet."

"I'm pleased to hear that this experience was an improvement," Ben says faintly.

"Significantly." A look of pride flashes across Ben's face. "So?" I say, lifting my pencil again in readiness.

"So what?"

"So, how was it for you?" I ask. "Purely in the spirit of scientific inquiry, of course."

"In the spirit of scientific inquiry . . ." Ben shakes his head. "It was . . . I don't know, Bea! It was . . . good."

"Good?" I make a note. "Could you expand upon that a little?"

"Very good," Ben says. "Are you writing that down?"

"Very good," I say slowly, and a warm feeling settles in my belly.

"Yes, Bea." He throws his hands up in exasperation. "Very good. Excellent, in fact. In the top five of the *millions* of kisses I have obviously experienced."

"Top five?" I pause, my pencil hovering over the page. "How gratifying. And without any practice . . . That must be a good sign. Perhaps I'm a natural talent." I look at the next item on my list. "Right. Technique."

"Technique?" Ben repeats mechanically.

"Yes." I push a stray curl behind my ear. "For example, there was . . . a thing you did to my neck that I found particularly enjoyable."

"Oh?"

"Yes." I touch the spot just underneath my jaw. "Here."

Very slowly, Ben reaches out and brushes his own fingers against my skin, and it's as if all the blood spontaneously rushes to my cheeks. "Here?" he asks softly.

"Y-yes." I'm surprised to find myself stuttering.

Ben moves closer, turning toward me. He brushes his lips gently against the place under discussion, feathering light kisses down the side of my neck.

"Like this?" he asks, pulling back slightly. His face is close to mine; his pupils are wide, turning his eyes a darker, navy blue.

"Yes," I say, my hand stealing up to touch the side of his face. "Like that. What about you?" I ask. "What do you like?"

In answer he leans forward and presses his lips to mine. His mouth is soft and delicious. He trails hundreds of those terribly lovely kisses along my neck, leaving me shivering. We kiss for a long while: slow, drugging kisses that have no beginning or end, that leave me feeling heavy-limbed and dreamy. It's strange how not-strange it feels, how completely right and good it is.

When we break apart, I am left staring at him wordlessly.

"Aren't you going to write that down?" Ben quirks an eyebrow, but his voice betrays a slight tremor.

"I'm not exactly sure how to write that down," I admit.

"Well," he says, "at least we know the kissing part of the experiment won't be a chore."

"No." I lift my fingers to my lips, which feel tender and swollen. "I suppose not."

Ben's book has dropped to the ground. I look at the notebook in my lap. It's certainly going to be difficult to keep a level head. "Is it always like this?" I ask.

"No, Bea." Ben lets out a slow breath. "It's not."

"Oh." I don't know if that makes me feel better or worse. "So . . ." I struggle for a moment, not wanting to push too much, but also interested in the answer. "I'm different?" I ask finally.

Ben takes my hand in his own, tangling his fingers through mine and squeezing gently. "I actually think you're sort of . . . extraordinary."

"You do?" I blink.

"Well, yes," Ben says. "I mean, you're completely maddening, of course, but you're clever and interesting and funny—sometimes even on purpose."

"Oh," I manage, completely reeling from this unexpected barrage of compliments. "Thank you."

"Don't go getting a big head about it," Ben warns quickly. "After all, compliments are part of the whole wooing thing. I'm contractually obliged to produce them. I'd be more than happy to sit here and list all your flaws, but that wasn't part of the deal."

"The feeling is mutual," I say, but I'm smiling. Even if the compliments are just part of the experiment, they're still nice to hear.

"Good." Ben clears his throat.

I am distracted from whatever he is going to say next by the now-familiar song of the hoopoe. Then, suddenly and without ceremony, the bird I've been so desperate to see lands on a nearby branch, fluffing out its soft peachy feathers, the long black-and-white crest fanned out impressively on its head.

"Look, Ben!" I exclaim, pointing.

My sudden movement must come as something of a surprise. He tips backward, there's a bit of comic arm-wheeling as he hangs, suspended for a second on the edge, and then Ben finally goes head over heels, falling into the fountain with an almighty splash.

I leap to my feet, dodging the tidal wave that his impact sends crashing toward me. Ben emerges from the water, spluttering indignantly, his face a mask of outrage.

"Oh dear," I say.

He stays where he is, sitting in the fountain, blinking at me for a moment. Rivulets of water stream from his hair, and he pushes it back and away from his face.

"Let me guess," he says finally. "There was a dragonfly?"

"Oh no," I say quickly. "A hoopoe, Ben, look!" I turn, but the bird has flown away. "Oh." I frown. "You must have scared it."

"How thoughtless of me," he mutters.

"I don't suppose you did it on purpose, but really, Ben, you are quite clumsy."

Ben glares at me. "I wasn't clumsy before I met you."

"I hardly think you can blame that on me," I say. "But if

your balance is off center, perhaps there's something wrong with you, medically speaking. You should get that looked at. Unsteadiness can be a symptom of many different things. How are you feeling?"

"How am I feeling?" Ben muses, lifting a hand to rub his chin thoughtfully. "How do you *think* I'm feeling, Bea?"

"Quite damp, I should imagine," I say, trying and failing to stifle a laugh.

Ben pushes himself to his feet in one swift movement and, like a sea creature emerging from the deep, he sends another wave of water crashing against the edge of the fountain.

"Now, Ben," I say coaxingly, "don't be cross. Look, I saved the most important thing." I hold out my hand to reveal his book, slightly damp but mostly unharmed.

Ben pauses, looking from my face to the book in my hand. "You," he says, almost to himself, "are the strangest person."

"Extraordinary," I remind him. "You think I'm extraordinary."

"Extraordinarily annoying," he says acidly.

"That doesn't really seem to be in the spirit of our agreement, Ben," I say sweetly. "And you were doing so well with the compliments." I'm taunting him now and it's fun, but the look on his face tells me it's also possibly dangerous. I absolutely wouldn't put it past him to throw me in the fountain out of some misplaced idea of vengeance. I edge away. "Well," I say brightly, "this has all been very enlightening, but I think I'd better be off," and I turn and stride away, ignoring the spluttered outrage that hangs in the air behind me.

CHAPTER TWENTY-FIVE

◆

The days that follow are dreamy and intoxicating and extremely educational.

Ben throws himself into the experiment with great enthusiasm, and there have been enough stolen kisses to fill two notebooks with observations. We have not yet tackled the subject of moving *beyond* kisses, but I have to say my increased awareness of both his body and my own has been rather thrilling.

It's late afternoon now and the light is heavy and golden. We're in the garden, and against my better judgment I'm allowing Ben to give love poetry another go.

"There's no romance in your soul," Ben grumbles as I press my lips together, trying and failing to stop the laughter from escaping.

"I think it's your reading style, rather than the words,"

I point out fairly. Ben is obviously relishing the role of romantic hero, and—as I feared—the overblown, high-drama, "raven-haired beauty" stuff only seems to make me laugh. "I enjoyed Filomena's poetry at the bonfire the other night."

Ben drops to his knees in the grass in front of me. "Ah yes." He smiles wolfishly. " 'Give me a hundred kisses. . . .' "

"A thousand," I correct him.

"Honestly, Bea," he murmurs, leaning in. "You're insatiable."

I am laughing as his lips meet mine.

There's a sound nearby: a foot treading heavily on a twig and an elaborate clearing of the throat. By the time Filomena comes into view, Ben and I have sprung apart, our clothes still slightly rumpled, the pink stain in our cheeks a dead giveaway.

From the smirk on Filomena's face, I can see that we're not fooling anyone.

"There you are," she says. "I've been trying to track you down."

"Have you?" Ben asks, aiming for nonchalance.

Filomena nods. "I wondered how the painting lessons were coming along?" She looks rather pointedly around us, where there is a noticeable absence of art materials.

"Painting, yes," I say, still trying to get my brain back in gear.

"Bea is coming along quite well," Ben jumps in. He gives me a look filled with mischief. "With a bit more practice I think she might do quite nicely."

"It was a shaky start." I nod, flashing him a dirty look. "Ben's teaching technique needed some refining. But things are definitely improving."

"Wonderful," says Filomena serenely. "I look forward to seeing the results. Perhaps Bea can contribute to the exhibition."

"Exhibition?" I ask weakly, looking between her and Ben.

"That's rather a grand description, I suppose," Filomena says. "Really it will be a big party, where we display some of the work created here over the summer."

"Oh yes," I say. "I think Leo mentioned it when I first arrived." It feels like a long time ago.

"I'd half forgotten about it," Ben says, almost to himself.

"I thought perhaps you had," Filomena says gently. "But this could be a good opportunity for you, Ben. Influential people come."

"Yes." Ben rubs his chin distractedly. "I know."

"And," Filomena says, "if Bea contributed as well, then I think Leo would be pleased." He nods. "I will leave you to it, then."

She turns and walks away, her hips swaying and her long, dark hair swishing gently around her waist.

Ben stares after her.

"Are you all right?" I ask. He doesn't reply, and I touch his arm.

"What?" he says, turning. "Oh, yes." He gives his usual carefree grin.

"Looks like you're going to have to produce a work of

dazzling talent, so that I can earn my crust around here," he says.

"Hope you're prepared to go hungry," I grumble.

An hour later we are both standing before canvases in our—now thankfully flying-ant-free—picnic spot. Once again I am halfheartedly attempting to paint the view in front of me while Ben gently corrects some of the many mistakes I make.

I sigh heavily, regarding the mass of marks and splotches on the canvas. "Is this any better?"

"Let's try another approach," Ben says, quite diplomatically for him. "Are there any particular artists that you're drawn to?"

I think about this for a moment. "Father used to have a nice Stubbs before we had to sell it," I say finally. "One of his horse paintings. It was above the mantelpiece in the drawing room. I liked that. It looked like—well, it looked like a real horse."

I expect Ben to be dismissive—even I can tell this is not exactly top-notch art critique—but he nods. "That makes sense," he says. "Stubbs studied anatomy, and his paintings are incredibly accurate, scientifically speaking." He gives me a lopsided smile. "He actually dissected horse carcasses and hung them from the ceiling of a barn, peeling back the different layers and making sketches of them."

"I didn't know that!" I exclaim. "That *is* interesting."

"You *would* find the dissected horse flesh interesting."

Ben pauses. "He wrote a book about it, *The Anatomy of the Horse*," he continues thoughtfully. "It was quite groundbreaking, apparently—the way it brought together art and science."

"Rather like us?" I say.

"Yes." He drops a quick kiss on the tip of my nose. "Like us. But with more dead horses."

I think for a minute. "Do you suppose drawing would help my anatomical studies?" I feel a real tingle of enthusiasm at this.

"I don't see why not," Ben replies. "Anatomical study made Stubbs a better painter; drawing might make you a better scientist. Worth a try, anyway. Why don't you find a suitable subject and see where it takes you?"

While Ben continues with his painting, I go off on a hunt for subject matter. While not squeamish about dissection, I don't like the idea of killing anything just for the sake of a drawing, but about forty minutes later I find a beautiful and categorically dead *Lucanus cervus* in one of the flower beds. Cradling the stag beetle carefully in my hand, I return to find Ben hard at work.

Sitting down on the blanket that we have brought with us, I pull a sketch pad and pencil from Ben's bag and set to work, carefully trying to capture the insect on the page. Looking so carefully at the insect is revealing an intricate world of minute detail that I haven't really seen before. I try to remember what Ben has said about form and perspective, and though the drawing I create is far from perfect, it is, at least, recognizably a beetle. I feel a huge sense of satisfaction at having observed so much, having learned so much, about the creature itself.

I look up when Ben comes to sit beside me. "Nice." He gestures to the drawing.

"Thank you," I say. "I haven't got the maxillary palps quite right."

"What exactly is a maxillary palp?" Ben asks, leaning over.

"These bits here." I point to the small feelers between the beetle's large, hornlike jaws. "They're sensory organs for tasting food. I never noticed how wonderfully complicated the whole jaw was before."

"Seems like sketching could be helpful for a natural historian." Ben leans back on his elbows. "Perhaps you can go to Vienna and draw those man-eating plants at the end of the summer."

"The plants are carnivorous, not man-eating," I say automatically, but my head is buzzing. No one has called me a natural historian before, and it leaves me feeling a bit breathless. It sounds so serious somehow, as if he's taking *me* seriously. "And I'm not a *natural historian*," I say. "I just enjoy studying it. I'm completely self-taught."

Ben shrugs. "So are lots of experts."

"I suppose," I say. "But to be able to study properly, to learn from true specialists and to attend lectures and demonstrations . . ." I feel something leap in my chest. "Well, that would be a dream."

There is a brief silence. I realize that I am bracing myself, holding my body taut as I wait for the dismissal, the cold water thrown over my enthusiasm.

"I understand," Ben says. "That's how I felt when I was studying art in Florence. Being immersed in it, surrounded by so much knowledge and expertise and trying to take some small part of that for yourself, to improve, to do better . . . it's a powerful thing."

I look at him in surprise. He does understand. At least, more than anyone else ever has.

"So why don't you go and study?" Ben asks. "At university, I mean?"

"My family would never approve." I twist my fingers together.

"You don't strike me as someone who seeks approval," Ben says dryly.

I shake my head. I could never explain to him what it's like at home. "We couldn't afford it anyway," I say instead. "University is expensive, and any money my parents have goes straight into the estate."

"What about a scholarship?" Ben presses.

"A scholarship?"

"Yes," he says, as if it's obvious. "You're clearly clever enough. I mean, you're the most intelligent person I know." He grins. "That head of yours contains so much knowledge I'm surprised it doesn't weigh you down."

"It doesn't feel possible." Saying the words aloud, I

realize that they aren't exactly true anymore. What seemed completely impossible in the insular world of Langton Hall doesn't seem as unlikely here.

"You could make it happen, Bea," he says with total confidence. He lies back and laces his fingers together behind his head, closing his eyes against the sunshine.

Impulsively, I lean over him and press a quick kiss on his cheek. The sweet, cut-grass smell of his skin is heady, making my limbs tingle, and I find myself thinking that if I could bottle it I might make a fortune. His eyes flicker open.

"What was that for?" he asks.

"I'm not sure," I say. "I just felt like it. Do you think that marks a new stage in our romance? I should probably record that."

Ben smiles, a slow, sleepy smile. "Oh, I don't know, Bea." He reaches up and pulls me toward him. "I feel like kissing you all the time."

By the time we get back to the villa the sun is starting to go down, and I feel loose-limbed, drugged on kisses. Ben holds my hand the whole way back, and I can feel myself grinning inanely at nothing in particular. This whole summer-romance thing really is quite enjoyable.

When we get to the terrace, Klaus is sitting with a drink. He looks up as we approach.

"Bea," he calls. "Your uncle is back."

"Oh. That's nice." I can't keep a hollow note from my voice. Uncle Leo being back feels like the end of something, and I wonder why.

"He's not alone," Klaus murmurs. "He has brought with him an Englishwoman . . . Lady Frances somebody." He glances at Ben. "And he has brought Sir Hugh."

There is a silence. I look at Ben's face and see that it is stony.

"Who is Sir Hugh?" I ask.

"No one worth talking about," Ben mutters, and with that he turns and strides toward the doors.

I look at Klaus for answers, but he is not giving anything away. We follow Ben inside. When we reach the entrance to the drawing room, Ben hesitates. I go in, but he and Klaus remain behind me in the doorway.

The drawing room looks like a carefully arranged scene from a painting. Everyone is gathered there, drinking tea, though the heat in the room is stifling. I stand silently for a second, taking it all in.

Hero sits on a sofa beside Uncle Leo. Her hands are folded neatly in her lap and she looks bored. Her hair is tidy, her dress perfectly pressed; she looks, I realize, like a demure young lady. Next to them is Filomena, a frozen smile on her face. Ursula stands by the window, her back to the rest of them, a cigarette held in one hand. Her posture is rigid.

In the chair nearest the fireplace is a woman who looks to be in her late forties. She is expensively dressed in black; a collar of glossy black feathers trims her dress. A necklace of enormous pearls circles her throat, luminous as tiny moons against her skin. Her pale hair is swept away from her aristocratic face, and her makeup is subtle. She looks very relaxed and is mid-sentence.

"And, of course, I told them that such behavior was simply unacceptable," she says, picking up a dainty teacup and taking a delicate sip. "My husband was the ambassador, after all, and I think I would know better than *them* what the fascist position would be."

"Hello," I say, taking another step forward.

"Bea!" Filomena stands and reaches out a hand to me. I think I see relief flicker in her eyes.

"There you are, Bea." Leo also gets to his feet. "Where have you been?"

"With Ben," I say simply, accepting a perfunctory kiss on my cheek.

"Just the two of you?" Leo's glance darts toward the woman by the fireplace.

"Well, yes." I am surprised. "He's been giving me art lessons, remember?" I add.

"Of course." My uncle's face clears. "Good to make the most of having these artist types about." His tone is jolly, but the words feel wrong somehow. I slant a look at Filomena, who is sitting again, with a frozen smile on her lips.

"Now, Beatrice," Leo says, "I've been very rude—may I present Lady Frances Bowling?"

I move obediently forward to shake the woman's cold, smooth hand. "It's nice to meet you," I say.

Her mouth lifts in an approximation of a smile. "I know your mother."

"Do you?" I ask. I've never heard her mentioned before.

"Yes, we came out together, oh, a hundred years ago now." Frances's voice is light, her tones well rounded. My uncle laughs politely at her joke.

"I didn't know that," I murmur. "How interesting."

"You're a Langton, of course," she says, looking at me as though sizing up a horse she might like to buy. "Good breeding always tells." Her gaze flickers to Ben, standing with one shoulder resting against the door frame, and Klaus hovering beside. "And bad blood will out."

I don't understand the slight, or why she's looking at Ben and Klaus like they have crawled out from beneath a rock, but I feel a strong shudder of dislike pass through me, and I eye the woman with distaste.

"You're right, of course," I agree. My mother would know that trouble was brewing from my casual tone, but this crowd is blissfully unaware. "But then, unlike so many of the aristocracy, my parents are not related to each other. Criminal what all this snobbish inbreeding has led to, don't you think?" My question hangs in the air like the challenge that it is.

A horrified silence is broken by the sound of laughter. Ursula finally turns away from the window. "Wonderful, Bea." She exhales a stream of smoke. "Wonderful." Her eyes snap around the room, landing on Frances with an expression of open dislike. "I think I need a drink," she says shortly, and she leaves the room, with Klaus in her wake.

"Lady Bowling and I met in Milan," Leo says quickly, his words spilling into the tense silence. "I suggested she and her friend Sir Hugh stop off here on their way to Rome. We're having a few people over for dinner tonight to welcome them."

"I see," I say. "So you are just . . . passing through?"

The smile Frances gives me is ice-cold. "Unfortunately, yes," she says in wintery tones. "Such a shame we won't get to know one another better."

"Yes," I agree with a smile that shows my teeth. "Such a shame."

CHAPTER TWENTY-SIX

♦

"Odious woman," Ursula hisses while pouring drinks. "These frigid fascist types make my blood boil."

Across the terrace, the fascist in question is serenely accepting a glass from my uncle. They are surrounded by people I don't know, a more polished set than we typically see at the villa.

"Who are all these people?" I ask.

Ursula snorts. "They're your uncle's friends," she says derisively. "Dull, dull, dull, and painfully bourgeois."

"I wonder where Ben is," I say. After the scene in the drawing room he slipped away, and he hasn't returned since.

"I'm sure he will be here soon," Klaus says. "He's probably just trying to get used to the idea of Sir Hugh being here."

"Who *is* this Sir Hugh?" I ask.

Klaus looks surprised. "No one told you?" I shake my head. "Sir Hugh Falmouth. The artist, you know?"

"Sir Hugh *Falmouth*?" I repeat, startled. Even I've heard of *that* Sir Hugh. His paintings hang in the National Gallery; we've got books about him in the library at Langton.

Klaus nods. "He is an old friend of Filomena's, I believe. He was caught up with Lady Bowling in Milan somehow, and Leo brought the pair of them back with him. I understand he has been resting after the journey." Klaus's eyes light with amusement. "I believe your uncle considers his visit quite the social coup."

In fact, Uncle Leo has been strutting around with the self-satisfaction of a peacock, and this does rather explain that.

"Gosh, even Mother and Father will be impressed when I tell them." It will, I think, be something about this trip I can actually share with them. "But why doesn't Ben like him?" I ask, puzzled.

"There is a history between them," Klaus says. "I don't know exactly what."

"I can't believe I'll get to meet Hugh Falmouth," I say wonderingly.

"Well, brace yourself," Klaus whispers, his lips close to my ear. "He's coming this way right now."

I follow Klaus's eyes and see that Filomena is approaching, her hand tucked into the crook of a man's arm. He looks about sixty and his hair is completely white, swept back from a high forehead. There is a roguish twinkle in his blue eyes. A silver-topped cane is hooked over the arm that isn't holding Filomena, though he moves easily—jauntily, even. He must have been startlingly handsome in his youth, and he still has a commanding presence. He is dressed impeccably in a light evening suit, and as I watch, he leans in close to Filomena to say something to her, something that makes a languorous smile break out on her lips. My uncle follows behind the two of them with Hero at his side. He is beaming from ear to ear.

"Ah, Beatrice!" Leo booms. "There you are!" He insinuates himself between Filomena and the dapper gentleman. "Sir Hugh, allow me to present my niece, Beatrice Langton—of the Northumberland Langtons."

It's such a strange, formal introduction that I hesitate, not quite sure how to respond. It feels like I'm being presented in an Austen novel, like I should curtsy.

"My dear." Sir Hugh solves the problem by stepping forward and taking my hand. "What a delight to meet you."

"Sir Hugh," I murmur.

"It's silly, isn't it?" The man himself chuckles, squeezing my fingers. "This *Sir Hugh* business. But I'm afraid that after the knighthood some rather shameless young friends of mine began calling me that, and then it stuck." I look down at my hand in his. He has lovely hands, I notice, neatly manicured and graceful.

"And these are the other young people we have staying with us," Filomena says, "Klaus and Ursula."

"More of Filomena's artists," Leo puts in.

"And you know Benedick," Filomena adds, glancing over my shoulder.

I hadn't noticed him there. He steps forward, and his usually expressive face is a blank.

"Hugh," he says quietly.

"Ah, Ben." Sir Hugh's voice is easy. "Filomena told me you were staying. What a nice surprise."

"I didn't realize the two of you knew each other," Leo says, his eyes traveling between them.

"Many years ago now, when Ben was just a boy," Sir Hugh says. "I knew Ben's mother—oh, a lifetime ago. How is she?"

An odd look passes over Ben's features. "She's dead," he says flatly.

"My dear boy," Sir Hugh starts, lifting a hand to his throat. "I am sorry to hear it."

Ben's hands hang by his side, and I notice his fists clench. A strange tension that I don't understand fills the air.

"How do you and Filomena know each other, Sir Hugh?" I ask quickly.

"Filomena modeled for me several times over the years." Sir Hugh's eyes light up as he looks over at her.

"When I was much younger," Filomena adds firmly.

"Alas," Sir Hugh says, "I cannot persuade her anymore." His glance drifts over to me. "I must say, my dear, that if you would agree to model for me while I'm here, I would be thrilled." His voice is silky, coaxing, but there's something in the way his eyes crawl over me that makes me shiver. "I think you are something . . . quite out of the ordinary," he finishes softly.

"Did you hear that, Beatrice?" crows Leo. "What an honor! I'm sure she would be honored, Sir Hugh."

"Oh, I don't think she would," Ben says at the same time that Filomena says, "She has her lessons. . . ."

"Filomena is right," I say, determined to have my own say in the matter. "Not to mention that I'd be an absolutely useless model. I cannot sit still." I put enough finality into my voice to indicate that the subject is closed, even though Uncle Leo's mouth is set in a straight line and I can tell he is not pleased.

"Not to worry," Sir Hugh says mildly. I see his eyes flicker to Ben, who is standing, still stone-faced, beside me. "You'll let me know if you change your mind?"

Filomena takes hold of Sir Hugh's arm again. "Come, Hugh," she says. "I want to introduce you to Felix—he is around here somewhere, and his miniatures are most charming. . . ." She disappears into the crowd, chattering away to Sir Hugh, who nods happily beside her.

"Well, Beatrice," Uncle Leo says, looking after them, his expression sour. "I think you've looked a gift horse in the mouth there. A portrait by Sir Hugh Falmouth . . . Any number of young ladies would jump at such an opportunity."

"I prefer to keep my feet firmly on the ground, Uncle," I say.

Leo shoots me a look then that reminds me so much of

my parents that I feel another chill run through me, and I cross my arms defiantly across my chest.

"Sir Hugh is a guest here, Beatrice," Leo says, and there's a note of steel in his voice. "I trust that I can rely on you to remember your manners." With that he turns on his heel and walks away. I exhale slowly.

I watch my uncle move through the crowd, and somewhere behind me I can hear Hero laughing at whatever Klaus is saying to her.

"Are you all right?" Ben asks.

"Oh yes," I say brightly. "I'm fine. Disappointing my family members is something of a full-time occupation for me."

"He shouldn't be disappointed," Ben says. "It's a very good thing that you didn't agree to model for Hugh Falmouth."

"Filomena modeled for him," I point out.

"And she didn't seem keen to repeat the honor, did she?" Ben looks at me.

"No, I suppose not," I admit. "And, to be quite honest, the man gave me the heebie-jeebies." I nudge him. "Not to mention that I'd be a complete disaster as a model. Can you imagine? I'd get bored and end up doing something outrageous."

Ben grimaces. "God, that's true." He runs a hand through his hair and sighs. "I'd almost feel sorry for the man."

"Hey!" I exclaim.

"*You* said it," Ben retorts.

"Just because I said it doesn't mean you have to agree with me," I reply, biting back a smile.

"I can't win." He's smirking now. "Even when I agree with you, it seems I'm in the wrong. It's a special talent."

"You're a very talented individual," I say. "Just too simple-minded for the subtleties of our conversation."

"Ah, *there* you are." Ben's dimples appear, distracting me. "I was worried that you were being a bit too nice to me."

"Trust me," I say cheerfully, "that's not something you ever need to worry about."

CHAPTER TWENTY-SEVEN

◆

The next day I am surprised to find Filomena in the drawing room, taking tea with Sir Hugh.

"Oh, sorry," I exclaim, checking my stride and coming to an abrupt halt. "I came in for my sketch pad."

"Not at all." Sir Hugh gets to his feet with a gentlemanly little bow. "It's lovely to see you again, my dear. Won't you join us?"

"Please do, Bea." Filomena gestures to the chair beside her.

I hesitate, but I am curious about Sir Hugh, and Ben's dislike for him. Ben himself has not been at all forthcoming on the matter, even muttering something about curiosity killing the cat, but I am a scientist and, as I pointed out to him, curiosity is one of my defining characteristics.

Which is probably why I say, "Thank you. A cup of tea would be lovely."

Filomena pours me a cup from the silver tea service on the table beside her. The tea is amber and steaming: a perfect taste of home. I settle into one of the hard-backed chairs.

"Filomena tells me you are having art lessons," Sir Hugh says genially. "I must say the villa is the perfect setting for such an endeavor."

"Yes," I agree, "although I'm afraid that my talents are wholly unworthy of this environment. I'm improving, however. Thanks to Ben." I reach for a plate of flat, pale biscuits dusted in crunchy sugar, bite into one, and allow it to melt on my tongue in a swirl of vanilla.

Sir Hugh laughs gallantly. "I'm sure you do yourself a disservice." I feel the familiar creeping boredom of polite social visits at Langton. I am not terribly good at small talk. I stir the tea in my cup, and the sound of the silver teaspoon chiming musically against the porcelain echoes around the room.

I reach around in my mind for something to say. "Have you been in Italy long?" I ask finally.

"For about two months." Sir Hugh sips his tea. "And before that in the South of France, before that in Vienna."

"But you live in England?"

"I do," Sir Hugh says. "England will always be my true home. But I find that travel helps me to create. Of course . . ." He smiles at Filomena. "It does leave me rather relying on the kind hospitality of others if I wish to avoid hotel living. When I learned that darling Filomena was staying here . . .

well, I confess I might have fished for an invitation. It's just so nice to catch up with old friends, isn't it?"

"I don't suppose there are any hotels quite like this place," I say, setting my empty teacup down.

"You are perfectly right," he replies, smiling. "It's truly something special. Filomena, my dear, you have fallen on your feet." His tone is pleasant, but something in his words makes me look up sharply.

"I am certainly very lucky," she says calmly. "As we all are, to enjoy Leo's hospitality."

"I know I am," I break in anxiously, not enjoying the ripple of tension that is suddenly palpable in the room. "If I was stuck at home now, I'd be lonely and cold and miserable— and here . . ." I spread my fingers wide to indicate the bounty around us.

"Here, you are having art lessons," Sir Hugh puts in.

"Well, there has to be at least one fly in the ointment," I say lightly, and Sir Hugh chuckles.

"I take it Ben is not a patient instructor?" he asks.

"Actually, he's an excellent teacher. Much as it pains me to admit it."

"Bea and Ben enjoy . . . what do you English call it?" Filomena smiles. "Bickering?"

Sir Hugh takes a sip of tea. "Benedick always did have the ability to charm. But also to rub people the wrong way."

I eye him speculatively. "You know him well, then?"

"I know his temper," Sir Hugh says, his tone suddenly serious. "A troubled young man, very troubled. Though a promising artist now, I have heard." He must notice my inquisitive look. "A sad story, I'm afraid. His mother, when she had him, was young and—well, she was *unmarried*—"

"I don't think Bea needs to hear all this ancient history," Filomena cuts in, and I am suddenly relieved. If I hear this story, I think, it should be from Ben.

I cast about for something else to say. "Are you staying here long?" I ask.

"That," says Sir Hugh, "is something I was just discussing with Filomena."

"I hope you will stay as long as you wish to!"

I didn't hear Uncle Leo come in, and we all turn around at the sound of his voice. Frances drifts into the room behind him and folds herself into another chair, crossing one leg over the other. Leo lays a hand on Filomena's shoulder. "It is an honor for us to have you both here," he continues, his smile engulfing Frances and Sir Hugh.

"You are much too kind," Sir Hugh says. "However, as I was explaining to your charming fiancée, Frances and I have an important dinner to get to in just a couple of days' time. I can say no more." His tone is light, teasing.

"But why?" Uncle Leo frowns.

"Ignore him," Frances says. "He's enjoying being mysterious. The truth is that we are attending a small dinner being hosted by Benito." I see Filomena's hand go to her throat in a quick, unconscious gesture. "My late husband was, as you know, a great personal friend of Mussolini's, and he is in Rome this week."

"An honor indeed," Leo says, his eyes wide.

"You have met him yourself?" asks Sir Hugh.

Leo looks rather wistful. "I haven't, no."

Frances nods. "A marvelous man, and so charming. What he's done for this country, well . . . we could use some of it back in England. Perhaps darling Oswald will be able to make some much-needed change there. You know," she says slowly, tapping her chin, "you could come with us, as my guests, if you wish. That way I could introduce you to the man himself—it's the least I can do after your gracious hospitality."

Leo looks like a child at Christmas. "Visit Rome to meet with Mussolini?" he breathes. "We would love to, wouldn't we, darling?" He turns his shining eyes on Filomena.

"What an opportunity." Filomena's voice is steady. "Regrettably, I must stay here with Hero and Bea." She smiles at him. "But you must go, my love. We will be quite all right here for a week or two without you."

Leo catches up her hand. "Best of women," he says. "And when I've only just got back as well. I truly don't deserve you." He turns to me. "Isn't she wonderful, Bea?"

"Wonderful," I agree, and I force a mechanical smile. I am slightly horrified by the whole idea of this visit with Mussolini. Nothing that I have seen or heard at the villa has made me feel any more inclined to the fascist cause. If anything, it has been the opposite. It's a problem that I have had to deal with before: questioning the judgment of the adults around you is not an especially comfortable experience. The idea

205

that my uncle could be wrong—dangerously wrong—about something so important is unsettling. I try to shake off the uneasy feeling that it gives me.

I look up, and as I do so I catch an odd look—almost of displeasure—flicker over Sir Hugh's face, his gaze moving between Filomena and my uncle.

"It's decided, then," Frances says. "We were planning to leave tomorrow—will that be too soon?"

"Not at all!" Leo claps his hands. "We like to seize the day in this house."

As he stands, I glance over at Filomena. The look in her eyes takes my breath away. It is a look of bone-deep sadness, a weariness that leaves her shoulders drooping, a tremble in her hands.

Half a second later the look is gone, and Filomena's face is serene once more, her shoulders back, her chin lifted. I would almost think I had imagined it.

CHAPTER TWENTY-EIGHT

◆

I think it's safe to say that everyone is relieved when my uncle and his new friends leave for Rome the next day.

Once more it feels as if the reins have been loosened, and over the following week the house fills up again as Filomena welcomes guests—more and more artists arriving in the buildup to the villa's end-of-summer exhibition. There are new faces and some that I recognize from earlier in the summer. Everyone seems very busy.

Although as a playwright she won't be presenting at the exhibition, Ursula has been caught up in her work as well, camped out in the summerhouse for days, and I'm surprised to find that I miss her. I go in search of her one morning, to discover her wild-eyed and disheveled, hunched over her desk. The piles of paper in the room seem to have multiplied tenfold, teetering precariously in corners, scattered across the floor, marked with the dirty rings from the bottoms of coffee cups.

She greets me without looking up. "Bea, hello. I think I'm finally getting somewhere," she says feverishly, her fingers drumming on the typewriter.

"Do you need a break?" I ask. "I thought you might like a swim?"

"Oh, a swim," she murmurs abstractedly. "Have fun."

I give up and make my way to the pool alone. Ursula is not the only one with her nose to the grindstone. There's been a significant increase in activity this week, and I have to admit that it has left me a little off balance. Everyone, including Ben, Filomena, and Klaus, seems driven by something, something that is big and significant. I have continued to improve in my sketching and have surprised myself with how much I am enjoying it—the way it teaches me to look at things with fresh eyes—but it's not the same.

I want what the others have for myself, I realize. The sense of purpose, the all-consuming passion for their work. I'm never going to feel like that about art, but it *is* how I feel about science. It's becoming harder and harder to imagine going home to my aimless solitude—or, even worse, to the stifling company of someone like Cuthbert. There's pleasure in studying alone, but I want to *do* something with my knowledge. I want a purpose, a vocation.

I think about it as I swim up and down the length of the pool, enjoying the coolness of the water as it twines around my limbs, the way I slip easily through it in my new bathing suit. I think about what my mother would have to say about this short, clinging, bright red costume. I know that the answer is nothing good, and that makes wearing it feel even better. I turn over and float on my back, my fingers splayed as I close my eyes against the dazzling sunlight that continues to dance behind my eyelids in scattered golden shards.

Finally, I drag myself out of the water and wrap myself in a towel. I sit on one of the sun loungers, untangling my long hair with my fingertips and relishing the sun on my skin, the way its warmth spreads over me in waves.

Eventually, I am joined by Ben, and I smile up at him sleepily as he drops into the seat next to me. His hair is ruffled, and his hands are covered in paint. There's paint on his cheek too. He's been working on something new, something that he's excited about, though I haven't seen it yet. Whatever it is, it makes his eyes shine.

"How does it work?" I ask him after a moment. "The exhibition, I mean."

He sprawls back in his chair. "Filomena hasn't held one here at the villa before, so I'm not exactly sure."

"But she's had them elsewhere?" I ask.

He nods. "Yes, on a smaller scale. I went to one a couple of years ago in Florence. It depends if she has a patron or not."

"A patron?" I frown.

Ben stretches. "Someone who funds the work. Like Leo."

"But Leo is Filomena's fiancé, not her patron," I point out.

Ben snorts. "Same thing."

I sit for a moment, absorbing that information.

"Filomena's circle of friends may be impressive, but they're all poor as church mice," Ben continues. "It's the rare artist who is appreciated in their own lifetime, Bea." He smiles grimly. "Not everyone gets as lucky as Sir Hugh."

"So the work goes on display?" I ask.

Ben nods. "In the house and in the gardens. Usually, Filomena plies everyone with drink, and there are a few moneyed types who turn up and buy things—collectors come to look for new talent. There are a handful of people coming to this one who I am hoping might offer me a commission. The summer's almost gone, after all. I need to start making plans."

He speaks lightly, but the words hit me with a force I hadn't expected. "Plans?" I repeat.

"Well, yes." Ben eyes me with something like amusement. "We haven't all got stately homes to return to. I can't expect your uncle to house me indefinitely."

"I suppose not," I say, my voice a little hollow.

"What's wrong?" Ben asks.

"Nothing." I shake my head. "Just thinking about the summer being over. Going home. I suppose it just feels like the end of something." I sit up.

"The end of a glorious summer romance?"

"The end of a very interesting experiment."

"You're only interested in me for my scientific possibilities," Ben grumbles.

"Perhaps." I smile. There's a pause. "Why did you ever agree to it?" It's a question I've been wanting to ask for a while.

Ben looks thoughtfully into the distance for a moment. "I suppose the idea was a bit of a novelty," he muses. "Whatever else you are, Bea, you're never boring."

"Oh," I say, somehow deflated.

"Of course, there was one other reason," Ben says slowly.

"What was that?"

"It was becoming very inconvenient, wanting to kiss you all the time." His voice is very neutral, matter-of-fact.

"*Did* you?"

"Yes, I did." He sighs. "Despite all my better judgment, against every measure of sanity I possess, I couldn't stop thinking about it whenever you were around."

"That's just how I felt," I say. "As if my brain and my body were completely disconnected and I kept having all these involuntary responses. I should note this down. Do you think it is something chemical?"

I look over at Ben now and catch my breath, because there's something glittering in his eyes that makes the air between us crackle.

"Something like that," he says.

Before the crackle can turn into anything more interesting, Filomena appears, wearing a strange expression.

"Is everything all right?" I ask, noticing that she is clutching a letter in her hand.

"Everything is very all right, Bea," she says, a slow smile spreading across her face. She sits down. "Now, how would you feel about a trip to Florence?"

"To Florence?" I repeat, in a daze.

"You've heard from Lili?" Ben perks up. "She's back?"

"I have"—Filomena nods—"and she is." Ben lets out a whoop of excitement. "There's a letter for you too, of course," she continues, holding out an envelope to him.

"Who is Lili?" I ask, trying to catch up.

"An old friend," Filomena says. "A very dear old friend of both of ours. And one who invites the two of you to stay for a couple of days."

"Me and . . . and Ben?" I feel a little flustered by this, by the casual way we have been paired together. "How does she know who I am?"

"I told her that Ben was giving you art lessons." She folds her hands placidly in her lap. "If one is to truly learn about art, then one cannot miss Firenze."

"I wrote to her about you too," says Ben abstractedly as he scans his own letter.

"Did you?" I ask, finding myself flushing with unexpected pleasure. "But won't my uncle mind?"

"You will be back long before he is." Filomena waves her hand in an airy gesture. "And I'm sure he would not mind."

I'm not so sure about that, actually. In fact, I'm starting to suspect that perhaps he has not embraced the relaxed bohemian lifestyle as wholeheartedly as it first seemed. Still, I'm certainly not going to turn down the opportunity to visit Florence. Far be it from me to start throwing obstacles in my own path.

"You can go for a few days and still be back in time for the exhibition party," Filomena says. "You'll love Florence, Bea." Her enthusiasm is unrestrained. "It is the *most* romantic place."

"It will probably be wasted on me, then," I say, and at that Ben lifts his eyes from his letter to meet mine.

"Oh, I don't know, Bea." The smile that he gives me is warm, and I feel it all the way in my bones. "I think even you might not be immune to the romance of Florence. In fact, I think you'll like it a lot."

PART FOUR

Florence
AUGUST 1933

BEATRICE:
For which of my good parts did you first suffer love
for me?

BENEDICK:
"Suffer love," a good epithet! I do suffer love indeed,
for I love thee against my will.

—*Much Ado About Nothing,* act V, scene 2

CHAPTER TWENTY-NINE

◆

"Tell me about Lili," I demand after we have settled in next to one another on the faded green velvet seats in the train compartment. The journey is only a few hours, but I am desperate to be there already.

"Lili is a force of nature," Ben says fondly. "She's American and she hasn't much money, but what she has she spends on art. She has a terrific eye, and her collection is beyond belief. She lives in this tumbledown house in Florence, and every artist of any importance, and quite a lot of no importance at all, have stayed there at one time or another."

"Including Filomena," I say.

"Right." Ben nods. "And—and my mother, and me." He smiles at my surprise. "We lived in Lili's house for almost two years when I was nine."

"Your mother was an artist too?" I say.

"She wanted to be," Ben says. "She was very young when she had me, with barely a penny to her name. She came over to Italy from England when I was still small and fell in with a group of artists in Florence who pretty much saved her life. They saved mine too, I suppose."

"Is that how you know Filomena?" I ask.

Ben nods. "She was a friend to Mum when she really needed one. And she taught me about art. She was the one who encouraged me, who told me I had talent. It was a wonderful time living with them. We were so happy. At least, for a while."

"And Sir Hugh?" I ask quietly. "Is that when you met him as well?"

I'm sure I feel him tense beside me, but his voice when he speaks is neutral. "Yes. My mother modeled for him."

I sense that's all he will say on the subject, and we sit quietly for a moment.

"So this is like going to visit family for you?" I say finally.

Ben nods again. "Lili and Gert are probably the closest thing I have to aunts."

"Is Gert Lili's sister?"

Ben smiles. "No, not her sister. Gert is Lili's . . . *lover*, I suppose you would call her. But a partner, really. They've been together for over twenty years."

"Oh, right," I say, reminded again of how far away I am from my parents' world. I find myself smiling, thinking about it.

"What?" asks Ben.

"I just can't imagine my parents' reaction to such a setup," I explain.

"But *you're* not shocked?" he asks dryly. "Not that I should be surprised. It seems that shocking you is an impossibility."

"Thank you," I say, pleased. "And, no, I'm not shocked. I'm not quite as naive as people seem to believe. I'm looking forward to meeting Lili and Gert."

"There are plenty of people who really don't like it. Lili and Gert move in bohemian circles where people won't bat an eyelid, but outside of their friends it can be different. . . ."

"Yes, I can imagine," I say. "It must be difficult, especially with what's going on politically. The fascists aren't precisely welcoming of anyone they consider different. Though my uncle seems quite excited about his meeting with Mussolini," I add dryly.

"I've heard him say that fascism is the future," Ben says.

"I'm sure he believes it," I say, "but I don't think he understands the real cost. Look at what's happening in Germany. Look at Ursula and Klaus. If you ask me, Mussolini is a dangerous man."

Ben leans back in his seat. "You may be right," he says. "You'll meet plenty of people in the next couple of days who share that opinion."

I glance over. "But not you?" I ask.

Ben shrugs. "I care about my work," he says. "I'm no fan of Mussolini, God knows. But I know plenty who are, and some of those people are likely to be the ones who can help me work." He frowns briefly and then his face clears. "All of this political fuss will probably come to nothing; the world will go back to normal. It's the work that will last."

The rest of the journey passes companionably enough. I ask Ben about some of the art we will see, and his face lights up as he describes the colors and textures, the genius of the old masters, and the startling, vibrant works of the new. I like listening to him talk about it; he makes it all come alive for me. In return, I pull out the detailed itinerary I have made of all the museums that I want to visit, detailing the collections at the natural history museum, telling him about the plants at the botanical garden.

"It's the third oldest in Europe," I say excitedly. "It was established in 1545 by a Medici, Ben. . . . A Medici!"

"*Everything* in Florence was founded by a Medici," Ben says. "And you've left off some of the best places."

"How will we do it all?" I ask despairingly.

"We'll manage," Ben says. "I promise, you won't miss anything on your preposterous list."

When we reach the station, Ben climbs down the steps and holds his hands up for the bags. Our eyes meet, and I grin, remembering how we first met. Ben grimaces, which I think means he is remembering it too.

No one has come to meet us, but Ben says there would be no point—he knows where he's going, and they'll all be waiting at the house anyway. The station is heaving, full of people shouting and shoving at each other. Parts of the impressive new structure are still covered in scaffolding, but above us soars a great glass roof.

"More of Il Duce's improvements," Ben says, gesturing around us.

"It's certainly very modern," I say, looking around at the imposing building.

I'm constantly distracted by the noise, the crowds, all there is to see as we walk out of the station and into a bustling piazza. Another explosion of sound greets us, as hawkers try to sell their wares from various stands.

"They used to hold chariot races in this square," I say. "Right up until the end of the last century." It's easy to imagine: with the square hemmed in by tall, stone-faced buildings, a sense of timelessness exists, hovering over it all as if we are both now and then, as if the line between us and the past is suddenly less certain. I can see it all here in front of me, and this nearness to history is dizzying, like walking straight into the pages of the sort of book I would read at home.

"Santa Maria Novella." Ben points to the church on the other side of the square. "Always my first stop when I get to Florence. Come on." He hitches the bags on his shoulder again and grabs my hand, weaving through the crowd. "This was one of my mother's favorite places," he says.

We push through the wrought-iron gate cut into the high walls and around the small, neat cloister behind. When we walk into the church, there's an incredible feeling of space and light. The high stone arches meet gracefully in a vaulted ceiling. The floor is laid in a checkerboard of black, gray, and white, rubbed smooth by a million footsteps. The muted colors of the walls and ceilings tangle with the brilliant stained-glass windows. Despite there being so much to take in, it leaves me feeling serene, as if the quiet and the beauty speak to something right at the core of me, as if I feel it right in my bones.

We go back through the cloister and enter another chapel, one that feels a million miles away from the huge white space we've just been in. Here, the walls and the ceiling are painted in earthy jewel tones crowned by a midnight-blue sky filled with saints. It's joyful, noisy, clamoring: a riot of color.

"It's incredible," I murmur, feeling suddenly a little shy. "I can see why your mother liked it so much."

Ben returns my smile and reaches for my hand again. I like the feeling of his fingers around mine. "Come on," he says. "Let's go and find Lili."

We wind our way down narrow cobbled streets, and it seems that every corner we turn in this beautiful maze leads to another scene so picturesque that even I, with my lack of artistic eye, am moved. The light here is golden, and it brushes lovingly against every surface like a kiss.

Finally, we come to a stop in front of a tall building with a terra-cotta roof. There are peeling gray painted shutters at the windows. Ben bounds up the three wide steps that lead to the front door and pulls enthusiastically on the bell, which I can hear clanging distantly inside the house.

"Open up, Lil!" he calls. "The prodigal son has returned!" He looks younger all of a sudden, and I can imagine him running up these steps as a small, scruffy boy.

A second later the door flies open, and Ben is being waltzed around by a lanky woman in a loose white shirt and slacks. Her bobbed hair is a light brown peppered with gray, and her tanned face is wrinkled and laughing.

"Ahhh! My boy, my boy!" she exclaims, pulling Ben's face down and kissing him on the cheeks. "You've grown another foot at least." She slaps him on the shoulder as though she's telling him off for it.

"And you must be Beatrice." She turns to me, her expression welcoming, her arms open. Her voice is warm and singsong American, and she pulls me into an enthusiastic hug.

Behind her I see a pretty, slightly round lady who looks like a Dutch porcelain milkmaid.

"Gert!" Ben manages before he's pulled into another smothering embrace. When he's released, Gert has wet eyes, which she dabs at ineffectually with a large white lacy handkerchief.

"Come in, come in!" she says, standing aside so that we can move through the doorway. "Let's not give the neighbors any more to talk about!"

I step through the door into a dingy hallway. The carpet

223

is worn, and there is a row of brass hooks piled at least three deep with coats and hats and scarves in various states of disrepair. Ben chucks our bags down at the bottom of the staircase and dives through a door on our right. I follow behind and catch my breath.

The whole bottom floor on this side of the house has been opened up to make one huge room. The walls are painted burgundy and the floorboards are stripped and polished. At one end of the room is a makeshift kitchen with a couple of counters and an ancient-looking stove. Copper pans hang from the walls beside a tall window that looks over a small green strip of garden. Fragrant, dried herbs hang in bunches from the ceiling.

At the other end of the room are several squashy sofas and some battered armchairs clustered around an incredibly long coffee table, which is in turn groaning under the weight of books and newspapers and magazines and dirty wineglasses. There's an aging piano in the corner, and the top of that is also covered in books.

The thing that takes your breath away, though, is the art. Jostling for space on the walls and illuminated by the beautiful light that spills through the windows are dozens of paintings in different styles. It's like the most ridiculous jewel of a museum. There are huge landscapes in heavy frames and there are napkins with ink sketches on them pinned up carelessly with gold tacks. Depictions of classical mythology rest alongside geometric shapes in bold colors, and the effect is dizzying.

"Let me give you the tour," Lili says, taking my arm. She guides me around the room, pointing to different pieces and telling funny stories about the artists who painted them: how they hogged all the hot water when they came to stay, or how they would only drink a particular vintage of wine and ate raw vegetables for a week. There are names that even I recognize, names like Picasso and Matisse. We stop in front of one painting. A white road curves through a trembling blue sky, full of arcs of light, and Lili says, "This was always Ben's favorite."

Ben comes to stand beside me. "Balla. This piece is genius. See how he captures the speed and urgency of it, the way the light crashes like waves across the canvas, pulling you along and through it."

I am distracted then by a portrait of a beautiful woman whose face looks faintly familiar.

"What about this one?" I ask. Ben's face stills; the enthusiasm dies from his eyes.

"That is a genuine Sir Hugh Falmouth original," he says.

"It's a portrait of Susie, Ben's mother." Gert wraps a plump arm around Ben's waist and squeezes hard. "That is why we keep it here. She was a real beauty."

"She was," I murmur. She looks like she fell out of a Renaissance painting, all golden hair spun like a halo, and delicately flushed skin. Still, there's something about the picture that I don't like. Her eyes look hunted, and her head is turned slightly away, as though she longs to escape the canvas. It's like seeing a butterfly pinned to a board.

I shiver, telling myself I am being melodramatic, but even as the others continue chatting cheerfully about the friends who will be calling in to see Ben, even as I accept a cup of coffee and settle into one of the sofas to hear stories of Ben's childhood, I still feel as if those eyes are watching me, crying out for help.

CHAPTER THIRTY

◆

After we have been sitting for a while, chatting and dunking biscotti into bitter black coffee, Gert shows me up to my room, which is small and papered with tiny yellow roses. There is an old brass bedstead and an ancient-looking travel case that acts as a nightstand. Gert bustles around, checking that I have all I need.

"We're so happy to have you here," she says at last. "We hardly ever get the chance to meet Ben's friends."

"I know Ben was excited to come and see you," I say. "He says you are his family."

"Oh, we are close." She nods. "He was such a lamb as a boy. So inquisitive." Her voice is soft and affectionate. "He was already painting and drawing when he came to us, but the way he flourished here . . ." She shakes her head. "He's got real talent."

227

"And you would know," I say. "Judging by all that beautiful work downstairs."

"It's true, we've seen it all," Gert says. "And Ben is capable of great things. We're both very proud of him. His work changed, of course, after his mother died." She looks up, her face open, her wide blue eyes guileless. "Has he spoken to you about her?" she asks.

"Not really," I say. "Just that she was very young when she had him."

"He will," she says certainly. "That poor boy has needed someone to confide in for years. Lili and I tried, but . . ." She smiles at me. "I'm so glad he's found a nice young lady at last."

"Oh, we're just friends," I say awkwardly.

Gert smiles serenely. Her expression is innocent, but I think she sees a great deal more than she's letting on.

When Gert and I head back downstairs, it's to find that several more guests have turned up to see Ben. In fact, over the next few hours a sort of rolling cocktail party takes place in Gert and Lili's living room. The bell jangles and jangles and people stream in, starting conversations right in the middle as though they've been here for hours. Lili reigns from one of the battered armchairs, and people buzz around her like worker bees around their queen.

Sometime after a delicious dinner of bread and stew has been handed around in chipped and mismatched plates and bowls, I am in the corner, deep in conversation with a beautiful man with dark brown skin, a French accent, and long-lashed, dancing eyes about the medicinal uses of lavender, when Ben squeezes through the crowd to us.

"Excuse me, Alphonse," he says, patting the man on the shoulder, "but I wondered if I could steal Bea away for a moment?"

Ben takes me by the hand, just as the scrape of moving furniture is heard and the wheeze of the record player begins. "Come on," he whispers, "quick!" and he tugs me through the crowd. As we dodge through the doorway, I look over my shoulder to see Gert and Lili leading the charge to the makeshift dance floor, their arms wound tightly about one another.

It's a bit of a relief as we make our way up the stairs, past the crush of people sitting in small groups, smoking and having intense conversations. As the crowd thins, the temperature cools and the noise recedes a little.

"This is quite a party," I manage when we make it to the top landing.

Ben laughs. "Gert and Lili wouldn't call this a party, Bea. This is just an average Tuesday night for them." He gestures back to the crowd. "This house is always absolutely full of people, so you'd better get used to it. Friends of friends, like-minded folk. They all find Lili and Gert. . . . People are just drawn to them, I guess. They're like the flame that all the moths gather around."

"I can see why," I say. "They're so open, so friendly. They remind me of Filomena."

"Well, she spent a lot of time with them too," Ben says.

229

"Come on. I've got something to show you." He reaches up to a cord that hangs from the ceiling and pulls open a trapdoor with a rickety ladder, which slides noiselessly down. "Follow me," Ben calls over his shoulder as he starts to climb.

I hesitate for only a second before following. When I stick my head through the trapdoor, I see that we're in an attic room, dark and poky and seemingly used for storage. There are lots of bulky objects covered in dust sheets. Ben is fiddling with the latch on the small window, and once he manages to get it open, he starts to squeeze through.

"Ben!" I gasp. "What are you doing?"

"Come on," he calls again, his voice a dare, a challenge I don't want to refuse. Tentatively, I poke my head out the window and see him scrambling along a broad ledge. There's a short wall on the other side, but it doesn't even come up to my knees, and on the other side of *that* wall is a sheer drop down, down, down to the tiny garden below.

With a sigh, and against my better judgment, I haul myself out on top of the ledge, holding my breath and determinedly keeping my eyes away from the wall on my right as I mutter the Lord's Prayer under my breath.

As I move to Ben's voice, the roof on my left flattens out into a platform, and this is where I find Ben waiting.

"You made it!" he says, and he holds out his hand for me, helping me to pick my way over the tiles. "There! Now, tell me that wasn't worth risking life and limb for."

"Oh, goodness," I breathe as I turn around.

"I knew you'd love it." His voice is smug, but for once I

don't care. Spread out in front of us like a divine offering is all of Florence, radiant under rose-tinted skies. The sun has almost done its work for the day, and it hangs just above the horizon, burning fiercely like a hot ember. The golden light has diffused into something pink and mellow, and the River Arno curls around a crisscross pattern of streets that stretch out for miles; in front of us and a little way into the distance, the Duomo glows softly like a beacon, welcoming us to the city.

I sit beside Ben in silence for a while, too full of it all to speak. It feels so big—endlessly big, I think, as if the sky has grown.

"This is my secret place." Ben's voice breaks the quiet. "I used to sneak up here by myself all the time. Mum never knew where I was; it drove her mad. Lili knew, I think, but she never said anything."

"Will you tell me about your mother?" I ask hesitantly. There's a pause.

"She was very beautiful," he says, and his voice is a little rusty, as if he's trying out the words for the first time. "That's the thing I remember most, actually—that she looked like an angel. Every day I feel like I remember a bit less, just pieces. How she smelled like lilacs in spring, how she could peel an apple in one long, curling strip."

He looks off into the distance and rubs his nose. "She was always nervous—highly strung, I suppose you'd say— but who could blame her when she'd been kicked out of her home at sixteen for falling pregnant with me? She loved me."

His voice is so soft now I can hardly hear it. "I remember that, at least." He clears his throat. "Somehow she got the fare together and we came to Europe. To France first and then to Italy. Someone gave her Lili's name, and she took us in, and then we lived here for a little over two years. It was home, or the closest to it I ever had."

"Why did you leave?" I ask.

"Sir Hugh came one summer to paint; Filomena was with him," he says. "He took one look at my mother and said he had to have her as a model. I think Filomena was relieved to get away from him. . . . Looking back, that should have been warning enough." His hands clench into tight fists, resting against his knees. "He seduced her. I was young still— I didn't understand. All I knew was that the house felt suddenly less safe, that Mum was shouting and crying a lot, that she was drinking a lot. And then we left with him. Not long after that, he left us. A few months later she was dead," he says dispassionately, his voice uncannily flat. "They put me in an orphanage. When I was fourteen I ran away, and I came straight back here. It was the first time I had seen Lili and Gert in two years. They hadn't known where I was. Didn't know about Mum. We all cried." He manages a weak smile.

"They scraped together money for me to study art," he says more briskly. "And then I went out into the world, traveling, painting, doing whatever odd jobs I could to pay my way. Four months ago I got a letter from Filomena inviting me to the villa to stay for the summer, and . . . well, here we are." He holds out his hands in a gesture that envelops the scene around us. "That's the whole sorry tale, or most of it, anyway," he says. "More than I usually like to share." The smile he gives me is crooked, and it cuts straight through me.

"Thank you for telling me," I manage, though the words feel inadequate. I know what he has trusted me with: a part of himself that he keeps shut away. We sit quietly together, our fingers entwined, my head on his shoulder, as the sun dips below the horizon and the first evening star dances overhead.

"You know, when I hid up here," Ben says after a while, pulling a paper bag from his pocket, "I would bring my spoils with me so that I didn't have to share them." He hands me a delicate white sugar mouse. "But I don't mind sharing them with you."

Something warm and heavy settles in my chest. I lean against him and he wraps an arm around my shoulders, pulling me so close that I can hear the steady thump of his heart. "I like that you're here," he murmurs.

"I like it too," I say, and when I reach up to kiss him, he tastes of sugar.

CHAPTER THIRTY-ONE

◆

When I wake up the next morning I take a moment to stretch gleefully in my comfortable bed. The dopey smile on my face remains from the night before, and I touch my fingers to my lips, remembering the kisses that Ben pressed to them.

Today we have a very full schedule, and I am eager to get started. I dress as quickly as possible and head downstairs. In the kitchen Lili is frying bacon, and Ben leans against the counter, drinking a cup of coffee. When I enter the room, he looks up, and a smile lights his face for a second before he gets himself under control. Lili glances between us, a knowing look in her eyes.

"Good morning," she says, flipping the bacon expertly. The smell of it sizzling in the pan, mixing with the scent of freshly ground coffee, is absolute heaven, and I place my hand over my stomach as it starts to rumble.

A deep, growling snore arises from one of the sofas, and I look over to find that a large, scruffy man who I don't know is sound asleep there. His legs are sprawled out, crossed at the ankles, and he still has his boots on.

"Don't mind Boris," Lili grunts. "He could sleep through anything. I do find most of these anarchists are actually quite lazy when they're not rabble-rousing."

"Is it usual for there to be an anarchist asleep on the sofa in the morning?" I ask.

"It is in this house," Ben says.

"Boris is a harmless dear," Lili says, cracking eggs into the pan with one hand and making the fat spit furiously. "He hasn't recovered from the Arditi being broken up." The Arditi were the anti-fascists—I know that much. "God knows he is right to be frightened."

"You think Mussolini is dangerous?" I ask. I take a sip of my coffee, leaning against the counter, my arm pressed lightly against Ben's.

Lili starts flipping the bacon and eggs onto plates. "Look at those young kids out there," she says. "Head to toe in black and that fanatical gleam in their eye, committing violence in the name of a charming dictator." She shakes her head. "You tell me that's heading anywhere good. Nationalism is like a sickness." Lili hands me my plate. " 'Italy first,' Mussolini says, 'let's rebuild the Roman Empire,' and they look at him and see hope for the future, but everyone seems to forget that the Roman Empire was built out of blood and bones."

And right now my uncle might be drinking tea with him,

for all I know. I catch Ben's eye and I know that he's thinking the same.

"A lot of people think he's charming," he says with an easy shrug. I'm struck again by how little these things seem to touch him. Lili's anger is palpable, but Ben is relaxed, already more interested in the breakfast that he's been handed.

"I suppose it's the same in England," I say. "Lots of my parents' friends seem quite interested in the BUF."

"That's the British Union of Fascists?" Ben's brow crinkles.

"Yes." I blow gently on my coffee. "It's all dressed up in so much civility," I say. "Like that horrible Lady Frances woman my uncle seems so enamored of."

Lili nods. "Evil can come under the guise of gentility. Things will get a lot worse before they get better," she says with certainty.

"Let's not talk about it this morning," Gert chimes in, coming through the door in a pale-pink silk dressing gown. She reaches up to peck Lili on the cheek. "We should be making the most of having Ben and Bea here with us for a few days."

We chat quietly about other things as we eat our breakfast, but I know I'm not the only one with half my mind still on our conversation. I remember again the newsreels I have seen of Mussolini shouting from a podium at wild crowds of people, leading military demonstrations of rows and rows of soldiers, stony-faced and obedient. Lili's warning sits in my stomach like a rock, and part of me knows she's right, knows that something dark and dangerous is wrapping itself in a death grip around this beautiful country. It may be easy to ignore, but it doesn't seem like something that's going to go away on its own, whatever Ben may say.

"So what do you two have planned for today?" Gert asks.

"A *lot*," I say, a surge of excitement thrilling through me.

"So much that we should really get going," Ben agrees. "Thanks for breakfast, Lil." He walks around to the other side of the counter and kisses Lili on the cheek.

She reaches out a hand and pats the side of his face. "We'll see you both later for a family dinner," she says.

Ben and I leave the house, stepping into the dazzling sunshine. Adrenaline thumps through my veins as I realize that we have the whole city to explore. It's that vertiginous feeling of freedom again, calling to me, reminding me that I'm far from home.

The city is a warren of side streets and we zigzag through them, heading for our destination. Ben is buzzing with excitement, almost giddy, and his enthusiasm feeds mine as we skitter through the streets, giggling like schoolchildren.

We walk for miles. Strolling through the Piazza del Duomo, I finally see the famous redbrick domes up close. As I stretch my neck, tipping my head up to the skies to take it all in, right up to the gleaming bronze ball that Leonardo himself may have had his hands on, the cathedral is like something from a fantasy. The white-and-green marble exterior looks like it has been spun from sugar in an eccentric confectioner's workshop, the fulfillment of a greedy child's wish. It is a ridiculous, delicious delight.

"It's so beautiful," I say.

"Like a wedding cake," Ben says, his nose slightly wrinkled.

I smile. "I was thinking a home for your sugar mice."

We keep moving, through to the Piazza della Signoria, where the town hall, the Palazzo Vecchio, looms—an impressive fortress, a palace complete with battlements at the top. In the square we pass a group of Blackshirts, none of them much older than me, and they are joking and laughing, though in their black shirts, ties, and hats they still manage to look sinister, like overgrown crows.

I look at them for a moment and catch the eye of one boy. He grins and shouts something in Italian that I don't understand.

"What did he say?" I ask Ben.

"You don't want to know," he says grimly, dragging me along.

"I would think you would know me better than that," I reply.

An exasperated smile tugs at the corner of his mouth. "Let's just say he was appreciative of your appearance."

"Ah." I turn over my shoulder and catch the boy's eye, then shout something back. The boy's mouth drops open in incredulity, and then, amid his friends' shouts of laughter, he begins to move to us.

"You've done it now." Ben sighs, tugging me down an alleyway.

We run, zigzagging a little, until he is certain we have lost our pursuer.

"And where did you learn that?" Ben asks. "I'm fairly sure they don't teach words like that to proper young ladies."

"Good job there aren't any of those around, then," I reply. "And I learned it from Ursula, of course. Such a poetic language, Italian." It's rankling a little that we fled so easily. The sight of the Blackshirts unnerved me, and a part of me relished the idea of a confrontation. I wanted to push back against something that I know in my heart is wrong. Doing nothing, running away, it feels . . . cowardly.

There's not too much time to dwell on this, though, as we have reached our first important stop, a pilgrimage to Ben's place of worship: the Uffizi Gallery. We turn down an unobtrusive side street and find ourselves walking the length of the narrow courtyard between the two wings of the museum; ahead is a tantalizing glimpse of the Arno and all around us the high walls of the old building, built for the Medici. Graceful pillars support a wide portico, where happy tourists buzz like little bees, and we join the swarm into the gallery.

Inside the museum there's a sense of calm. It is already very obvious to me that the people of Florence hold the business of art to be a serious one—sacred, almost—intertwined with the iconography and the churches and cathedrals that stand shoulder to shoulder here. We clip along the endless, light-filled hallway, one side given over completely to windows. We stop along the way to examine the delicate busts and statues, and I marvel at the way that the softness and warmth of flesh and cloth can be depicted in chill, pure white marble.

We duck into the galleries that lead off the hallway, and the artwork that's on display is almost comically famous. There's Botticelli's *Venus* rising from her shell, and Titian's *Venus of Urbino* with her frank stare and the little dog curled at her feet. There are paintings by Michelangelo, Rembrandt, and Raphael. It is nearly overwhelming, but Ben is the perfect guide, pointing out little details and explaining different techniques that the artists used.

In one room we find several works by Caravaggio, and Ben is amused by my bloodthirsty enjoyment of his depiction of Medusa—a screaming, severed head with twisting serpents instead of hair.

"I always liked the idea of Medusa having serpents instead of hair," I admit. "At least she had company." I tip my head to consider the painting. "Snakes were probably better than most of the humans she encountered, anyway."

We stop outside the Uffizi so that Ben can buy us both gelati, handing over a fistful of coins for the two small dishes. I've never eaten gelato before, and mine is pale green and tastes of sunshine. "Pistachio," I murmur, spooning the smooth, sweet ice cream into my mouth and closing my eyes as it melts on my tongue. "It's wonderful."

We walk along, eating our gelati and watching the world go by. We're by the river now, and the sunlight dances on the blue water, leaving spots of light glittering like sequins scattered on the surface. We cross over the Ponte Vecchio, the famous bridge lined with higgledy-piggledy rows of shops, mostly jewelers, their wooden shutters flung open for business.

When we turn down another narrow street, full of life and car horns and crowds, and past the Pitti Palace, I feel my heart speed up. There has been one place I've been longing to go since I heard we were coming to Florence, and we're about to arrive. We continue to make our way down the road, which grows narrower and narrower, until we stop in front of an unassuming facade with a small stone plaque beside the door. "Museo di Fisica e Storia Naturale," I breathe. "The Museum of Physics and Natural History." I dance from foot to foot.

"I've never been." Ben looks down at me. "It's your turn to be the guide now." I grab his hand, tugging him through the doorway and down the long, dimly lit stone passage beyond.

Inside the museum is a treasure trove: dozens of rooms crammed with all sorts of fascinating exhibits. Others might have been horrified by the gruesome anatomical wax models that fill several of the rooms, but Ben listens with interest as I explain that they were used in the eighteenth century to teach medical students. "They're incredibly accurate because they were copied from real corpses," I say as we linger over a waxwork heart.

Ben's eyes light up. "I would love to come back and sketch some of this."

"So would I," I admit. "I feel like Stubbs with his horses."

"So we can tell your uncle that I made an artist of you after all." Ben grins. "I'm sure he'll be relieved to know he got his money's worth." The words have a slightly bitter ring to them, and I look up, surprised, but Ben has already moved on to another model and is asking me what the names of the various veins and arteries are.

I take him into more rooms, rooms filled with entomological collections. "Of course you want to spend your time with the bugs," Ben grumbles, but I'm not listening.

There, on one of the long wooden drawers, is a label: *Collezione Rondani*. "Camillo Rondani's collection," I whisper, awed as I pull out the drawer, slowly and with a muffled shushing sound.

"Who was he?" Ben asks.

"He was an expert on Diptera, or—"

"Flies." Ben cuts me off. He flushes at my surprised expression. "You mentioned it the other week. I looked up what it meant."

That warm feeling in my chest is back, and I try to fight it down, to keep a lid on the thing that is growing inside me with every day we spend together, the thing I don't want to name. I try not to beam at him like a moonstruck ninny, like so many girls have probably beamed at him before.

"Yes, flies." I clear my throat. "He also wrote some fascinating things about insects in Sicilian amber."

"Like what?" Ben asks.

I walk around the room, pointing things out. I like that

he's interested, and that he doesn't mind me knowing so much more than him about this. He asks me just as many questions as I asked him in the gallery. Mother and Father always told me that a man wouldn't appreciate a woman who had more education than him. I smile. Ben seems to appreciate me just fine.

At the end of the day, when we return to Lili's house, I am relaxed and happy. Ben holds the door open, and my body brushes against his as I walk through. He catches me and kisses me before we go inside. This is dangerous, I know; this is playing with fire.

And yet, as I look up at him, I feel ready to burn the whole place down.

CHAPTER THIRTY-TWO

◆

The next day we return to the natural history museum, where Ben makes quick, vibrant sketches, and where I attend to my anatomical studies. I'm particularly proud of the drawing I do of the human digestive system, based on the wax figures.

"Isn't it fascinating, Ben?" I ask. "To think all of this is going on inside us right now. That our bodies work so perfectly."

"It's . . . something." Ben admits.

"Beautiful," I breathe, looking at the cross section of a forearm, the bones, muscles, and arteries all intricately bound together.

Ben laughs. "Is it any wonder you weren't won over by the traditional romantic gestures?"

"You're not going to start reading poetry again, are you?" I ask suspiciously.

"Philistine." Ben shakes his head and goes back to his own sketching.

Later that evening we have dinner with Lili and Gert. They tell me stories about Ben when he was small, about the time he brought an injured pigeon into the house and kept it secretly in a box in his room.

"I only found out by following the little trail of bread crumbs," Lili laughs. "We wondered where all the bread had been going. By the time Ben let him go, he was the fattest pigeon in all of Florence."

"Bea would have liked him," Ben says. "She would have known his name in Latin, *Pigeonus maximus* or suchlike."

"*Columbidae*, actually," I correct him with a smile. "I did the same thing once, with a sparrow. But my mother found out and she was furious. She wouldn't let me keep him, despite the fact that—as I pointed out—a big creaky wreck like Langton Hall was probably full of rats and bats and other far less savory creatures."

"I'm surprised that didn't win her over," says Ben.

"I was too," I agree. "But then you never can have a logical argument with her."

"It sounds like you and Ben would have been good friends, then," Gert puts in.

"Yes," I say. "I think we would."

Ben shakes his head. "Oh, I doubt Beatrice would have had much to do with a ragamuffin like me." The words are said lightly, but there's something underneath them that I don't like.

"Well, it's a good job you found each other in the end," Lili says firmly.

My eyes meet Ben's across the table. "Hear, hear," he says, raising his wine in toast. We all clink our glasses together.

Later, after the candles have burned down and we've cleared the table, Ben and I sneak up to the roof. I'm fairly sure that Lili and Gert know that we come up here, but they haven't said anything about it, and as long as we preserve the illusion of propriety, they seem happy to leave us to it.

As it has every evening, the view momentarily deprives my lungs of air. Stars wheel overhead, and, with the lights burning in the surrounding windows, it feels as though we are suspended among them. Settling into the nest of blankets and cushions that we have built, Ben hands me a paper bag full of sweets that we chose together this morning. This too has become tradition, and I rifle through until I find one of my favorite sweet violet pastilles.

Sucking on a cinnamon sweet, Ben eyes me thoughtfully. "So," he says. "We're heading back to the villa tomorrow."

"I know." I draw small circles on the blanket with my finger. "I can't believe we're leaving Florence already. I really love it here."

"But you love the villa as well," Ben points out.

"Yes," I agree, lifting my head to meet his eye. "But it's been different to be here. With you. I mean, things feel different between us," I finish a little awkwardly.

There's a pause as we look at each other for a long moment.

"There are only two weeks until you go home," Ben says carefully, breaking the silence.

I feel a twist in my gut. I nod. "I know that too," I say.

"And our experiment will reach its conclusion," Ben says. "Do you feel it has been a success so far?"

I consider the question. "Well," I say, "when one considers the objectives, I think we've done quite well."

"The objectives?" Ben offers me another sweet, and our fingers graze as I take it.

"You promised me romance. And there have been flowers and boiled sweets and"—I grimace here—"poetry."

"I seem to remember Ursula mentioned kisses." Ben grins. "I think we've done all right on that front too."

"She also said that she thought you would be a satisfactory lover," I say.

Ben chokes on his sweet. "What?" he finally manages after a significant amount of spluttering. "I don't remember *that* part of the conversation."

"I don't think you were there," I say.

"Oh."

"Is that something you would be interested in?" I ask.

He stares at me.

"This whole thing did start when I said I would like to

take a lover," I point out. "It seems like that would be the logical conclusion."

Ben runs a hand through his hair, rumpling it in a way that I find very attractive. "That's true," he says slowly, "but I wasn't sure if you actually wanted to. . . ."

"Oh." I wrinkle my nose thoughtfully. "I suppose I should have been more direct."

Ben lets out a shaky laugh. "You're very direct, Bea; it's one of my favorite things about you. I just didn't want you to feel like there was any pressure . . . like I expected . . ."

I decide that the easiest way to halt this slightly stumbling conversation is to stop his mouth with a kiss.

"Violets," he says a little unsteadily. "You taste like spring."

Laughing, I pull him to me again. He kisses me back, and his hands reach up to frame my face, cradling my jaw and pulling me closer. I'm on my knees now and so is he, our bodies pressed tightly together. My own hands rest lightly on his shoulders, and as I move them to his chest I feel his heart thundering. He lowers me to the roof and I twine my arms around his neck. The kiss is desperate, tender, hungry, sweet—I never knew that a kiss could be like this, that it could be so many things all at once.

His clever fingers skim down my side to rest at my hip, and I shiver against him—it's an unconscious movement, one of expectation and delight. I feel meltingly hot, as though something is burning me up from the inside out.

Finally, he breaks away from me, his face suspended over mine; his blue eyes seem almost violet now, the color of larkspur. "Are you sure?" he asks gently. "Do you want to?"

"Yes," I say, reaching for him, smiling against his mouth. "Please."

PART FIVE

Villa di Stelle
AUGUST 1933

———

Sigh no more, ladies, sigh no more,
Men were deceivers ever;
One foot in sea, and one on shore,
To one thing constant never.

—*Much Ado About Nothing*, act II, scene 3

CHAPTER THIRTY-THREE

◆

As we travel back to the Villa di Stelle, I know that something is different between Ben and me. The events of last night are seared on my brain, and I confess I have been quite distracted all morning. As knowledgeable as I thought I was about the mechanics of lovemaking, I could never have anticipated the torrent of emotion that came along with it. It was more than I could ever have prepared for.

"More than satisfactory," I told Ben as he laughed, pressing kisses against my skin.

I feel changed now, as though something has altered not just between the two of us, but in me, forever. I just don't know exactly how to talk to him about it. Instead, I concentrate on the scenery slipping past the window, the way the world rushes past us, each view a fleeting blur, instantly replaced by another. I smile across at him and he smiles back, my own giddy happiness reflected in his eyes.

I find my thoughts drifting, and I dare to wonder, for the first time, if this experiment with Ben might not last only for the next two weeks. If there's a way it could stretch out beyond the summer, stretch out interminably into some rosy vision of the future. The idea is as paper-thin and fragile as the wings of a butterfly, and as it flutters gently awake, I hardly dare to hold it still in my mind. Could it be possible that Ben is thinking the same thing? I don't know. Everything I knew about him before this trip told me that such a thing would never happen, but there's something different now; I know there is. In Florence, I have seen him differently. With his guard down, without the smooth facade.

"I'm sorry that we had to leave Florence," I say a little awkwardly. "I really loved it."

"Yes," he agrees. "It was nice to be back."

"Will you . . ." I hesitate, clearing my throat. "Will you go back there when you leave the villa?"

There's a pause. "I don't know," Ben says slowly. "Hopefully I will have a new commission by then."

"Oh," I say, picking at a loose thread on the seat beside me. Of course. It's the exhibition tomorrow. I can't believe I forgot.

As the train leaves the city further and further behind, it feels as though our new closeness is unraveling, as though we're going to go back to how we were before. Perhaps I'm being a fool, trying to convince myself that I'm different, that

I mean something more to him than a few stolen kisses. Perhaps it's all in my own head.

No, I think. It has always been there between us—something electric and exciting, right from the start.

"I don't want the experiment to end."

The words are out of my mouth before I know I'm going to say them, but I'm not sorry. I sit up straight, my chin high. To stay quiet would be the easy thing. To let the possibility of happiness slip away without even trying to fight for it . . . that's the coward's way. And whatever else I am—stubborn, difficult, argumentative, perhaps—I am no coward.

"Bea." His voice is quiet, and I try to look calm and collected as I meet his eyes. He leans forward, and I do too. He takes a deep breath; the silence between us is like a real tangible object, it's so thick and heavy. "I—" he begins.

"AREZZO! AREZZO!" The call comes up the corridor and I jump in my seat, on edge and flustered.

"We're here," Ben says unnecessarily, getting to his feet. The moment is gone, and I wonder how on earth to get it back, what exactly he was going to say. There's no chance to talk now, not as we're swept up in the bustle of getting ourselves and our bags out onto the platform.

We walk through the waiting room and the ticket office without saying a word to one another.

Klaus is waiting for us outside the station. He leans casually against a flashy new convertible car—sleek and expensive as a racehorse—and waves when he spots us walking toward him.

"Hello!" I exclaim. "Where on earth did you get that?"

Klaus leans forward and kisses me quickly on both cheeks. "Ah, it is your uncle's newest toy," he says, opening the door for me as Ben climbs into the back seat.

"My uncle?" I say, puzzled, as Klaus slips behind the wheel and starts the car up.

"Yes." Klaus nods, something I can't place in his voice. His smile is mechanical. "They came home early."

"They?" This can't be good.

"Your uncle has brought his guests back with him for the exhibition," Klaus replies.

"His guests?" I repeat. "Lady Bowling?"

"Yes." Klaus pulls out of the station. "And Sir Hugh."

I look up at the rearview mirror and meet Ben's eye there. It seems that the perfect bubble we've been living in has well and truly burst.

CHAPTER THIRTY-FOUR

◆

"You have to be careful, Beatrice," Uncle Leo says earnestly. "Think about your reputation. You can't just go gallivanting off to Florence without a by-your-leave or a proper chaperone. Your parents entrusted me to take care of you, and to have you spend your time here in a way that they would approve of."

I gather that despite Filomena's best efforts to paint the trip in the most respectable light, it hasn't gone down well with my uncle.

"I did have a chaperone," I say.

Leo frowns. "I know Ben is a tutor of sorts," he says, and I suppress a nervous giggle. "But he's still a young man, Beatrice. He's hardly the most appropriate escort."

He has changed, I think. The relaxed and cheerfully scruffy man who greeted me when I arrived in Italy has been slowly fading away. His clothes are smarter. He's more but-toned up, and his face is cleanly shaven with a thin mustache above his top lip. It has coincided with meeting Lady Bowl-ing, perhaps, but I think it was always there. The bohemian patron was no more than an act.

Having arrived home with less than twenty-four hours to go before the big exhibition, Ben has been kept busy with his work, which means I haven't really seen him. This is probably for the best, with Uncle Leo finally paying attention to my comings and goings, but I find—much to my surprise—that I miss being with him, even though we have only been apart for a few hours. It is quite disturbing.

The artists are all working hard. There's a feeling of breathless anticipation in the air, and I find myself drawn into their nervous excitement, all the while envying their sense of direction and purpose. Klaus ropes me in to help with the hanging of his work in the house, fluttering anx-iously like a moth bumping up against a glowing window-pane. To please my uncle, Filomena insists that I show some of my own work, the product of my art lessons. I'm not sure the sketch of the inner workings of the forearm is exactly the sort of ladylike accomplishment Leo was hoping for, but I'm proud of it and I place it in a quiet corner where it's unlikely to draw much attention.

I escape to my room for a moment to read and to look through the rest of the sketches that I made in Florence. I compare them to the first drawing of the stag beetle and re-alize how much I have improved. When Filomena first suggested the lessons, I saw them only as an inconvenience, but they had real value. It was a gift that she gave me, in more ways than she could perhaps have anticipated.

Through my open window I can already hear the sounds of people arriving at the villa—shouted greetings and bursts of laughter and the clatter of footsteps through the halls. I know that I need to turn my mind to getting ready. Besides, the sooner I join the party, the sooner I'll see Ben.

The thought of a party back home would have me full of dread. I remember the disastrous dinner party that led to my coming here. Already it feels like so long ago—as if it happened to someone else, someone who has nothing to do with the girl who arrived here six weeks ago.

I go to my wardrobe for something suitable to wear. Unfortunately, there are no dresses in with my new clothes. I run my fingers along the rail, and my hands brush against my old dresses. There's nothing in my new Italian wardrobe that would fit in at Langton Hall. These beautiful colorful scraps would be as out of place as a butterfly in the damp, dark hallways of my home. Mother and Father would also never throw a party like this one; they would never open up the house to whoever wanted to come. There would be a guest list, a seating plan, the same slender circle of approved acquaintances rolling through the door again and again. I close my eyes for a moment, thinking of my home and of my parents and feeling a pang that I am finding so much happiness being away from them.

When I open my eyes again, I find comfort in the room

around me. This room, which is warm and full of light, is friendly, already familiar, already so much my own.

With a sigh I drag out the best of my old dresses and button myself into it. It feels tight and restrictive.

There's a knock on the door. It's Ursula.

"Can I come in?"

She looks ethereal in a dress that is a column of spun gold, her eyes heavily lined in dark kohl. Like a nubile Egyptian queen.

I sigh. Taking a deep breath, I open the door more fully.

Ursula looks at me for a long moment, her nose wrinkled, and her mouth a moue of distaste.

"What is it?" I fold my arms defensively across my chest.

"Why," Ursula asks heavily, "are you wearing . . . *that*?"

"You make it sound like I'm wearing a potato sack."

"You might as well be," Ursula says bluntly. "That dress doesn't fit you, Bea. Not in any way."

"Well, unfortunately, it's all I've got," I reply. "But thank you for filling me with such confidence."

"I think we can do a little better than this," she says slowly. "Wait here."

I sit on the bed, my posture rigid thanks to the restrictive nature of my dress. Several minutes pass before Ursula bursts back into the room, her arms full of black material.

"Are those Klaus's clothes?" I ask as she dumps them on the bed.

She hushes me impatiently, rifling through my wardrobe for a white silk shirt. "Put these on." She hands me a pair of

Klaus's trousers. They are black and edged down the side with inky black satin ribbon.

"Is this a *tuxedo*?"

"For goodness' sake, Bea, are we going to stand around talking about it all day?" Ursula grumbles, sifting through the items on the bed. "Haven't you ever heard of Marlene Dietrich?"

I shrug, and the movement is accompanied by a loud ripping sound, as the seam on my shoulder splits quite dramatically.

"Looks like you can't wear that horrible dress anyway." Ursula is gleeful. "So we might as well get on with my plan."

I wriggle out of my dress and put on the white shirt and the trousers. Considering that Klaus and I are very different shapes, the fit isn't so bad. "They're a little big," I say, pulling at the loose waistband. Ursula threads a thin belt through the loops on the trousers, pulling it tight and cinching them at my waist. The effect is to make them fall, straight and wide and not a million miles away from the loose-fitting trousers that I've been wearing around the villa for the last few weeks.

She also hands me a black waistcoat, tucking and pinning it at the sides so that it hugs my body. Then, she stands in front of me, frowning in concentration as she ties a black bow tie around my neck.

I accept this patiently, but I'm certain that I'm going to look ridiculous. When Ursula finally turns me around to look in the mirror, I realize this isn't the case—but I also wonder if I dare to wear it.

There's nothing *really* improper about the suit, I suppose—it's not that far away from how I've been dressing this summer. But somehow it looks a little improper on me. I look . . . *womanly*. I'm so used to folding myself in, trying to make myself look smaller at my parents' parties. This outfit won't let me hide. This outfit doesn't make me small.

I certainly don't look like the pretty, willowy figures in the fashion magazines that Mother still keeps in the house, but I like the way I feel in this suit, like a grown-up, as if the clothes I have been wearing for years were a costume, forcing me into a part I didn't want to play. The trousers are loose, light, the silk shirt a whisper on my skin. I can move. I can *breathe.*

"Well," Ursula says finally, with a dry chuckle. "That's certainly an improvement."

"You don't think it's too much?" I ask, twisting from side to side in the mirror.

"Oh, I think it's just right," Ursula says, circling me with a critical gleam in her eyes. "Or it *will* be, as long as you don't start curling yourself over like a . . . a sad shrimp."

"A sad shrimp?" I repeat, smiling.

"Yes. That is what you were like when you came here," Ursula says firmly. "Stop doubting yourself. It's boring. The outfit is perfect and you will wear it and Ben's eyes will fall out of his head. You look delicious."

"Delicious," I repeat, feeling a tingle as the compliment registers. "All right."

I start to pull my hair into a braid.

"Oh no you don't!" Ursula lifts a finger. "Leave your hair down."

"Do you think?" I ask, eyeing my curls.

"Yes, I do." Ursula is firm as she comes to stand behind me, reaching up to untangle my hair with surprisingly gentle fingers.

"Thank you for helping," I say. "It's nice to have someone to get ready with."

"Isn't that what girlfriends do?" Ursula asks a little sharply after a moment. "Gossip and share lipstick and things?"

"I don't know," I say honestly. "I've never had a friend like that before."

"Neither have I," Ursula replies, her expression guarded.

"I don't have any lipstick to share either." I catch her eye in the mirror and smile tentatively.

A similar smile appears on Ursula's lips for a second. "Now, that," she says, reaching for her gold bag, "is something I can *certainly* help with."

Ursula paints my lips a dark, berry red and lines my eyes with smoky kohl.

"Well?" I ask, as she steps back to survey her handiwork.

She nods. "You will do," she says. "Are you ready?"

"I am," I say, taking a deep breath. "All right. Let's go."

CHAPTER THIRTY-FIVE

♦

As we make our way along the hall I can hear the murmur of conversation, and music drifts through from the garden. We descend the staircase and I feel nerves fluttering through my body. Clustered below us is a crowd of people, mostly my uncle's age, looking closely at some of the paintings that hang in the hallway.

"Promising," a man mutters to his companion. "Filomena always did have a good eye."

The majority of the noise seems to be coming from outside. A couple of people glance up and catch sight of us; I feel my step wobble, and for a second I think I'm going to do something mortifying, like tumble head over heels down the staircase. Ursula slips her arm through mine, and I look down at her in surprise. She gives me a sort of rueful grimace, as though she can't quite believe that she's doing it herself.

"I feel like everyone's looking at me," I say.

Ursula snorts. "Darling, if anyone's looking at *anyone,* then they're looking at me." She untangles her arm from mine and smooths down the sides of her dress, flashing a man nearby such a dazzling smile that he blinks owlishly, looking more than a little stunned. An expression of satisfaction crosses Ursula's face.

"Oh, this is going to be fun," she breathes, drifting gracefully forward and leaving me to follow.

We head straight outside, and I was right in guessing this was going to be like no party I've been to before. The whole garden is lit by candles—there must be thousands. They're dotted along the paths, they twinkle in glass lanterns in the trees, they stretch out endlessly into the night, and the picture that they make takes my breath away. As I pass one of the trees, I realize that there are small mirrors hanging there, reflecting even more dancing flames back to one another, multiplying the candles by infinity. It's a magic trick that casts a spell over everyone who sees it, and each new arrival gasps in delight as they step into this wonderland.

Nestled within this constellation are easels holding paintings, and plinths supporting graceful sculptures. The candles stretch down the avenues, luring visitors further into the garden, where more treasures are offered up on display. There's a buzz in the air as people cluster around the works, their voices loud, animated, their movements sharp, as they sketch shapes in the air or talk about form or color. They use words like *cobalt, malachite,* and *azurite:* words that have a little bit of magic clinging to them, words that feel completely at home here.

The long table that we usually gather around is piled high with offerings from Rosa, and I pluck a green olive, fat as butter, from a dish, enjoying the salt taste of it on my tongue. I see the others—Hero dressed in shell pink, her heart-shaped face glowing with pleasure at the scene, and with her are Klaus and Ben. Klaus's dark hair is slicked back, and he wears a sharp, light-gray suit. His dapper look is completed by a jaunty red bow tie.

Ben, on the other hand, has already discarded his suit jacket. He is wearing slightly crumpled cream trousers and a matching waistcoat over a white shirt, sleeves rolled up and open at the neck. My eyes catch on that spot at the base of his throat for a second, and I feel a flare of heat in my belly. His golden hair is rumpled, and there is a hint of stubble on his face.

"Bea!" Hero exclaims. "You look so . . . *different!*" She stares. "Beautiful."

"Oh, don't." Ursula rolls her eyes. "You'll make her blush again, and her face will clash with her lipstick."

Klaus comes forward and bows elaborately over my hand, pressing a fleeting kiss to the inside of my wrist and looking at me with such naked admiration that it makes me squirm.

"Your cousin is right, Bea," he says softly. "You are so striking tonight that you leave all the other women in the shade."

Ursula snorts. "Not *all* the other women, thank you." She juts out one hip, her hand resting on the curve of her waist, candlelight flickering over the gold dress.

Klaus chuckles. "Too true, sister of mine—forgive me. No one will ever accuse you of hiding in the shadows."

I dart a look at Ben and find that he is watching me, his expression inscrutable.

He steps forward and presses a long kiss to my cheek. "Beautiful, Bea," he murmurs, his words caressing my ear and sending a shiver of awareness through my body.

We share a look then, and I know. He sees *me*. He knows me. And he thinks I'm beautiful.

We move across the terrace accompanied by Hero's high, breathless stream of chatter and Klaus's animated answers to her questions. The excitement of the evening has got hold of us all. We're giddy with it. And why not? We're in fairyland. It feels unreal, like a dream.

A sound breaks through my daze—the scattered, bird-song sound of a fiddle striking up a tune. I hadn't noticed the ramshackle band setting up, and when they pick up their instruments, the air hums with excitement. A lithe, graceful young man with a flashing white smile lowers a bow to his violin, and a wild and joyful melody skitters through the air to howls of approval. The crowd begins clearing a space for dancing immediately.

"Well . . ." Ben lifts an eyebrow. "Surely you didn't get all dressed up like that to stand around. Will you dance with me?"

"Of course," I say, stepping into the circle of his arms. "I'd love to."

CHAPTER THIRTY-SIX

◆

Ben holds me close while we dance, and I think about what a good thing it is to twirl around in someone's arms under the stars. I've never been particularly interested in dancing before, but it suddenly seems like a wonderful idea.

"Whoever invented dancing should get a medal," says Ben, echoing my thoughts.

"I think we've always danced," I say dreamily. "Homer wrote about dancing in the *Iliad*, you know. That's almost three thousand years ago. But every society must have danced long before that, though of course it's harder to find evidence."

"Perhaps dancing makes us human," Ben suggests with a smile.

I pull back a little. "Oh no, Ben," I say firmly, "plenty of birds dance. After all, one only has to look at the grebe . . ."

I stop because Ben is laughing, holding me so close that I can feel the laughter rumble in his chest. I look up at him, and his eyes are crinkled around the edges.

"I'm just glad we're including dancing in the experiment," he says.

"What are your observations?" I ask.

"I observe that your cheeks are flushed"—he runs a finger down the side of my face—"that your eyes are sparkling, and that we haven't stepped on each other's toes. I would call that a success."

His arm is tight around my waist and my hand rests on his shoulder, the fabric of his shirt soft against my fingertips.

The music changes and Ben twirls me suddenly, setting the world spinning around me, a kaleidoscope of light and sound. The melody is shrill and exciting, a heady cacophony of sound, full of life. Some of the songs that follow have words, and the Italians burst into a loud, enthusiastic singalong that I ask Ben to translate for me. I'm not sure if he is teasing me or if the lyrics really are as scandalous as he claims, but either way it's a very interesting lesson in social behavior.

"I should go and talk to people about my work," Ben murmurs reluctantly in my ear. "Will you save me another dance later?"

"Perhaps," I say.

With a rueful smile, Ben drops his hand from my waist and takes a step back. The air that rushes between us is cool, and I feel curiously bereft, as if my body is registering the absence of his touch.

But then, after Ben, I have another dance partner and another and another. "My dance," they say. "My dance, my dance." I've never been so much in demand, and I try to concentrate on enjoying myself. After a while I forget to try, caught up in the easy excitement of the crowd.

I notice that Klaus chats easily with the musicians in between songs, paying particular attention to the handsome violinist. The two of them smile at one another in a way that is warm and intimate. How interesting.

I feel like a spinning top as the music rings out and the lights blur around me. After a while I find myself in Klaus's arms, and he greets me as though we've been apart for months, pressing warm kisses to my cheeks. Finally, after yet another dance, I've had enough, and I leave him with a new partner as I head off in search of food and water.

I come across Hero sitting at the dining table, her chin in her hand, her eyes on the decadent scenes unfolding in front of her. She looks as though she's at the pictures, watching quietly from the darkness as the light spills to her.

"Are you having fun?" I ask, sitting down in the seat beside her and reaching for a hunk of bread topped with oily tomatoes and sweet-smelling basil leaves.

"So much fun," Hero breathes. "Isn't it wonderful, Bea? You'd never see anything like this in boring old England."

"Certainly not the England that we inhabit, anyway," I agree, licking my fingers.

"I hope we never have to leave here," Hero says. Something sad comes into her eyes. "I think . . . I think maybe Pa is getting homesick."

"Perhaps it's just spending time with Lady Bowling and Sir Hugh," I say in what I hope is a comforting way. "That's bound to remind him of home. When they leave, everything will go back to normal." The truth is, I suppose, that Leo feels separate from all this. It's as though he's already back in the polite drawing rooms of England.

"I suppose." Hero doesn't sound completely convinced. Her gaze strays to Klaus, who is now twirling Ursula around, her gold dress rippling like a beacon. I can already see several other men prowling around the edge of the dance floor waiting to pounce once the song ends. "Klaus is handsome, isn't he?" she asks, changing the subject with a moonstruck sigh.

"He is," I agree.

"And Ben, of course," Hero adds fairly. "He's handsome too."

"He certainly thinks so." I laugh.

"I think we've already established how handsome you find me, Miss Beatrice Langton of the Northumberland Langtons," Ben's voice chimes in, his tone containing an edge of mockery, and he drops into the chair on the other side of Hero, pouring himself a glass of wine and knocking it back in one swift draft.

"Arrogance is not at all attractive, *Benedick*," I reply primly.

"You might be handsome, Ben," Hero says slyly, "but I think my cousin is the most beautiful girl here tonight. Don't you?"

"I know *I* do," a voice with a heavy Italian accent pipes up, and a polished-looking man in his late twenties bows his head. "Would you do me the honor, signora?" He holds out his hand, but before I can reply, Ben is on his feet.

"I'm stealing her away, I'm afraid," he says, and with that he practically hauls me out of my chair and off away from the crowd. I can hear Hero's stifled laughter.

"That was very rude," I say.

"That man is a notorious womanizer," Ben replies. "I was being protective. Chivalrous."

"Oh yes, chivalry, I'm sure that's what it was. Wouldn't want to spend time with handsome, notorious womanizers," I scoff. "They are truly awful. I am perfectly capable of looking after myself, thank you."

"I know you are; I was trying to protect *him* from receiving a black eye."

"Honestly, you accidentally punch someone in the face just *once,* and you never hear the end of it," I complain. "And you barely even had a bruise."

I look over to where Klaus is once again in conversation with the handsome musician, their heads close together. Something invisible crackling between them.

"I know you said that Klaus was flirting with me before," I say carefully, "but I wonder if he might not be more interested in your company than mine."

A flash of surprise appears in Ben's eyes. "So you know about that, do you?"

"I've been making some observations," I concede.

"Well, as it goes," Ben says, "I'm not Klaus's type."

"Mmm," I murmur in agreement. "Not like the violinist over there."

"You *are* observant. . . ." Ben smiles. "But you should know that Klaus's interest in the violinist does not preclude him from being interested in you."

"Oh really?" I say. "He's attracted to men *and* women? How interesting."

"Anyway," he says, tugging at my hand, "enough about Klaus. I have something I want to show you."

"Are you just trying to get me into a dark corner?"

Ben gives me a long look. "Maybe later," he says, pulling me further down the path into the garden. "I want you to see my work."

"Oh!" I exclaim. "I would love that." *Hopefully I can manage something better than "nice" this time,* I think.

The noise from the crowd recedes as we follow a path lined with candles. Ben leads me to the fountain, where ropes hung with lanterns cast the space in a warm, golden glow.

There, standing on three easels, are the most beautiful paintings I have ever seen. They are alive with swaths of bright color, and though they are not faithful reproductions, it is easy for me to recognize them.

"Anisoptera," I murmur, standing in front of a canvas of dazzling blues and greens and purples. "A dragonfly." I turn to the next painting. *"Gonepteryx cleopatra."* This canvas is all saffron, gold, and cinnamon. "The Cleopatra butterfly." And, finally: *"Upupa epops."* The hoopoe, the bird I longed to see the most, its striking black-and-white comb displayed in geometric shapes against coppery peach feathers. "I can't believe you painted them." Somehow Ben has captured the freedom of the creatures, their beauty, and the way they move.

"I was thinking of you," he says. He touches the painting of the dragonfly. "The first time you came here to the fountain." He turns to the next canvas. "And our terrible first attempt at a romantic picnic." He rests a hand on the final one. "The fountain again . . . after you pushed me in."

"Those don't seem like the happiest memories," I murmur, still spellbound by the paintings in front of me.

"Oh, they were," Ben says quietly. "They were with you."

I turn to look at him, and for some reason there are tears prickling at my eyes. "I love them," I say simply. "Thank you for painting them."

Ben swallows. "It looks like the great experiment has helped us both. I think it's some of my best work."

"I'm glad," I say, forcing myself to sound cheerful. "I wouldn't want to think that I was the only one who experienced positive results."

I think he's going to make a joke, something sly about the "positive results," but instead he smiles, a slow, sweet smile.

"No," he says. "You're not the only one."

My heart thumps irregularly in my chest. "You're being very romantic now."

"I suppose you bring it out in me," Ben replies, and his face is difficult to read.

I clear my throat. There's a strange tension building between us. I think it's because there is so much unsaid.

I know that there are lots of things I want to say, but for some reason it is proving difficult. Ever since Florence, things have been different between us. It's not just what happened physically; something else is happening here—something messy that has to do with feelings. Something that is very much supposed to be outside the scope of our experiment. I don't usually have a problem with sharing my opinions, but in this case I feel incredibly vulnerable—like my emotions are something tender and new.

"So," I say finally. Unfortunately, I don't seem to have any more of the words in that sentence to hand.

"Bea," Ben begins. He takes a step to me.

"Ah, here you are!" a hearty voice exclaims. It's my uncle, and Sir Hugh and Lady Bowling are with him. As they walk into the glade, his eyes dart between me and Ben, and a look of displeasure crosses his face. "Beatrice, you mustn't be out here unchaperoned; it's most improper."

"Is it?" I ask blankly, thrown by this sudden intrusion into what was a very private moment. I feel as though I have been running at great speed, only to be pulled up short, and I am struggling to catch my breath.

"You must know it." Leo sounds impatient now. "Ben is hardly a proper escort for a young lady."

Ben turns. "Aren't I?" he asks, his voice flat.

Leo looks uncomfortable for a moment. "Well, I didn't mean . . ." He trails off. "That is to say, of course there's nothing *untoward* going on. Just that appearances are important, aren't they? We can't be too careful when it comes to a young lady's reputation, particularly a young lady of Beatrice's social standing. After all, Beatrice's parents expect us to, to . . ."

"Naturally Beatrice's parents expect her to maintain a certain *standard*," Frances says. Her eyes are on Ben, her disdain obvious.

"And what sort of standard is that?" I ask, matching her icy tones. "Because as far as I can see, they entrusted my care to my uncle, and I am merely socializing with his invited guests." I fix her with a level stare. "Not all of whom are being as polite as Ben."

"Beatrice!" Leo stares at me, aghast. "I'm sure Benedick here understands what we're saying. He knows the way the world works. A young man of his . . . *background* is hardly a suitable chaperone for a girl like you. Art lessons are all right, on the grounds, but this . . ."

"I was just showing Bea the work," Ben says, and his tone is expressionless.

"And very interesting it is." Sir Hugh breaks in here. While we have been talking, he has been examining Ben's paintings closely. "Quite a fresh approach, Benedick. This is promising."

"Thank you, sir," Ben says quietly.

"Well," Uncle Leo says, looking around anxiously. It

strikes me that he enjoys pleasing people, and that in our current group there is no possible response that will appease everyone. "Perhaps we should return to the party."

But as he speaks we are joined by other guests, and one draws Ben aside to talk about his work. Leo takes the opportunity to pull my hand through the crook of his arm. I am still frozen, barely able to take in what has just happened—the way a perfect golden scene has been so shattered.

I look back at Ben, and it's as if a door has closed.

"Ben—" I start to say.

"You should go, Beatrice," he says, and I think only I hear the harsh note in his voice. "I wouldn't want to do anything to further compromise your reputation."

His face is a smiling mask as he turns to speak to the newcomers, answering their questions and accepting their enthusiastic praise, and I am left reeling by his coldness.

"It looks as though Ben is getting on very well," my uncle says, in what I think is supposed to be a comforting tone. He pats my hand. "Best for everyone that he focuses on his work, eh?"

By now we're back at the center of the party, and the music is still skittering through the air, its cheerfulness at odds with my own emotional turmoil.

"My dance, I think," says a voice, and in a daze I twirl into another pair of arms, trying to ignore the hollow ache in my chest.

CHAPTER THIRTY-SEVEN

◆

The next morning, I lie in bed, trying to organize my thoughts. Clearly things with Ben have reached some sort of turning point that needs to be addressed. It's no use being cowardly about it, I realize; it is time to face up to my own feelings.

The experiment has been over for me for a while—what is happening now, as far as I'm concerned, is very real. But does Ben feel the same? I frown. He hasn't said so—not in so many words—but I think he does. With a pang I remember the rules we established, the last being that I must not fall in love with him. A qualm of doubt passes through me. Finally, I decide that I simply can't take it anymore and run down the stairs to find him.

A raised voice from the drawing room causes me to stop. It is Ursula, I realize, and she sounds upset.

I follow the sound of heated conversation and find a group gathered, frozen before me like the denouement of a play. My uncle sits beside Hero, who looks miserably down at her hands. Frances and Sir Hugh are there too, and Filomena, so still she seems carved from stone.

Ursula stands in the middle of the room, Klaus at her shoulder. Her jaw is set and her eyes are cold. "I have said all I have to," she says quietly. "And I think now Klaus and I will get our things together and leave."

"Leave!" I exclaim, making my way to her. All seven sets of eyes snap in my direction. "Whatever for?" I catch Ursula by the arm. "What has happened?" She turns away from me and I follow. "Can I help?" I ask in a low voice.

"No, darling," she says softly, and her hand covers mine in a most un-Ursula way as her eyes flicker away again. "It's clear that my sort are not welcome here," she says in a louder voice.

"Not *welcome*?" I frown.

"Now, that's not—" my uncle starts up, his cheeks turning red.

"Oh, really." Frances's languorous tone cuts across his bluster, her voice a savage chip of ice. "All I said was that Herr Hitler's theories about racial and cultural purity were *interesting*. I, personally, have nothing against the Jews—but one can rather see his point when it comes to protecting certain values."

"You are an ignorant woman. You do not know the first thing about what you're saying," Ursula flares.

"Ursula," Filomena murmurs, holding out her hand, though whether it's to stop her from talking or to offer support it's not exactly clear.

"I think things are getting a little heated," Leo says, clearly flustered. "As Lady Bowling said, this isn't a *personal* issue. There's no need for you to take such offense."

"I assure you that it is very personal to us." Ursula's voice is needle-sharp. "This is how it works, don't you see?" She looks around at us all. "The bigotry and the hatred . . . It doesn't come in like a hammer and hit you over the head. It's insidious." Her contemptuous gaze lingers on Frances. "It's a well-dressed lady in a drawing room, drinking tea and talking about 'certain values.' That's how they get you; that's how they worm their way in, rotting the apple from the inside. And you don't see—none of you will see until it is too late."

She's magnificent in her anger, ten feet tall, and her words are a call to arms. It feels like we should all be on our feet applauding.

"How very . . . *dramatic*," Frances says instead.

Ursula smiles then; it's not a nice smile. "Until it's too late," she repeats, and then she turns and leaves the room, Klaus following behind her, his face pale. I stand frozen to the spot.

"I—I—" Leo stutters. "I can't tell you how sorry I am, Frances."

"Now, now, Leo," Sir Hugh says soothingly. "We must make allowances for the ardor of youth, eh?"

"She's the playwright, yes?" Frances asks, and my uncle nods. "In that case," she continues, "painful as it may be, it is perhaps best that she *does* leave. An association like that might be bad for you. Her sort of work is being banned in Germany." Her tone is even, as though she's talking about the weather. "These are uncertain times."

Leo looks thoughtful. "Well then, I suppose my announcement is quite timely." He turns to me. "I'm sorry to have to cut your stay with us a little short, my dear, but spending so much time at the British Embassy in Rome with Lady Bowling and her charming friends has made me terribly homesick."

A freezing sense of dread begins to creep through me. I look at Hero, pale and silent on the sofa.

"What do you mean?" I ask.

"I have arranged for us to return to England. I'm going to take Hero back with me to Suffolk and get her some proper schooling. I've been irresponsible since dear Thea passed, selfish. I see that now. Frances too will return—we will escort her back to Kent on our way."

She bows her head slightly to him, like a queen acknowledging a favored courtier.

My head is reeling. "You're going back to England?" I say. "When?"

"The passage is booked." Leo smiles, as though delivering joyful news. "Within the week. I've already written to your parents. They'll be delighted to see you."

"But—but—" I stammer, my heart thumping. I look

wildly around the room, at Filomena's grave, calm face. She does not meet my eyes. "What about Filomena?" I burst out.

Leo looks a little uneasy and begins clearing his throat noisily. Filomena rises and comes forward, graceful as always.

"I will stay behind and see that the house is closed up properly. Then I will join Leo."

"Exactly," Leo wheezes gratefully. "Exactly right, join us later, once things are a bit more settled." He beams at me and at Frances. I look at Hero again. She hasn't said a word since I arrived. I don't think she's even moved.

She's not surprised, I realize. She looks sad, yes, but re-signed. I think back to her behavior over the summer—her restlessness and frustration, her urgent need to take in all this loveliness, as though it might all be over too soon. As though she expected something like this.

"So," Filomena says brightly as she moves across to the door, "I think I will go and begin the preparations."

"More tea, Frances?" Leo asks.

"Certainly, thank you," she replies. They return to their chitchat as though nothing has happened. I remain, stunned and unmoving, where I stand. Then, through all the noise in my brain, one thought crystallizes.

I need to find Ben.

CHAPTER THIRTY-EIGHT

◆

I spend hours combing the grounds, starting with the fountain, but I can't find Ben anywhere. When I finally track him down, he is in about the last place that I expect him to be.

He is in Filomena's room, and though his back is to me, I can tell from his rigid posture that he is angry.

Filomena is folding clothes and packing them carefully into a set of suitcases laid out on the large four-poster bed.

"You can't go with him," Ben says firmly. "You can't."

"What's going on?" I ask, my voice low. I shut the door carefully behind me.

Ben swings around to face me, his eyes blazing. "She's leaving. She's going with Hugh," he says.

I freeze, unable to take it in. "Filomena—why? I don't understand."

"Yes," Filomena says. "I will go with Hugh, because he

284

has offered to take me with him." She gives me a small smile. "And because I have nowhere else to go. I am fortunate that Hugh is here to offer at all."

"But I don't understand!" I exclaim. "You're going to join my uncle and Hero in England."

Filomena sits on the bed. "I said that because it is what Leo wanted me to say." She shrugs. "He is not a man who likes disharmony. So I give him this: a peaceful separation at the end of our time together. I know he would not like a scene. But I also know what he means when he says that he is going back to England. It means that my time is up."

"But not Hugh," Ben pleads. "Please, Fil. You know what kind of a man he is."

"Yes," she says, and her eyes spark. "I know what kind of a man he is, Ben. And I can take care of myself."

"Like my mother did?" Ben asks. "Women are objects to him, that's all. Disposable objects."

"I know you are only trying to help," Filomena says gently, so gently. "And I loved your mother. . . . Despite what you might think, I love you too. I am grateful that you care. But I know who he is and I know who I am. And I am not her."

There is a silence, and then, without another word, Ben turns and leaves the room. I go to follow him.

"No." Filomena's voice stops me. "Leave him, just for a minute. He will want you, but not now."

"How can you be so calm?" I ask her, rage rising inside me. "How can you stand this?"

She shrugs again, that shrug of world-weary resignation.

"It is not a surprise to me. I knew that my relationship with Leo would come to an end; it was only a question of when."

"Because you didn't love him?" I say, thinking back to her detachment around Leo, her refusal to discuss a date for the wedding.

Filomena gives me a look full of pity. "Because he didn't love me," she says quietly. "Only the *idea* of me, for a while."

I understand, then, what has been just out of sight for me this summer, the thing that wouldn't sit smoothly. I thought Filomena's feelings were not as strong as my uncle's. Now, I realize, she was simply bracing herself for this moment.

"He is not a bad man, Bea," she continues, taking my hand and setting her rows of gold bracelets jangling. "But he is weak. He allows himself to be swayed by others. He embraces what he admires. For him, I think I was a . . . What do you say? A novelty. We were happy together, for a time, very happy, and that must be enough."

"That's not enough," I whisper. In that instant I see my uncle for what he is: a weak-willed man, easily led, afraid of confrontation. Not bad, not wicked, but foolish.

"Listen, Bea," Filomena says. "Before you go, please listen to me."

I lift my eyes, meeting her steady gaze. She reaches out and presses my hand between her own. "I meant what I said to Ben. I will go with Hugh, but on my own terms. I am not afraid to be alone, because I know that I am strong. I know what I want: my art is what drives me, what gives my life purpose. It is art that I prioritize above everything else, not a man." Her voice is low—hypnotic, almost—and I feel her words in my bones. "You are so strong, Bea," she says. "You have so much in you, such joy, such a gift for life. Your drive and your intelligence should not be squandered in isolation. Go into the world and make your mark on it. You are brilliant. Do not let anyone make you feel less than that. Not your parents, not anyone."

For a moment it is as if I have been struck. My ears ring and I feel dizzy.

As Filomena's words settle, I realize that they are only confirming a decision I have already made. I can't go back to my life as it was. I can't molder away, dragged down by the estate and its problems.

I want a life of my own. I want to go to university and to learn. I want to travel and see the world. And, for the first time, I am not afraid to make that happen. I meet Filomena's eye and nod, once. She squeezes my hand again, and there is a world of understanding in her gaze.

"Go," she says.

CHAPTER THIRTY-NINE

◆

I find Ben by the fountain. *Our* fountain.

He stands, looking down into the water.

"Are you all right?" I ask tentatively, placing my hand on his shoulder. He relaxes a little against my touch.

"I don't know," he admits, and then he lets out a deep sigh. "Filomena is right. She can look after herself. I was angry. I *am* angry, but not at her." He gazes down at his hands and then up at me. "I'm glad we get to see each other again, before I leave."

I feel the ground tilt momentarily beneath me. "You're leaving," I repeat.

"I am," he says. "I'm hardly going to stay and make nice with Hugh and that witch Lady Bowling, am I?"

"But what about me?" I burst out.

"What about you?" Ben's words are hard. "You're leaving too, aren't you?"

"Well, yes, I suppose." I flounder.

"So what are we talking about, then?" Ben runs an impatient hand through his hair. "Your uncle is taking you home, Bea. The summer is over. The great experiment is over."

"But that's not what I want." The words are torn from me before I can think about them. "Is it what *you* want?"

Slowly, Ben shakes his head.

Happiness floods through me, leaving my body warm, tingling. I feel a grin spreading across my face. "You could come with me," I say eagerly. "Come back to England with me."

Ben laughs, but there's no humor in the sound. "Oh, your family would love that, wouldn't they? You turning up with me in tow. Your uncle already made it very clear how they would look upon any connection between us."

"I don't care what they think," I say. "I'm surprised that you think I would."

"Are you?" Ben asks, rubbing his brow in a gesture of frustration. "I know you, Bea. You're the one who told me that you want to please them, to make them happy. I know it's important to you, whatever you say."

"It is," I say, confused. "It *was*." I struggle to find the words. "If I try and fit in their world, I'll end up making us all unhappy. Things have to change." I take a deep breath. "I'm going to school," I say. "It's what I want. It always has been. I think I'll study medicine. Find a way to help people, actually make a difference."

Ben smiles, a real smile this time. "That's wonderful," he says. "*You'll* be wonderful, I'm certain."

"And you could come with me," I say again.

"And do what?" Ben asks. He turns and walks restlessly away, before turning back again. "Look, I've been offered a commission in Spain. It's an important one, one that could mean big things for me. You have your life to live, Bea, and I have mine. I don't want to go back to England, but you should." He gives a small smile. "It's the rational thing to do."

A sense of numbness is spreading through my body; it's as though his words are coming from far away.

"I know that," I manage. "I understand it logically, but I—I don't feel rational about you."

I find myself suddenly swept into a kiss that is frantic, wild. It's a kiss that says so many of the things I've been struggling to find the words for. It's ferocious, all-consuming, and almost painfully intimate. It feels as though I've been stripped back to something shining and elemental. As if I have shared my whole self with Ben, and he has shared his whole self with me. Our bodies coil around each other as if that's what they were made for, as, I suppose, they were. It's a kiss full of longing, of tenderness, of sorrow, and by the time we break apart I am trembling.

"I don't feel rational about you either," Ben says finally.

"But that doesn't change the facts. We always knew it was just for the summer. That's why we put the rules in place."

"'You must not, *under any circumstances whatsoever,* fall in love with me,'" I say dully.

"Right."

"You'll go to Spain, will you?" My voice is bitter; I fling the words at him angrily. "And what will you do there? Paint? Flirt with women? Ignore what's happening in the world around you? It's not just me you're running away from, you know. You're burying your head in the sand, too afraid to look at what's going on. You'll take a commission from whoever pays you, no matter what they stand for. Don't you see that these people, all these rich patrons who will happily have dinner with a dictator—they'll hurt the people you care about. Ursula and Klaus. Gert and Lili." He flinches at that, and I wonder if I've hit home. "You're afraid," I say, and to my surprise my voice is steady. "Too afraid to stand up for what you want. What you believe in. Do you think I care about your background? Do you think I wouldn't fight for you, defend you? You're a coward. You're a coward and you're turning your back on something that could be real."

There's a long pause. Anger and sadness and hurt and a million other emotions rush through me, and I see them all reflected in Ben's eyes.

"Maybe you're right," he says finally, with practiced nonchalance, though his voice is hoarse.

And that's it. I want to punch him in the nose and I want

to kiss him senseless. I've done both, and at the moment I'm not sure which one would be more satisfying.

He puts a hand to my cheek. "I didn't mean to break the rules," he whispers. "But I couldn't help it."

And then, just like that, he's gone.

CHAPTER FORTY

◆

As I stand on the deck of the boat, I watch the white cliffs of Dover come into view with mingled emotions. I'm not the same girl who left England, who turned her back on those cliffs and experienced her first taste of freedom. My heart is battered, bruised, not quite as open as it was before. *I managed to acquire all that experience I so badly wanted*, I think, with a rueful grimace. It's funny how much older I feel than just a couple of short months ago. How one summer can change a person so dramatically.

I wouldn't take it back, though. Even the sharp pain in my heart that tells me I'm alive, more alive than I have ever been.

My uncle is somewhere belowdecks, fawning over Lady Bowling. I wonder what will happen now, if he will change again, become something else to please someone else. He's inconstant, I realize, turning with the tide.

I clamber up onto the rail, and it's easy, thanks to my trousers. I left my old clothes behind me at the villa, along with the girl who used to wear them. I'm stronger now. I know what I want and I know how to get it. I am going to squeeze every last drop of joy out of the life that I have. I'm not going to make myself less than I am.

These are the tangible outcomes of my experiment, outcomes that stretch beyond Ben and me. In my bag is a notebook that contains several lists—there are lists of birds I have seen, there are lists of kisses that Ben and I shared, and there's the list of things I want to do when I get home.

"What's that in your hand?" Hero asks, coming to stand beside me at the rail.

The flower was sitting on top of my suitcase before we left. I hold it now, gently, between my fingers, while the wind tangles around me. Its delicate white petals, unfurled like a star, are velvety soft to the touch. The scent of it is heady, intoxicating.

I don't know where it came from, but I know who it came from.

"*Gardenia jasminoides,*" I reply.

"What does that mean?" Hero wrinkles her brow.

"It means love," I say, and I let go, watching the gardenia dance across the water.

EPILOGUE

England
JULY 1937

I know you of old.

—*Much Ado About Nothing,*
act I, scene 1

"We have guests arriving," my uncle says, coming into the room with a telegram in his hands. "Including some old friends."

"Oh?" I say, lifting my eyes rather grudgingly from my textbook. It may be the summer break, but that's no excuse for falling behind on my studies. Mother and Father used all the emotional blackmail at their disposal to get me to visit Leo and Hero in Suffolk for a couple of weeks, but as I told them, the examination period at Oxford is not something to be taken lightly.

At least it means I will escape their matchmaking efforts—I hear poor Cuthbert Astley is due a visit, and my parents still find the idea of him a compelling one. If I had hoped that my scholarship to study medicine would quell their urges to interfere, then that hope was rather swiftly revealed to be a naive one. After all, as the saying goes, a leopard can't change its spots. (Though, of course, a leopard's spots *do* change significantly as it matures into adulthood.) I may have changed that summer, but my parents didn't, and they're still very much a work in progress.

Still, it is certainly easier to bear now that I have a life of my own—one not confined to the drafty hallways at Langton.

And last week I overheard Mother talking to the vicar.

"Of course, Beatrice is practically a doctor," she said. "Top of her class." The words, carefully casual as they were, betrayed a tremor of pride that left me stunned.

"The Lord works in mysterious ways" was the vicar's sour rejoinder.

"Who are the guests?" Hero leaps to her feet, dancing excitedly to her father. In moments like this she still seems so young, and despite her eighteen years I see my little cousin, the one who asked over and over for the tale of the toad.

Perhaps her youthfulness is down to the way Leo dotes on her. Thankfully, his association with Lady Frances Bowling lasted a scant few months, and after a—mercifully brief—flirtation with Mosley's British Union of Fascists, Leo seems to have given in to a happy bachelorhood, devoting his attention to his daughter.

"An old army friend of mine, Peter—and his brother John," Leo says.

Hero's nose wrinkles. "I don't know them," she says.

"Peter did meet you as a baby," Leo says. "But it wasn't them I was referring to. They're bringing a group of youngsters with them who have been out fighting in Spain."

"Oh?" I lift my eyes. "It will be interesting to hear how things are going over there. I'm glad that there are people who have enough conviction to actually *do* something."

"Yes. Terrible, all these fascists. Not the thing at all," Leo agrees fervently, and I smile faintly. "Though I'm not sure about these young people getting tangled up in things that don't concern them."

"Oh! If I were a man, then that's where I'd be," I say with certainty.

Leo looks vaguely horrified by this statement.

"But who *are* they?" Hero asks, regaining his attention. "You said they were old friends."

"Daresay you might not remember them," Leo says, "but you met them years ago when we, ah, lived in Italy. Artist chaps."

The book drops from my nerveless fingers and hits the floor with a thud. I bend to pick it up, hoping to conceal my confusion.

"Klaus?" Hero squeals, delighted.

"That's the fellow." Leo beams. "And another." He consults the telegram.

"Signor Benedick, perhaps," I say, my voice perfectly calm.

"Ben!" Leo exclaims. "That's it. They'll be here any minute, as it happens. Seems the boy at the post office took his time about bringing this over."

With comedic promptness, a horn sounds outside. "Ah!" Leo jumps to his feet. "Here already." And he leads the way through the house to the front door and the crunching gravel driveway, Hero and me following behind.

From the shadow of the doorway, I watch as the doors on the two cars open and several men spill out. Among them I spy Klaus, still dashingly handsome, though his face is more serious than I remember, and then—the last to emerge—there is Ben.

My heart is thumping so loudly that I can't hear what

299

they are saying. I study Ben closely. The golden hair, the clear blue eyes crinkling in laughter. He seems taller than in my memories, and he's definitely thinner. His face is tanned; his clothes—even by his standards—are exceedingly worn. There is something different about his face—it has sharpened. A man's face, perhaps, not a boy's. He's saying something now, something that makes them all laugh, before he is cut off by Hero flinging herself down the steps and into Klaus's arms.

I step into the sunshine. "I wonder why you're still talking, Ben," I say, proud that my voice contains not a single tremor of emotion. "It seems nobody is listening."

His eyes snap up to meet mine, and it's as if the past four years fall away in an instant. "Hello, Bea," he says softly, moving to me. "Why so disdainful?" The look he gives me is a challenge.

"Why not?" I ask lightly. "When there's so much to be disdainful of." I run my eyes lazily over his body, finally meeting his gaze.

I don't know how long we look at each other, but a tingle of bone-deep recognition spreads through me. Slowly, Ben begins to smile, a glitter of appreciation in his eyes.

I feel an answering smile on my lips.

Oh yes, I think. *This is going to be fun.*

The End of the Beginning

ACKNOWLEDGMENTS

I have a lot of reasons to be thankful and a lot of people to thank for making the book that you are holding in your hands. It's still staggering to me that something can go from a slightly vague, tingling idea in my brain to a beautiful, real, tangible book, and there's just no way it would happen without a whole team of people.

My agent, Louise Lamont, should really get the credit for this one. It makes so much sense that after years of sending each other GIFs and pictures from *Much Ado* to commemorate and celebrate different milestones, we would make this joyful book together. Thank you so much for everything you do, thank you for making my job so fun, and thank you for not making me put in more fascism. *Benedick-dancing-in-the-fountain image*

To my editor, Gen Herr, thank you as always for being a

friend, an encouragement, and the person I trust the most. Thank you for taking the tangled, unfinished mess that was the first draft of this book and helping me make something I love. I could not have done this one with anyone else; it's your book, too.

Thank you to so many others at Scholastic for their hard work and for just generally being so supportive and sweetly enthusiastic about my work that it kept me going. In particular, thanks to Harriet Dunlea, Kate Graham, Emma Jobling, and Pete Matthews for all their hard work. Thank you to Sophie Cashell, Lauren Molyneux, Lauren Fortune, and Sam Smith for cheering me on when I really needed it. Thank you to Jamie and Yehrin for joining forces again to make something so beautiful. I couldn't ask for a better team.

Thank you so much to the incredible readers, bloggers, and authors who have supported me over the last couple of years in ways that make me feel quite teary. I so appreciate you all. Special thanks to Amy McCaw, Chelle Toy, Jo Clarke, Liam (@notsotweets), and Claire (@thechesilbeach) for the unfailing Twitter support—where would I be without you?! To human sunbeams Alice Broadway, Melissa Cox, Lauren James, Katherine Woodfine, Maggie Harcourt, Laini Taylor, Ella Risbridger, Lucy Powrie, and Lucy Strange, thank you, thank you, thank you for being so generous with me—I respect your opinions hugely, and your words about my first journey into YA meant everything and made this book possible.

Thank you to my friends and family for their unfailing

support. My mum and dad continue to be the model for proud, supportive parents, and I would be lost without them. When this book comes out, it will be only a couple of weeks before I gain a new sister, and I couldn't be happier that my little brother found his person. I love you both! Special thanks have to go to Mary Addyman, who brings joy and laughter and cake into my life whenever I need it most. Biggest, best thanks of all to Paul. This book is special for lots of reasons, but partly because *Much Ado* was something we had in common from the beginning. This one is yours, because I really do love nothing in the world so well as you.

And finally, thank you very, very much to my (future) close personal friends, Emma Thompson and Kenneth Branagh. When I was sixteen, I watched your adaptation of *Much Ado About Nothing*, and it opened up a completely new world. You made Shakespeare come alive for me, and in doing that you changed my life.

LAURA WOOD is the award-winning author of *A Sky Painted Gold*. She lives in a cottage in the English countryside and recently received a PhD from the University of Warwick, where she taught about nineteenth-century literature, feminism, and children's literature. When she's not traveling to far-flung places, she enjoys watching old movies and swooning over good romance novels.

LAURACLAREWOOD.COM